THE WANDERERS
BOOK ONE

THE WHISPERING WALLS

by J. E. Hunt

Carius Books

Text copyright © 2009 by J. E. Hunt
Illustrations and cover art © 2009 by J. E. Hunt

Excerpt from *The Wanderer* courtesy of Tim Romano
Find the full text and his excellent translation via
http://tinyurl.com/thewanderer

All rights reserved. Published by Carius Books in Alexandria, Virginia U.S.A.

No part of this publication may be reproduced or stored in a retrieval system or transmitted in any form or by any means, electronic, mechanical, photocopying, recording, or otherwise, without written permission of the publisher.
Reviews and critiques are welcome. For information regarding permission in these contexts and others, contact information@cariusbooks.com.

The author has made every effort to provide accurate Internet addresses at the time of publication, and neither the publisher nor the author assumes any responsibility for any errors or changes that occur after publication. Further, the author and publisher do not have control over and do not assume any responsibility for third-party Web sites or their content.

ISBN 978-0-9825665-2-7

First Edition, January 2010

This book was typeset in 11.5pt Adobe Garamond Pro.
The jacket is composed of original artwork, images in the public domain, textures from highresolutiontextures.com and grungetextures.com, and brushes from obsidiandawn.com

Nis nu cwicra nan
þe ic him modsefan minne durre
sweotule asecgan. Ic to soþe wat
þæt biþ in eorle indryhten þeaw
þæt he his ferðlocan fæste binde,
healde his hordcofan hycge swa he wille.
Ne mæg werig mod wyrde wiðstondan
ne se hreo hyge helpe gefremman.
Forðon domgeorne dreorigne oft
in hyra breostcofan bindað fæste,
swa ic modsefan minne sceolde
— oft earmcearig eðle bidæled
freomægum feor — feterum sælan.

—*The Wanderer,* c. 597

Book One:
The Whispering Walls

Part One:
Tergiver

1

And they would send me to find you

Tergiver's forehead was hot like the candle at his elbow when he opened his eyes and found a shadow creeping across his unfinished letter. He caught his nineteen-year-old face reflecting on the windowpane, and he looked away to the burning hearth, where Charlie swung a sword against imaginary enemies that attacked with random pops of the fire.

Charlie was thin and blond, and he stopped, poking his sword absently into the tip of his shoe. "Are you still writing that? It's your third letter and we've only finished the first day of the tournament. Let's practice for tomorrow."

"I need to write this now." Tergiver was unmoved. His short black hair and handsome face were growing brighter and more distorted on the darkening glass beside him. He pulled the quill from the ink with a jerk and said, "You know he always wants every detail."

Charlie kicked at his sword for a moment, then whirled around to face an assailant that had sprung from the shadows with a sharp crack.

The words wavered on the page as Tergiver stared in exhaustion, knowing that his father was no more interested in the tournament than he was in learning to read. His eyes fell closed briefly, then drifted to the warm cup of cider that Charlie had brought earlier. It sat on the sill against the cold window, breathing steam intermittently and patching the glass with soft shapes that advanced and retreated in waves. He felt heavy. He heard no sound in the room save the quiet crackling of the fire. Then he sat up in alarm. Charlie was gone.

Across the room, two small beds stretched their feet against the hearth, and a pile of muddy clothes lay alone in the corner. Suddenly, a sharp hissing sound whipped across his right ear and stopped with a drabbing smack, as the flat of Charlie's sword splattered itself in the candle. It splayed warm wax all over Tergiver, who started away and tipped over backwards in his chair. There was a howl of laughter as the chair back knocked against the floor, and Tergiver saw Charlie standing over him upside down, holding his stomach and wiping watery eyes. Tergiver righted himself angrily, but then, unwillingly, he too began to laugh. He pulled his sword from the tabletop, scraping it across the wood, and said in a mix of jest and violence, "Alright, scourge ... guard yourself."

He lunged forward. Charlie parried the blow, then returned it. For almost an hour they fought, shuffling and stomping their feet across the dusty floor, swinging, clanging, and scraping their swords, throwing sweeping arcs and swift jabs. The window blackened against the darkness outside, and firelight climbed the walls, glowing bigger and brighter and throwing the young men into heavy orange relief. Their long black shadows cut each other cruelly as they scrambled across the hearth. Tergiver was tall and well-built, but as he shifted away from the fire, Charlie's shadow grew twice as large as his own.

They were skillful in their play, but as Charlie feigned a swing to the left, then attacked right, Tergiver deflected the sword sharply into the stone mantle, which coughed low as the blade raked across it, leaving a visible scrape.

"Hold on, wait!" cried Charlie. His face grew grim and disappointed as he rubbed his thumb over the scratch. Tergiver paused briefly, then lunged again, stopping his sword at Charlie's shirt. Charlie batted it away and began to work Tergiver toward the door. Tergiver understood, and as he made a quick feint toward Charlie, he opened the door behind him with his free hand and stepped backwards over the threshold into the brisk night air. Then he parried Charlie's last blow high and hard into the doorframe, dislodging a small chunk of wood. Charlie's face sharpened under his blond bangs and he set his sword down to show that he was finished.

Then he examined the wood. "You shouldn't have done that. This isn't my father's old barn; we will have to pay for it."

Tergiver leaned on his sword, pushing it deeper into a pile of dead leaves. Then he walked forward into the edges of the firelight and replied with arms outspread, "You shouldn't have attacked me, Charlie. You know there is no measure for my speed and power, or …"

Charlie's face warmed as he rolled his eyes up to the black sky behind Tergiver, "Or your overwhelming charisma — I know."

Tergiver stepped into the threshold and said, with a conciliatory lift of his hand, "At the end of the tournament tomorrow we will know our placement in the king's service, and since we've already made it into the final thirty-two, we're sure to get positions of importance — as well as good stipends — we'll be able to pay for whatever we want."

They passed over the next part of the conversation, which they had already argued many times in their friendship. Tergiver would say that Charlie's family had too much money to worry about such little things as a scratch in a door, and Charlie would argue that it did not give them license to be irresponsible. To avoid this, Tergiver said, "Let's climb onto the roof. I bet the wall is lit up by now."

The young men left their swords in the room and went outside. They walked along the edge of the inn, which consisted of a single row of rooms that ran parallel to the horizon of shedding trees in the west. Near the northern tip of the building stood a large elm with thick, knotted limbs that rose high above the rooftop. Tergiver ran forward and scrambled up the tree, disappearing over the sloped shingles before Charlie could pull himself onto the first branch. Tergiver's head reappeared against the night sky. He held a hand out to Charlie and hauled him up roughly.

A cold wind swirled about the roof as they gained their footing and leaned forward, placing their hands against the steep, rough shingles for balance. Charlie climbed carefully. To his left he saw scattered campfires warming scores of young men in their late teens, and he heard their voices as they laughed, made bets, and boasted of their parts in the day's tournament. Tergiver kept his eyes forward, staring up the slope, eager for the first glimpse of that which lay beyond it.

After a short distance, the two friends paused in wonder. Before them, the prodigious rock towers of the West Gate stood as enormous voids against the illuminated range of clouds.

They climbed higher and saw the base of the towers bulging out of the menacing face of the city wall, which appeared beyond the roofline. Tergiver and Charlie sat down at the top, staring up at the wall, which looked like a broad black wave poised to fall on anyone who came too close. Its battlements swelled outward in high piles, dotted with pointed spires, and a few torch lights slid across the stone walks, left and right, like distressed ships riding perilous crests.

After a while, the moon waxed full over the city, and slices of it shone through the intermittent cloud cover to light the wall in pallid streaks. Tergiver and Charlie sat without speech, watching the single torches move among the fixed ones. They traced the wall to their right, eventually losing it in the engulfing darkness as it curved away to the south and swept around the east of the city in a protective half circle.

The elm swayed and creaked loudly at their backs, and stray leaves joined them on the ledge for short periods before jumping away into the wind.

Tergiver's eyes followed the line of torches to his left, all the way up to the far north side of the wall, a towering rock cliff that stood a hundred yards higher than the massive, stony castle below it.

"How do you suppose it feels to be on that wall right now, protecting Murmilan, waiting for something to happen? Nothing would dare come if I were up there."

Charlie leaned back on his palms, "I still don't see why you want to stay. You've seen the castle with my father and it's always the same. Put me on a ship and let me see the world."

Tergiver made a friendly smirk, "You would get lost in a month, and they would send me to find you."

Charlie smiled and the moon vanished under a swell of grey clouds.

The noise from the campfires around the inn subsided momentarily, and Tergiver and Charlie imagined that they heard the faint sound of the crashing water that poured itself over the black, skyward cliff that served as Murmilan's north wall.

"Well," said Tergiver, "this time tomorrow we'll know, won't we?"

Charlie gave a sympathetic look and replied, "Listen, if you don't make it into the King's Guard, I promise to save a spot for you on my ship — when I have one. Every captain needs a cook."

They laughed, but Tergiver's ebbed away quickly. "I'll make it."

2

A GOBLET TURNED BETWEEN HER FINGERS

High in one of the West Gate's unlit towers, Baelin stood pensive and still in the wavering moonlight, gripping the stone ledge and tracing the city streets with his eyes. At his left, the castle spread its imposing bulk of pinnacles, cornices, and circular windows against the backdrop of the cliff. The Great South Gate stood opposite the castle at the other end of the city, and Baelin saw that its towers were still lit with bright fires. The East Gate was dark, lit only by the moon, which gleamed in the tiny lake that covered the city's southeastern corner, and glossed with pale blue the countless shops and carts that huddled against the west wall below Baelin. All three gates were closed tight, baring clenched iron teeth against the besieging darkness.

Baelin's thick eyebrows sat heavy on his face as he closed his eyes. The faint sound of shuffling feet on the stone staircase below had caught his attention. It grew louder and soon disturbed the dust a few feet behind him. He released his hands from the window and turned around to find the tall, wiry form of Anson, another member of the King's Guard, standing at attention and barely visible.

Anson stood a head taller than Baelin, and said in a light voice, "Sir, Herrick has requested your presence at the banquet."

Neither of these men had reached the age of twenty-four, but Baelin's face had gained hard lines with each increase in rank he had earned during his six years of service. His countenance was mature, serious, and discerning — an unconscious display of his achievements. Anson looked five years younger than he actually was.

Baelin descended the spiral steps alone and walked out onto the broad, arching bridge that formed the top of the West Gate. It was paved with rough cobblestones, and its parapets and machicolations filtered the moonlight into complex shadows on the road below.

He walked northward, knowing why Herrick had called for him, and he was not eager to go. Along the sloping path he heard the low chatter of guards at each station, the snapping of ambitious torches in their sconces, and owls hooting to one another in a grove of trees to his left. The black stone wall met the cliff at a flight of stairs that shot steeply up to a high platform. At the top, Baelin met another guard whose red cloak shone grey and orange in the flickering firelight.

The guard recognized him immediately and asked, "Who passes?"

"A servant to his highness."

"Evening to you, sir." The guard stood aside and allowed Baelin to descend onto the long slant of steps that were cut into the cliff.

He left the bleak stairway and ascended one of the arcaded walks that emerged from the pavilion, where the water that plunged over the cliff crashed noisily into a wide pool. A lawn sloped upward from the pavilion to a tiny guard post at the back of the castle. Baelin acknowledged the man stationed there, and entered the castle through a pair of broad, oaken doors.

The hinges groaned as the doors fell shut, and Baelin's cheeks warmed as he took the sloping stone hallway to his left and walked toward the center of the castle. He passed a handful of revelers who checked their behavior on seeing him, and after a few moments, he arrived at a green marble archway that was lit by double rows of bright torches, and which served as the rear entrance to the castle's Great Hall. There the fragrance of sap and burning elm logs hung about the air, and an ornate ceiling disappeared in the darkness above.

As he stepped forward, a breathless voice caught him from behind and held him as if by the chain of his cloak, "Baelin, wait for me!"

He stopped and briefly closed his eyes. Then he turned to find Princess Agatha catching her breath. Her dark-brown locks spilled over her shoulders as she leaned forward, panting and resting a hand on her thigh. She held out a small, pale hand to hold Baelin in place, then straightened herself with a deep breath and smiled at him with her enormous blue eyes. "Good," she said, "I didn't think I was going to catch you." She checked herself to make sure she hadn't wrinkled her long blue dress, then she cradled Baelin's arm in her elbow and led them into the Great Hall. "Now I can tell my mother we were talking in the hallway and that is why I am late." She smiled, satisfied, and Baelin gently removed his arm from hers.

Agatha and Baelin walked together down the middle of the hall, watched by the assembly of marble statues that guarded the numerous snaking hallways that skirted away into the castle through ornate archways. They walked through straggling coteries of gossiping men and women, all of whom stopped to greet and bow to Agatha. She acknowledged them absently, staring forward to the wide doorway at the end of the hall, from which music and light rushed only to pale and fade at the threshold. Inside that chamber, the banquet for the retiring members of the King's Guard had begun. Agatha spoke casually, "So, Baelin, has Herrick arrived yet? I thought I saw him earlier."

Baelin's eyebrows furrowed deep in hesitant patience, and he reminded himself that duty to his king and captain mandated his courtesy. "Yes," he answered, "I have been summoned to him."

Their steps echoed away into the noise of the crowd, and before they reached the door, Agatha leaned her head forward and stepped into his path, thrusting her long curls into his field of vision. "Why don't you like me, Baelin? You're only a few years older than me, not fifty, so you don't have to always address me like one of my father's boring councilors. Tonight is supposed to be fun; you can wait until tomorrow to walk around like you're about to die."

Baelin clenched his jaw and nodded forward, indicating that he simply wanted to continue into the room. The noise grew much louder as they approached the open doorway. In a weak gesture of friendliness, Baelin made a meager but sincere bow to Agatha and stepped aside for her to enter the long banquet chamber.

Agatha brightened when she saw the royal table. She scampered over to it, skipping a step. She did not notice the four colossal fires burning opposite one another in the head-tall hearths of each wall, nor the swirling golds, reds, and greens of the dancing troop to her right; nor did she notice the music or the musicians that accompanied them. If she had, she might have also seen Borleaf, a bald, stalwart, aged warrior with a greying auburn beard and arms as thick as birch trunks, twirling and laughing among the dancing girls and clapping his huge hands together. Of the four retiring guards honored by the ceremony, he was the most important. Borleaf was the current chief of the King's Guard. He was calculating, careful, and watchful, a man with a keen mind and heavy hand, though none of these traits could be seen at present.

Instead, Agatha's eyes were set on his replacement, a man who watched Borleaf with guarded amusement from his place at the high royal table, which sat upon a wide stone dais in the near corner of the room.

Herrick slouched almost imperceptibly in his chair and folded his hands together near his lips. He had sandy blond hair cropped handsomely around his head. His strong shoulders and square jaw belied the natural intelligence hidden in his liquid green eyes, which appeared drawn and disturbed on Agatha's approach.

She cast a quick, knowing glance at Herrick, who tried to look as if he hadn't seen. Then she stepped lightly to her seat on the king's right, and sat between her parents.

The table was made of thick ironwood inlaid with gold filament, and the intricate silver glasses and heavy plates that sat upon it reflected the firelight in their polish. Glancing quickly and unsurely at her father, the princess met his kind and deep eyes.

"Good evening, Agatha," he said, with a warm voice and a smile.

"Good evening, Father," she replied happily, picking up a goblet, relieved that he had not recognized her tardiness. Over her right shoulder, however, the queen's wide face moved back and forth, distressed and wan, gawking at her with round eyes.

Tugging Agatha's shoulder toward her, the queen said in a voice nearly as loud as the music, "Oh! Hello! It is my daughter everyone!" She laughed in abrupt, insecure gaffes as Agatha reddened and sank into her chair. "Now look who is late and has missed all the beautiful speeches!" The queen spoke with an odd inflection that pitched itself high at random. "You must tell your father you are sorry, Agatha; tell him you are sorry or I will not eat another bite at this table tonight. I mean it! Tell him!"

Agatha stared sideways into a red tapestry that hung on the far wall, too embarrassed to try the excuse she had contrived.

Then, as if she had forgotten her thought, the queen cleared her throat and smiled wide at no one in particular. Queen Rose was a large, garrulous woman whose pale face was always ornamented with her own selection of discordant colors. She addressed the entire table this time, causing her abashed daughter to shade her eyes and look away. "Now, have we introduced everyone? Oh! I do not know, I do not know. Let's see, Agatha, this is Herrick, and there by your father is Councilor Marscion, and then Councilor Robert, and here ..." As she said each name, she squinted narrowly and made a garish smile at her daughter.

"Mother!" cried Agatha desperately.

The king was conducting a gravid discussion of royal successions and lineage with the councilor on his left. He broke away from it and reached across his daughter to touch the queen gently on the shoulder. "Dear Rose," he said, "I believe everyone is quite familiar. Would you like Agatha to pour some wine for you?"

Those at the table began to speak freely again, happy to have escaped the scene. Arranged at the table were the royal family, twelve high-ranking members of the King's Council and Guard, and those honored in the evening's ceremony. On other occasions, the queen's introductions had lasted much longer. Her attention, however, snapped immediately to the subject of wine, and for the remainder of the night, she claimed that the vineyards of Murmilan were "completely and utterly incomparable."

Baelin had entered behind Agatha and walked a wide sweep around the room. He noticed a pair of agitated servants loading logs into one of the fires, and knew they would soon take their unspoken quarrel outside to be settled in the cold. He noticed how the dancing had scattered the great rugs and bear hides to the corners of the room; he saw who was drunk and who was angry. He took a quick inventory of the trophies, tapestries, and polished weapons that were mounted on each wall, including the pair of crossed scepters that were fixed directly below two grand, oval windows that sat high and black, gathering frost. He noticed a pair of large hounds standing at attention before the seats of two children and wagging their tales humbly for a scrap. He saw Borleaf, twirling and laughing with the crowd, and he noticed his captain, Herrick, brooding with his shoulders turned away from Princess Agatha. Baelin watched Herrick's eyes carefully for any inducement to action. This was common; Anson might have been sent to fetch him with only a look, and Baelin entered on the same terms.

As he approached the table, it seemed that Agatha looked younger or smaller than she had in the hall, but he could not decide which. Suddenly, the queen interrupted her speech about Murmillian wine with a quick, frozen smile aimed directly at him. "Hello!" she said through wide eyes, "have you just arrived?"

Baelin feigned an unconvincing smile and bowed in the anticipation of her next thought. "Highness, my name is Baelin, and I have come to speak briefly to Captain Herrick. I do not wish to interrupt your dinner and sincerely thank you for your leave to speak with him immediately."

The queen looked away, unsure of how to reopen the conversation. Baelin turned to Herrick with a blank face and nodded, "Sir?"

As Herrick motioned for Baelin to come closer, Agatha leaned forward slyly and spoke across the queen's plate, "Herrick, will you be on the field at the tournament tomorrow or will you join us in the gallery as Borleaf did?"

Herrick's impassive face concealed the struggle behind it, "Please excuse us, highness," he said, and whispered something nearly inaudible into Baelin's ear.

Agatha sulked angrily as Baelin nodded and turned to leave the room. "Oh, it's highness today," she muttered to herself, slouching a bit in her seat and turning a goblet of wine between her fingers.

The music stopped and drew applause from the tables around the room. Those who had been dancing yelled for it to begin again. A jester in bright-colored clothes ran across the floor and tumbled into a stack of empty wine barrels, prompting laughter from everyone who saw it. The musicians took this as a cue to begin a fast-paced jig, which eventually set the jester spinning and rolling so wildly that he spun himself headfirst into the stone dais, where he sat still for several minutes after giving a painful bow to his cheering audience. Borleaf had left the floor and stood exchanging stories with the other retiring Guard members. On the king's left, Councilor Robert was trying desperately to hold Councilor Marscion's attention.

Robert's thin, balding head poked almost unnaturally through his white robe, which fit him like a shell. He said, "It is hard to believe, hard to believe that Charlie's already old enough to be in the tournament. When you have children — though I do have just one — the years seem to flutter away so quickly."

Marscion's stern blue eyes set pleasantly in his face as he leaned over his plate, hanging a full head of wiry black hair between his face and Robert's. Robert was markedly older, but Marscion's face showed deep lines and rigidity, attributable to either age or hardship, or both. Marscion apologized and turned his head back toward Robert, asking him to repeat what he had said. Though his head was turned slightly, his eyes remained fixed on Herrick.

Robert continued, "He's always wanted to sail, but I think he's the kind of young man that would make a fine councilor one day — not sure where I get that idea." Robert laughed as if he had made a joke. He was conversing more with himself than with Marscion, who continued to watch Herrick's conversation with the king, wishing he could hear it over Robert's unending soliloquy. "— He's a good influence on him if you ask me, but they're both solid young men, and I trust …"

Herrick bowed formally to the king, disregarding Agatha's attention, and exited the banquet hall.

Marscion watched King Wiston's eyes follow Herrick to the door and rest on the empty space he left behind. He pretended to listen to Robert for a few more minutes, then excused himself and hurried out into the vaulted Great Hall. He moved quickly to the center of the floor, where he stood still and examined every doorway, and peered into every corridor that led away from the heart of the castle. For a moment, he stood like a sentry with too much area to watch at once. Several parties from the banquet stumbled past him to find their quarters, and then he disappeared between two statues into one of the dark hallways.

Herrick pushed open a set of wide, east doors and stepped out into the enveloping cold. He walked with his head forward, and a heavy, intricate sword bounced softly on his hip, hidden in a plain sheath. Pulling his cloak closer about his shoulders, he walked alone through a thick, but brief space of towering evergreens called the Pine Wood, which stood between the castle and the northern side of the East Wall. Ascending the narrow stairs in the cliff, which were directly opposite their counterparts, he climbed to the East Wall and walked toward the first spire. The pines below him shivered in an inconstant wind, and the torches placed at intervals on the wall created rings of light against the iron merlons on which they hung. The cloud cover had slowed and irregular shafts of light began to pour onto the floor of the city.

Herrick entered the spire and climbed the winding stairs to the top, where he found Baelin standing beside the window, barely visible in shadow. Herrick sat down against the stone wall, and Baelin sat opposite him. There was a short silence as the cold gathered and settled around them. Then Herrick spoke into the darkness, "In strategy or battle I have never hesitated; my judgment is clear whether in service or sport. I have no regrets. But here — here I am truly conflicted, Baelin. I face a perfect enemy, brilliant and beguiling, one that is actually convincing me that the loss of everything I have worked for … is the very thing I want. No soldier yearns for defeat, and yet, I do. I am becoming ever more convinced that my driving philosophies may be misguided. But you know all this already, and I would hear what you have to say."

Baelin sat quiet and still for several minutes, his head silhouetted against the window. With a steady voice he replied, "First, I am honored by your candidness, and I promise to answer the best I can, as my duty binds me. Second, I know that even if you find my words unfavorable, you are fair, and will not turn anger against my honesty."

Herrick grinned slightly in the darkness, an expression Baelin could not see, and a brief puff of wind shuttled through the tower. Herrick answered, "Please, Baelin, no more of that talk; speak plainly. I've given you my trust and I am asking this in good faith."

Baelin felt a touch of shame at having questioned his captain, and began, "Well, I will not make judgments on demeanor or spirit, which every man sees differently — although you know my opinion on that already — but, sir, even understanding that you have overcome the difficulty of the arrangement, I do not wholly believe that she has the feelings which you say she has been inclined to show you."

"Did you not see her tonight?" replied Herrick incredulously. Then he said, almost to himself, "I didn't think she could keep it a secret at all. She might have had a crier announce it to everyone at the banquet."

"Sir," replied Baelin, still hesitant, "I haven't spent as much time in the castle as you have, but I am familiar enough with our royal family. Unlike you and I, who have had duty to strengthen our bodies, and trials to sharpen our minds, I do not believe our

Agatha is much beyond grasping and crying for every pretty thing she sees, especially the ones she thinks she cannot have." Baelin paused, grasping for his next thought, and Herrick stretched his legs along the clean stone in front of him. "There is also your succession to Borleaf's post. Everyone knows that he is stepping down early because you have his confidence, but if your focus were to waver because of this, would his confidence remain? Sir, numberless soldiers have lost themselves to such preoccupations. It is wise to remember their mistakes and not knowingly repeat them. My opinion is that it might be unwise to give up your ambitions for a girl who will most likely grow tired of you by next summer." Baelin stopped again, attempting to frame his final thought, "The king has often said that to rule, one must first rule himself. This is what I think, sir."

Herrick sat in silence for several minutes, staring at the slow, dark clouds behind Baelin's head. Then Baelin spoke again, adding one last thought, "Although, sir, even if I am wrong on this point, she remains our only heir — but I will put aside that question, as you ask. You — and Councilor Marscion for that matter — seem to have a way of accomplishing the impossible."

Herrick suppressed a laugh in the darkness. "Marscion … Marscion is lucky at times, but that is all. I doubt he could dress himself in the morning without the help of servants. Take a look at the gallery and tell me what you see."

Baelin turned slowly and looked down toward the castle and the high, ornate gallery that jutted out from its center and overlooked the grassy lawn below. On it was a man in a white cloak, glaring conspicuously over the lawn and scanning the walls with wide sweeps of his head.

"Is he there?" asked Herrick.

"Yes," replied Baelin, bemused. "What is he looking for?"

Herrick shook his head in the shadow with an amused resolve. "I suppose he is looking for a reason, Baelin, I don't know — a reason to prove his importance, a reason to bring some charge against me, perhaps. You know he was the only one who did not support my replacing Borleaf. Maybe he doesn't know what he's looking for. Honestly, I would sooner worry about our queen than Councilor Marscion. But it is late and I am being unkind. No matter how conflicted my thoughts, I should take more care. Thank you for your advice, Baelin, and thank you for being a friend. You are relieved for the night. Get plenty of rest for tomorrow; there is nothing like judging your first tournament."

Baelin raised himself to his feet, said, "Thank you, sir," and vanished down the stairs.

Herrick remained on the floor, staring out the window into the open night, evaluating Baelin's words, and examining his own doubts.

A gentle wind pawed at Marscion's white robe as he stood high on the gallery that hung level with the top of the surrounding walls. He strained his eyes to inspect every dark corner of the city, from the wall's towers and many curving paths, to the Pine Wood, to the East Gate, across the tiny lake, to the Great South Gate, to the buildings nestled together in the west. Beyond the West Gate, he saw a hoard of tiny lights, some of them blinking as young men stomped them out and settled to sleep in preparation for second and final day of the King's Tournament.

3

NOT ALL ENTRANCES ARE EQUAL

The innkeeper's rooster hopped onto a low branch of the elm tree and crowed a long, screeching alarm that pried Charlie from sleep. He shuffled himself in his covers and rolled onto one elbow, lifting his head against the dim morning light. He kept his eyes closed for a moment, then opened them halfway. "Hey, Tergi," he mumbled, "how long have you been up?"

Tergiver's arm was draped over the back of his chair and his head leaned heavy against the milky window. Spread before him were several sheets of paper filled with neat brown ink. His candle was now a short, waxy dish on the edge of the table, giving a muted glow. He yawned deeply, seeing Charlie doing the same, and then widened his eyes forcibly to restore his face from its involuntary slump. "I couldn't sleep," he said, "but I'm not tired; I'll be alright."

Charlie raised himself out of bed, stretched, and glanced at the scratch in the mantle. Holding one hand against his right eye, he said through another yawn, "You didn't stay up all night, did you? Remember that time when you —"

"I said I'm fine, see...." Tergiver stood up straight and the quill fell unnoticed to the floor. A wash of light hit Charlie in the face as Tergiver stepped away from the window. Tergiver pulled the chair away from the table and sat down to lace his boots. "I'm going to run out and see if the gates are open yet; about an hour ago there were a lot of people moving on the walls."

"You were outside an hour ago?" asked Charlie, "It must have been freezing."

Tergiver finished lacing his boots and replied with an edge, "I said I couldn't sleep." He pulled his torn woolen mantle from a hook and walked out into the blue morning, sending a puff of chilly air into the room behind him. Charlie watched his form vanish across the still-whitening, frosty window. Tergiver had not slept for two days.

Charlie dressed himself and ate a piece of bread from his pack. He folded his clothes carefully and placed them in the corner. Then he made his bed and walked to the window. He gathered Tergiver's pages into a stack without reading them, and blew out the candle, which was burning low and close to the table surface. Then he picked up Tergiver's quill from the floor, put it into the ink bottle, and glanced out the window.

Ten minutes later, Tergiver appeared hastily in the doorway. He found Charlie practicing a defensive thrust, calm and shadowless by the cold fireplace. "Charlie, let's go! The gates have been open for a while and people are already going in! Throw me my sword — No! Bring it!"

Charlie smiled warmly and pointed with his own sword to Tergiver's, which was older, slightly rusted, and leaning against the chipped doorframe. "You should go on to the gate; I'll be there after I lock up." Charlie moved slowly to find his shoes. Tergiver agreed impatiently and ran off. Glancing around the room one last time, Charlie pulled a small bag of coins from his pocket and placed it on the table beside a carefully written note:

> We are sorry about the door
> — and the scratch on the mantle.

Turning right out of the door, Charlie crunched across the frost-covered grass and saw a long, distant line of wooden carts piled high with fruits, clothes, barrels, and bags stuffed with all sorts of merchandise to be sold at the festival. The line ran westward for a hundred yards, curving past tall oaks, and thinning as it rose over a massive wooden bridge in the distance. When he reached the elm at the building's edge, he turned the corner and saw the line curve directly to the West Gate, where it waited patiently between the towers. Men and dogs scrambled about the motionless line of carts as Charlie approached the massive black wall in the morning chill, wrapping his brown mantle around his shoulders for warmth. He passed several groups of men his age, and they cheered and wished him good luck. Before the gate he saw ten guards in red cloaks checking carts and conversing with everyone who entered. The iron gates hung tight and high above them, creating a hard mesh curtain in front of the stone bridge, which arched up and over the gate. The day dawned quickly, and the crowd was eager and talkative. Tergiver was not in sight. Charlie waited for a moment and decided that Tergiver had probably already entered. He walked toward the gate until a hand grabbed his shoulder from the crowd. He turned to find Tergiver inspired.

He had obviously been running, and he said between large breaths, "The South Gate, The Great Gate, today we have to enter, through there!"

Charlie glanced incredulously at the massive West Gate before them, then looked back at Tergiver.

Tergiver's lack of sleep showed in his reaction. His body felt hot and hollow, and even against the chill he felt a twinge of fever pass through his forehead, "Do it, Charlie!" he growled, "It's the last day!" He grabbed at Charlie's arm, then immediately let go and apologized. "I'm sorry. Come on, let's go through the South Gate, it would be grand; we'll never get to do today over again."

Charlie watched his friend's mind fluctuate, in a single moment, from hurried excitement, to anger, to self-abasement, then back to excitement again. He did not respond, but watched to see what Tergiver would do next. Tergiver paused, pleaded briefly with his eyes, and then turned and ran along the wall toward the South Gate. Charlie stood still as the churning crowd rambled around him, then he ran to catch up.

Tergiver arrived breathless at the entrance to the southern gate. Charlie caught up quickly, and they walked together to the front of the line where a short, stodgy guard greeted them. "Good morning, gentlemen, and good luck today. Perhaps we will see one of you in our ranks come this evening, perhaps both."

Tergiver's eyes shone proudly as he stiffened his gait and marched past the guard into the city. The Great South Gate was structurally the same as the others, but its wide opening framed a majestic scene. The castle rose into center view over their heads, pitched against the high black cliff, which poured out streams of gold in the rising sun. Tergiver and Charlie emerged from the gate and began to walk along the wide path of elegant green marble that ran all the way to the trimmed castle lawn. The entire path was guarded on both sides by the skeletons of magnificent Dogwood trees, whose rich, red leaves had dropped and scattered to form a swirling maroon carpet on the ground below. Stopping on the path, Tergiver breathed deeply. The air filled his tired body with a pleasant chill, and he felt the light breeze scattering the fallen leaves across his shoes.

Then they walked slowly, watching every movement of the crowd: the great number of brawny, mustached men setting tentpoles in the ground, the women bustling about the morning marketplace with baskets, the jumping and running of chickens and children, and the stamp and smell of livestock driven from place to place by muddy farmhands with well-worn ropes and sharp sticks. High in the distance, large reddish birds soared in the cold air and scanned the ground for prey.

The annual King's Tournament was the centerpiece of a grand festival that lasted three days. Each day, the city filled with travelers, merchants, dignitaries, and peasants — the rich and poor from every kingdom within forty miles of Mure Castle. Most people came from towns within the kingdom of Murmilan itself, or from the city of Talus, which sat just across The Silver Channel, a narrow body of water that marked Murmilan's eastern border.

The noise of the crowd excited Tergiver's blood, and he sucked in a large breath of air and released it loudly. His face was tense, but his reddened eyes were full of promise. Charlie looked to him occasionally, happy simply because his friend was happy.

As they approached the castle lawn, they met a few of the young men who were to compete with them. Charlie and Tergiver said hello, and they boasted, laughed, and gibed each other, working out their nervousness as the crowd swelled around them. There were steep wooden stands on both sides of the sallow lawn, and they were filling quickly with families and spectators.

After an hour, when the sun had risen fully above the East Wall, a monstrous, bearded man in a red cloak marched out of the main entrance of the castle, flanked by two imposing guards. The figure's approach drew the young men into a fast line. His giant bald head reflected the sun, and the wrinkles on his forehead deepened as he counted the men. Finally, he said in a low voice that straightened the backs and shoulders of the entire group, "Follow me." The line broke into clumps that followed the three guards in reverent silence.

In a quiet, windowless stone room just off the Great Hall, thirty-two stiff wooden chairs faced the front. The shortest of the guards, though still larger than most of the young men in the room, closed the door. The shoulder of his cloak bore the crest of Murmilan, a powerful red kite, descending with wings and talons outstretched before a tricolored shield. The entire emblem was woven in silver. He walked to the front of the room, stood straight, and addressed the young men, "Welcome, gentlemen. My name is Herrick. I am the Captain of the King's Guard under Borleaf."

The hairs rose on Tergiver's arms, and he cast an excited look to Charlie, who was sitting peacefully, as if he were at home having dinner.

"As you may know, last night we said farewell to four members of our ranks. You may also know that our loss has become your opportunity. Your performance yesterday in the physical and mental trials has earned you a place here today, where you will again compete, and where you will again be judged. This afternoon we will choose the four of you most suited for our work. The rest will go on to the honorable service of your choosing in the King's Army or Navy, with a rank conferred to you at that time."

Charlie made a subtle smile as he imagined himself sailing away on one of the king's great ships. He knew, however, that Tergiver's only ambition was to wear a red cloak, and Charlie's smile leveled as he grew nervous for his friend.

Herrick continued, "Anson will give your instructions for today's trials. Listen carefully because he will not repeat himself." He motioned to the tall, blonde guard who nodded knowingly to the group, inspiring in them a quiet excitement and the confidence that he would lead them well. Then Herrick motioned to the larger, more imposing guard at the front, and then back to the group, "But first, you are honored today, as the retiring chief of The King's Royal Guard has come to address you. Give him a respectful audience. He is a great man; he has been my mentor and a noble friend."

He turned to the bald giant whose crest glimmered in woven gold in the corner, "Borleaf, sir?" The young men sat frozen in awe as he walked to the center of the room and began to speak.

"Agatha," said the king, "this is not something you may choose to give up."

Father and daughter stood in a many-windowed chamber high in the easternmost wing of the castle, holding still before a polished silver mirror that stretched to the ceiling. The bright sun lit every corner of the room, while the queen rested heavily in a nearby chair, falling in and out of sleep. Servants busied themselves about the family, fussing over their clothes, hair, and crowns in preparation for the royal appearance on the gallery.

Agatha's face was sour in the mirror. Her thin, circlet crown sat crooked on her head, and her lips puffed outwards in restrained anger. Her fingers tugged gently at her thin, ruby necklace. "If it is mine, I should be able to rid myself of it, like a scarf that itches me; I should be able to cast it off; I don't want it!" She moved her arms stiffly to her side to avoid the poking pins of a seamstress.

Her father replied in a grave, loving voice, turning his head to look on her, "Do you love me, Agatha?"

Her eyes grew larger and rounder at the question and she lifted her eyebrows in a plaintive expression, "Of course! You know I do; why would you ask that?"

"I ask because I would know if your love is something that I, though I would never wish to, might cast off from myself, finding it inconvenient, or contrary to my purposes?" He held his eyes on her, awaiting her reply.

The princess shifted her head on her shoulders and sighed loudly before reciting a thought she had rehearsed in private that morning. "That is unspeakable, for my love is not to be given or taken away by anyone but me," then her voice carried a pinch of bitterness, "though by certain arrangements some still try to coerce or bury it."

The king looked forward at Agatha in the mirror and said, "Whether you want to accept the people outside matters not to them. They love you as their princess. They also know that to me, you must be daughter and son. Therefore, they have planted seeds of love for you as their future queen as well. Even if that love is contrary to your young purpose, you should be assured that it is the stronger and more important of the two. When you have a child, perhaps, you will understand that sometimes your loyalty to others must come before your own desires. But, my daughter, it would benefit you to understand it now." A brief shade of sadness fell across his face and hung there for a moment; but it dissolved quickly and he regained his commanding, noble countenance.

Agatha had looked away. Her face reddened, and she eagerly wanted to kick away the woman kneeling at the hem of her dress. She had been stirred hot by the word "young." She turned away from the woman with a dramatic fling of her hair and said, "Is something labored in the heart for so many months still young to you? This is not just a passing want of youth; it is serious." She turned to look at her mother, who was asleep and drooling on a white, ermine-lined robe. "But what would you know of it, being so burdened with her? Surely it wasn't out of love that you chose her. No," she paused to recover her affect, "you must have cared little for love, and for yourself, probably taking her for some worthless alliance or petty gain, of which I know not."

The king's eyes grew furious as he turned to his daughter, and yet his voice was steady, "Your life, which you so despise, was gained by it. So too was established a greater security and peace for your people, upon whom you now pour that same contempt with which you trample the honor of your own mother."

Agatha stood speechless as the queen snapped awake and began smiling at everyone in the room.

The general din of the crowd outside crept up and over the windows sills and entered nervously to chatter and gossip in corners of the room. The king stood pensively in the mirror, looking at himself, and then at Agatha. His expression cleared as if he had reached a silent conclusion, and he said, "May I ask you a few questions, Agatha?"

Though he did not have to, he waited courteously for her reply, and she nodded in acceptance.

"Do you understand that with their love, our people have expectations as well?"

She nodded again.

"Ours is a proud kingdom, and its people demand royalty and wisdom from their family, or else they would rule themselves. Agatha, do you also understand that if it became possible for you to pursue this man, you would necessarily strip both him and yourself of all rank and royal dignity, and lose your people's love?"

She made an inscrutable expression that seemed to end in a look of fearful uncertainty, so the king continued, "Such a union would be without the consent of the people, whose needs must be considered first. There could be no other way."

Agatha stepped away from those attending her and slumped in a purple velvet chair, looking hurt. To her, the words sounded like a threat. Her father knelt beside her and said softly, "Let us both lend greater consideration to these things, for our actions affect thousands beyond ourselves, and neither of us should rush our judgments. Will you be satisfied with this for now?"

Agatha stared at her own scowl in the silver mirror, which distorted it into an expression that made her feel uncomfortable. Then she examined her father's face briefly before looking away, "For now."

"Very well," said the king, noticing new movement in the mirror. "Now let us do our duty."

The attendants left, having finished their work, and Marscion entered the room in his white councilor's robe. He bowed and smiled heartily at Agatha in the mirror, but his face wilted as he caught her expression. Composing himself, he paused, letting the growing swell of the crowd in the windows introduce his thoughts. "Sire, the people are hungry for your appearance. If it would please you, Queen Rose, Princess Agatha, let us go at once to the gallery."

King Wiston held out a hand to his daughter, who raised herself using the arms of her chair and walked ahead to wait in the hall. Then he gently woke his queen, who had nodded to sleep again, and helped her to her feet. To Agatha, the short walk to the gallery seemed to last for hours. She looked ahead constantly, searching among the heads of council members and ranking guards, but she did not see Herrick.

The broad commotion from below smashed like surf up the castle walls and pitched to a thunderous level, seeming to rumble the heavy chairs in the gallery across its marble floor. Marscion emerged first and saluted the cheering crowd, which filled the stands and overflowed into every corner and crack of the near city. He saw in the distant lake several makeshift rafts, upon which spectators balanced and yelled excitedly. The wide lawn of yellow grass in front of the castle and directly below the gallery was clear and empty in preparation for the final stages of the tournament. Next, a few of Marscion's fellow council members came out into the sunshine, followed by several high-ranking officers of the King's Army, Navy, and Guard. Then, as Agatha stepped onto the platform, the people raised a roaring cheer. She shrank from it, remembering: *"This is not something you may choose to give up."*

The noise was even greater as the king of Murmilan stepped forward onto the platform and waved to the people with grand, stately gestures. He answered their love with his own, and they considered him the embodiment of honor, courage, strength, and wisdom. As the hurricane of voices reached its peak, King Wiston raised a hand, and one by one the people fell silent, until it seemed there was not a man or woman's voice to be heard whispering in all of Murmilan. The king stepped forward to the marble railing and looked across his city, silent within its wide belt of high black stone. Then, as everyone in the crowd held their breath, he stretched out his arms and bellowed in a deep, stentorian roar, "Let us begin!"

The crowd resumed its pitch immediately, and more than one spectator slipped excitedly from his raft into the lake. From a wide door below, a blare of horns shrieked across the cool air. The thirty-two young men, led by Borleaf, Herrick, and other red-cloaked Guard Members, took to the field and stood in a tight formation before the deafening stands. After a brief instruction from the guards, the men split into groups and took their positions.

Throughout the many events, the crowd cheered for its favorites, applauding scores and cleverness, and reacting in collective anguish and disapproval to mistakes and misses. For the whole of the morning, the men took turns riding, shooting, and solving problems before the crowd and the king, burning all the while to impress those who would decide their lifelong positions at the end of the day.

The sun had risen to its zenith and shone brightly on the field. The sky was a deep, cloudless blue. As the last round of archery ended and the group returned to the center of the lawn, the noise of the crowd rumbled within the walls and seemed to hang and crash over the field. The last and most popular event was about to begin — the rounds of individual combat, which would give them one champion to celebrate above the rest.

4

Sinking petals

Charlie and Tergiver shifted their feet on the yellowed grass of the lawn, rubbing their hands together to keep warm. They waited for instructions from a new guard who had just appeared out of the castle to roaring cheers. He moved with a quiet, serious demeanor that gave him an air of unquestionable authority. Before the man had quite reached the lawn, Charlie leaned over to Tergiver and whispered, "That's Baelin. My father says he's good friends with Herrick, and one of the best guards we have — he won this tournament when he was only sixteen."

Tergiver straightened his shoulders.

Baelin stepped close to the group and instructed them, raising his voice over the noise of the crowd, amplifying his already authoritative presence. "You will remain together here until summoned. I will call two men at a time. When you come forward, take up a saber from the table and stand opposite your opponent until I command you to begin. Now, listen carefully," he paced back and forth in front of them, seeming to search their faces for intent, "Your object is to score one touch or to dislodge your opponent's saber while retaining your own. When this is done, the first portion of the fight is over. Are there any questions?"

There were none.

Unintelligible chants soared from raucous sections of the crowd.

"For the second and third parts, you will grapple with your opponent, and a pin of both shoulders to the ground will count as a score. Any combination of two scores will end the match, and the loser will retire immediately to this section of the field." He pointed to an area of the grass near the stands, which was sectioned off with a long brown rope. "The winner of the match will proceed to this section," and he pointed to a similarly marked area to his left. "There are thirty-two of you, which means the champion among you will have to defeat five men. You should sit; you will need your strength. Wait here until I call."

Baelin walked away from the young men, who sat down on the grass under the high midday sun. Charlie leaned back on his elbows and smiled at Tergiver, who was nervous. Baelin stood twenty paces away, behind a table that held two blunt sabers. He saluted to Herrick and Borleaf, who were now seated among dignitaries and nobles on the side of the field. Then he saluted high to the king in the gallery, and turned to face the participants. He paused, imbuing the crowd with an excitement that tore through the stands and brought everyone to their feet. The combatants felt their hearts pulsing wildly. Baelin shouted in a clear voice that carried under the crowd to reach them, "Perren! Charlie! Approach!"

Charlie sprang to his feet and walked quickly to the table. His opponent was taller than he, a wiry young man with long brown hair. Under Baelin's direction, they took up their sabers and began. Perren leapt straight at Charlie with a running attack. Charlie parried lightly, spun to the side, and scored a touch on a quick riposte to Perren's outstretched arm. The crowd shouted their approval as Baelin stepped between them, recovered their weapons, and bade them begin again. Charlie had noted Perren's excellence in the other events, but as he dodged another hasty, miscalculated onrush, he could tell that his opponent had never had a training partner. Charlie swung fast about his back, carrying Perren's right arm in tow, and he turned him lightly across his leg to execute a quick, elegant pin.

Baelin shouted sternly, "Match!"

Charlie helped Perren to his feet, saying, "Final thirty-two, Perren, you still did great. Wish me luck." Perren, who was embarrassed and fighting tears, did wish him luck and walked to the loser's area with his head lowered. Charlie walked humbly to the winner's spot and sat down in the thick air of cheers and applause. He saw his father, Robert, standing among the other councilors and dignitaries, smiling and pointing proudly to his son. Charlie could hardly feel the ground under him and he missed the next two names, only noticing that they had started when their sabers clashed together with a loud clink.

Tergiver paced impatiently as his name was passed over repeatedly. After a long while it was apparent that he and Bronston would be the last to fight in the first round. The loser's section had grown more content and upbeat with each addition, and now it formed a boisterous cheering section. When Charlie had trod alone into the winner's section after the first match, Tergiver had watched with envy, and even though the loser's spot was now lively — even joyous, he began to loathe it, feeling that it was now somehow watching him out of the corner of a sinister, odious eye. He stared at it and felt his stomach sour.

Baelin called, "Tergiver! Bronston! Approach!"

To the amusement of the crowd, Tergiver ran to the table. He had been standing since Charlie had won his match, and though his nose and face were cold, his legs were shaky and hot. Tergiver rotated the saber back and forth eagerly as he waited for Baelin's signal, and Bronston stared menacingly at Tergiver through deep hazel eyes, flexing his heavy arms in intimidation. The order was given, and the two, having studied the others, began circling defensively. Then Tergiver struck with a combination that would have cost Bronston a quick score had he not retreated carefully. After a bit of rumbling from the crowd, the two came together again in a series of close, vicious strikes. Tergiver was the stronger. As their sabers clashed once near the hilts, Tergiver followed through with a forceful stroke that ripped Bronston's saber from his hand and sent it flailing into the air to eventually scatter a group of onlookers at the edge of the field.

In the second part of the match, a surge of energy and fear coiled in Tergiver's arms as he grappled with his brutish opponent, who was fiercer for having gone down a score. Again, Tergiver prevailed, wrenching Bronston sideways with a brutal twist of his wrist and hammering him into the ground. The crowd applauded and sent tiny scraps of paper into the air to mingle with the drifting leaves. The first round had ended.

The loser's section welcomed Bronston, who tenderly nursed one of the arms he had flexed at Tergiver. There were sixteen left. Tergiver joined Charlie, who patted him on the back and commended his hard fight. Tergiver did not give any response, but sat, breathing heavy and staring at the table intently as one who had narrowly escaped death and turned to reflect on the scene.

Baelin immediately called forth two combatants to begin the next round, "Charlie! Tergiver! Approach!"

The applause and cheers that opened the second round were louder and more focused, as the crowd had attached itself to favorites. Charlie, having won the first match so quickly, had the loudest supporters. Before he could offer a hand to Tergiver, his friend had regained his feet and begun to walk slowly to his place at the table, still breathing heavy from his last fight. In his ready position he did not look at Charlie, but dared to do something none of the combatants had done; he looked Baelin in the eye. His anger at having been called so soon and without rest was chiseled in a minacious leer, to the astonishment of all who saw it. In the months to come, those guardsmen, including Baelin, who had seen Tergiver's face, remembered it well and afforded him respect or safe distance, whichever they felt more prudent at the time.

Charlie picked up his saber and stood opposite Tergiver with a half smile and eyebrows that rose as if he wanted to make a light joke. Instead he pointed his saber at Tergiver and said under shining eyes, "Alright, scourge … guard yourself!"

Baelin was as bewildered by this spontaneous show of bravado as he had been at Tergiver's brazenness. He stood bemused, assessing this strange pair for a moment, then shouted, "Begin!"

The sun glinted off their sabers as they immediately came together in familiar form, Charlie, with quick slices that Tergiver parried hard away, and Tergiver with weighty thrusts that always just missed their moving mark. Their fight went longer than any had gone in the first round. The crowd thrilled at the misses, bold parries, and skillful combinations that were countered perfectly, as if the entire fight had been scripted. Tergiver began to fatigue, and the lack of sleep crept warmly into his shaking limbs, making them heavier.

As the crowd again raised its collective voice to a roar, Charlie dropped to one knee and skillfully exploited Tergiver's attack, a move that earned him the score and a deep scratch that ran the length of his forearm.

The sound grew dim in Tergiver's ears. Though he felt it, he did not hear the score announced, and he barely heard Baelin's commands for them to part. His mind wavered in dizziness, rejecting the failure that darkened his periphery, but he still felt it shaking his arms and legs. He returned his saber to the table and turned to face the loser's section. Then he turned to look at Charlie and heard Baelin's voice, as if from far away, "Begin!"

It was not until Charlie took him gently by both shoulders, as if to wake him, that Tergiver regained his mind. Then suddenly he raged like a threatened boar and turned on Charlie with a violent show of strength, ripping him sideways over his leg and falling on top of him, driving him down into the lawn, hard on one shoulder. As Charlie inhaled deeply to regain his breath, Tergiver drove his elbow into the wounded shoulder, pinning Charlie to the turf in agony.

Then Tergiver backed away, desperate and anxious, his strength springing from deep reserves of fear: fear of losing, fear of shaming himself and his father, and a fear of disgrace at the condescending hands of privilege and wealth that Charlie had always represented.

Charlie got up as fast as he could, holding his shoulder, and as soon as Baelin sounded the command, Tergiver attacked again. Charlie dropped to a knee and tripped him, then jumped onto his back. Tergiver was still charged with fury, and Charlie found himself twisted as if he had been caught in a powerful, swelling wave, rolled and pinned again with Tergiver's bony knee in his chest.

Baelin cried "Match!" and separated the two with powerful arms.

Before Charlie was to his feet, Tergiver did something else no one had dared; he spoke directly to Baelin. With flared nostrils, he said between heavy, sweating, threatening breaths, "Call me again."

Charlie tried to clear his head as he walked to the loser's section, where several hands clapped him on the back. Perren, who appeared to have fully recovered from his own disappointment, embraced him. "That was a brilliant stop-thrust you pulled to score that first point!"

Charlie thanked him in a voice that sounded a bit fragile, but he soon recovered his strength. He requested a salve for his forearm, and sat down to cheer his friend.

Tergiver was not allowed the next match, and he brooded alone in the new winner's section — the original spot where the thirty-two had begun. In time, seven others joined him, and the third round began.

The crowd was in awe of Tergiver as he dismantled his next opponent, raging like a blinded animal, silent and without mercy. Then he dragged himself across the lawn to sit again, looking wearied and lifeless. The high sun had given the grass a dusty yellow hue, and in it Tergiver felt discolored and weak.

When only four combatants remained, Tergiver faced a muscular, large-boned boy named Peter, who scored a lucky hit with his saber as Tergiver slipped on a thin patch of grass that was worn smooth from the fighting. Tergiver's strength, however, was at its end. His body began to collapse from the lack of sleep, and his anger and fear could no longer sustain him. He made frustrated mistakes, and Peter caught him in a hold from which he was unable to escape. Soon after, Tergiver was out of the competition.

The crowd stood and rejoiced in Tergiver's performance, and his new peers quickly cleared a space for him at the front of their section. Even some members of the council rose to applaud him from the high gallery.

He spoke to no one. He stared forward in exhaustion. The noise faded in and out of his ears in quiet bursts, and as he nodded his sweat-soaked head down between his knees, his eyes fell shut, and he slept through the rest of the matches.

Tergiver awoke groggily to the feeling of Charlie pulling on his arm. He was still on the grass, surrounded by the other beaten contestants. Peter sat in front of him. Tergiver leaned to one side and saw Baelin turned toward the king, holding high the arm of the champion, a dark, broad-shouldered peasant from the coastal town of Tholepin Bay, which was five miles northwest of the city. The champion stood exhausted, sweaty, and scraped, but his light amber eyes beamed in the afternoon sun and he could not stop smiling. Baelin turned him to the guards and dignitaries and then to the crowd, who collected all the noise they had left and spent it on one last roar. The crowd then spread out from the stands, some crossing the field to speak to the young men, some to form lines for food, and some to explore the shops and carts scattered about the west buildings. Still, no one went far, as the final announcements were pending. On a signal from King Wiston, Borleaf, Herrick, Marscion, and several high-ranking figures retired to select the four young men who would have the privilege of wearing the red cloak of the King's Guard.

Robert had been the first to spring from his cushioned seat. He jogged quickly across the field to embrace his son. He and Charlie recounted in detail his first, quick fight, and then they recounted the hard match with Tergiver with just as much pleasure. Robert pulled his white robe away from the grass and knelt beside Tergiver, offering to pull him up.

Tergiver stood on his own, silent and aloof, pondering the decision that was being made somewhere in the castle.

Robert held him by the shoulder and smiled with large eyes, "Tergiver, your father, were he here, would be so proud of you — the top four!" Robert mussed Tergiver's hair as if he were his own son. "Charlie tells me you were not even close to your top form. Well done, my boy, well done! I don't mind telling you that I put in the strongest recommendation I could for your appointment to the Guard, but I'm proud of you no matter what."

Charlie stood beside him and tried to offer encouraging words. "You made it to the top four you know, and you've done well in everything else, both yesterday and today, I think you have a good chance. There are four spots."

Tergiver still said nothing, but stared at the door from which the verdict would come, as if it took all the strength he had to remain on his feet.

Half an hour passed, during which a swarm of workers erected a wooden platform on the lawn. They set it at an angle so it would face the west stands as well as the high gallery. The sun began to lean toward the west, and short black shadows crept hesitantly from under the stands.

Finally, a door opened and Borleaf, Herrick, Baelin, and Marscion, emerged from the castle, followed by two more guards. The four men stepped onto the new platform and took their seats. The crowd settled anxiously.

Marscion stood and came forward to the edge of the platform. The people cheered in anticipation, and after letting the excitement swell, Marcion raised his hand to silence them. "Good people," he began, "today you have witnessed the determination and talent of the finest young men born of this great kingdom of Murmilan." The crowd agreed loudly with applause and shouts. "The participants in this year's tournament will approach the platform, and face their king." The group did as commanded, leaving their families and friends, and lining up before the platform. "As it pleases your highness, these men before you shall have their pick of service to you, with honors and offices awarded to them in either your far-reaching navy, or your mighty ground forces, O King."

King Wiston stood tall and gave a brief, loving look to his

daughter before proclaiming to the joy of the crowd, "So be it." Charlie's eyes were giddy and he laughed in happiness. Tergiver's were iron.

Marscion continued, "Today we also honor four members of this excellent group, that they might join your Royal Guard, to protect you and this, your great city." A sound like a proud wave surged excitedly from the citizens of the city. Marscion waited for it to subside then said, "I ask the noble Borleaf to come forward and bestow this honor on the men we have chosen."

Borleaf strode to the front of the platform as Marscion sat down and folded his white robe over his legs. He commanded the young men to face him, and they turned, obeying him absolutely. He wasted no time, and spoke the names everyone waited eagerly to hear, "Michael from Tholepin Bay, come, if you would serve the king." The champion came forward, eager and lit with pride, and stood in awe of Borleaf, whose mouth turned up slightly into the edges of a warm, welcoming grin. The crowd cheered and sang Michael's name for those who had not heard, celebrating it all across the city. Tergiver's heart raced as Borleaf announced the next name, "Oneas from Murmilan, come if you would serve the king." The face of his father was prominent in his mind, and he found he could not breathe as the next name was called, and it was not his, "Peter from Eastport ..." Applause came heavy and surrounded the platform. Then, streamers of bright ribbon dropped from castle windows as Borleaf called the last and final name, sending the crowd into a furor and officially ending the tournament, "Talias from Tholepin Bay, come if you would serve the king."

An hour after the last name had been called and the new guards taken to their celebration, after the crowd had dispersed and the cleaning begun, Tergiver picked up his feet and walked despondent, numb, and alone across the rough dirt road that ran between the Pine Wood and the lake. The East Gate was open, and he lumbered through it, out of the city.

Agatha sat disconsolate in her chamber, resting her head in her hands. She was high in the east side of the castle, and the weakening afternoon light shone in four bright windows that overlooked the Pine Wood and the East Wall. Her chamber was dressed in rich reds and golds, and the floor was of polished white stone. A row of lighted candles wrapped its way around the entirety of the chamber walls.

At her feet lay three silk dresses, and she sat despising them all. Her hair curled around her fingers in lazy spirals as she ran her nails upward over her forehead. There was a knock at the door and she ignored it. It came again and she bellowed, "What?"

Marscion opened the door cautiously and beheld her. He spoke in his characteristically low, formal voice, "I have come to review your duties for tonight's ceremony; may I enter?"

The princess sighed and her hand dropped to her side lethargically, letting her hair fill half of her face, "Sure."

Marscion closed the door behind him and walked carefully over an embroidered green rug to take a chair from the desk and sit across from Agatha.

"You should know that your part in the ceremony bestows a great honor on the new soldiers."

Ignoring his words, she pulled her hair away from her face and looked up at him with angry eyes, "Is it right or fair that some people have such control over the lives of others? Is there one thing I can choose for myself?"

Marscion answered thoughtfully, but there was a tired edge to his voice, as if he had been forced to recite his answer a thousand times before, in a thousand other kingdoms, to a thousand other sad princesses with the same complaint. "Agatha, they will never control your courage or your honor, those are yours. Nor can they give you any great happiness, or take it away, unless you let them. Your people are an inexorable entity, and you may choose to hate or love them, that is up to you. However, you cannot make them disappear, nor can you change the rules which have governed their whims and every kingdom since time began." In these last words, more than the others, his tone disintegrated into an air of affected rote.

Then he waited for Agatha to begin working their conversation in a certain direction, and she unknowingly complied. "So," she said, "is Borleaf giving out cloaks to the new Reds in the ceremony, or is he passing that duty on to someone else?"

Marscion ignored the question, which he knew to be a pretense. He raised his eyebrows in small surprise that Agatha had introduced the subject so soon, and though it displeased her, he moved ahead to the end of the conversation she was trying to begin. "If you would accept my counsel, look beyond Herrick. I was, of course, referring to him when I mentioned the rules that govern us, but there is more that you should know. Herrick is … peculiar, and in my opinion, unstable — and this is only the first reason."

Agatha reacted with mild shock, as if her innocent question had been twisted unfairly. She knew, however, that Marscion would not be fooled, and she wanted to hear more about Herrick. "What are your other reasons, Marscion?" she said flatly.

He continued the bored tone with which he had concluded his first statement. "Let me address the first and obvious question. Though Herrick and his father arrived before me in this kingdom, I have ascertained enough pieces of his history to assure you that there is no hidden virtue or pedigree in his veins. You will be disappointed if you entertain any such simple, degrading peasant fantasies, for you have already achieved everything to which they aspire. You, Agatha, deserve a much richer story." Then Marscion began to break from his normally careful patterns of speech, as if he felt a great personal importance in expounding on the subject. "No, while Herrick has indeed elevated himself to a high rank, he is honored by that rank alone, to be quite sure. Furthermore, if we examine his behavior, we find that he holds meetings with lower guardsmen in the middle of the night, he is found in odd places at unreasonable hours, and he wastes your father's resources on pointless, secretive excursions. I tell you, the man has something to hide, Agatha, but much worse, he is often insolent to the king, your father, for I can see the great consternation that Herrick causes him."

"That is not true!" cried Agatha, "Herrick loves my father and he is loved in return. He serves him well and even better, I think, than Borleaf. You should not forget that he now protects this entire castle and you with it."

Marscion did not acquiesce under the pressure, but challenged her, "Then, highness, what do you make of his attitude toward you? Does he return your obvious affection, or do we all watch him spurn you? Before you welcome an animal not fit for a royal table, you might learn first whether he would even come." Agatha buckled, but allowed Marscion to continue. "Because your sovereignty and virtue compels me, I will tell you something that has concerned me in the past, but now concerns me even more as Herrick takes full control of The Guard. Many of his own men, and the majority of the council, do not trust him."

Agatha's unrepentant glare created fear in Marscion's eyes.

"Now you lie. I know you are the only one who did not openly welcome his promotion — and you are not to refer to the captain as an animal!"

Marscion recovered quickly, fearing that she might command him to leave before he could repair the damage he had done. He assumed a conciliatory posture, and said with affected humility, as he was accustomed, "It is very much my own opinion I admit, but even if we agree that he is a loyal man, you are still too noble, too good, high-blooded, and beautiful to be a match for him. I believe he knows that, and that is why he treats you as he does. He may also know that things often go poorly for young men who court the daughters of royalty." Agatha's stern expression weakened at this.

Then Marscion looked upwards as if he were wrestling with a difficult decision, then said softly, "I will tell you a secret now in the hope that I may regain your love and confidence. Know that I only speak freely with you about Herrick because your father has employed my counsel on the subject. He is a wise and strong-willed man, your father, and we have disagreed on many points; however, I believe that in this situation he has decided wisely, both for your good and for that of the kingdom. I should not tell you this, and I trust you will keep it to yourself, but your father has ordered a royal schooner, *The Dolphin*, to be prepared in the royal anchorage at Tholepin Bay. It is to carry an envoy to your mother's home across the North Sea. Now, I know that land to have several princes of distant but relevant relation, all noble and suitable matches for you. Of course, no one will force anything on you, but my hope is that you would consider first the diamonds you have not seen, before settling on the poor bronze that presents itself to you in the moment. Please remember that you must not tell anyone of this, for he has not given us any details — and much less has he given his leave for me to tell you. The purpose of this vessel is indeed my conjecture, but princess, it is plain under these difficult circumstances. I can tell you with certainty that it stands ready even as we speak, and it leaves in three days."

Marscion knew better than to touch her shoulder or arm, so instead he leaned as close as he dared, and said, "Agatha, please take this as a sign of his love. He does not want you to throw off your royalty in a youthful mistake, nor have to live your life regretfully deprived of the important honor you received at birth. There could be nothing worse."

They sat together in silence for several minutes as Agatha watched a series of birds alight on the long ledge outside her closed windows and chirp mutely against the glass. Marscion concluded by offering his advice again, still in an understanding, fatherly tone, "Try to think on him no longer. You are noble-hearted, and though it will be difficult at first, I know you will be able to bear it."

Agatha discovered that as long as her grief was visible to Marscion, he would continue to give her advice that she did not want. In the hope of making him leave, she sighed resolutely and nodded her head in agreement. Then she thanked him for his confidence, assured him that she would tell no one of the ship, and requested that he leave her, as she wanted to have a walk in the garden alone before the banquet.

Marscion suddenly remembered his original duty and said in a tone that strove to reinstate his usual attitude of attendant objectivity, "Of course, but first I should review your duties for tonight, highness."

"Marscion, I have done this for as long as I can remember; if there is nothing new, I would like to be left alone now."

Princess Agatha maundered sadly down the east arcaded walk, staring at the dark rock face before her. Halfway down the path she leaned against one of the stone arches and gazed across the wide, back lawn, on which sat the four odd-shaped statues. This lawn, called The Queen's Shadow Garden, consisted of four works of stone and glass, which, according to the height and position of the sun, produced distinct images on the manicured lawn below. The day had been steadily fading and the sun leaned hard and yellow to the west. On the grass below the nearest statue, the shadow-shape of an ascending kite stretched its long wings, reaching farther eastward as the day grew old. When the sun had risen that morning, the same sculpture had cast the shadow of a pointed crown on the other side of the lawn. Agatha held her eyes lazily on this sculpture, beholding the black wings that were reaching ever closer, moving slowly and threatening to pin her where she stood.

    She left the melancholy arch and ambled down the walk toward the pavilion, which stood surrounded by the sparkling, thunderous pool. Carpets of fine moss covered the ground that stretched from the end of the walk to the black cliff, skirting the lively pool in bright green. On each side of the pavilion, crawling pink rosebushes wound tight around the marble columns that supported its roof. Agatha broke off a stem and walked absently forward to the edge of the platform where the smooth grey marble met the circular pool of the same color at her feet. A few yards away from the cliff, hundreds of gallons of water plunged deep into the pool, raising sparkling foam that chased itself through thin rainbows that hung perpetually in the air.

    The spray rose up to meet her from the water and it was cool on her face. Agatha did not look up at the falls, yet she felt crushed beneath their driving force and noise. She did not look at the cliff that climbed to the sky above her, but still she felt hemmed in by it. Beset by stone on all sides, she leaned against a wide marble column and began to pick the petals from the rose stem, dropping them and watching them fall, twisting into the bouncing ripples of the deep grey pool, where they undulated on the tiny, harsh waves before disappearing under the floor at her feet to be carried away in darkness.

When the stem was thorny and barren, she dropped it too, and watched it sink away into shadow. Agatha stood long, watching her face and the colors of her dress swerve on the surface of the water; then she turned away and wandered back inside.

By the time she reached her chamber, children were discovering tiny pink petals surfacing in the lake where they splashed and played.

5

WALLS THAT WHISPER TERROR TO ONE, HOPE TO ANOTHER

Robert and Charlie walked proudly through a long, narrow hallway that ran west to east through the length of the castle. The walls were adorned with rows of tall, elaborate paintings of councilors and diplomats in scenes of noble service. These were interrupted by a regular pattern of torches and thin wooden doors that marked the councilors' private offices. The middle point of the hallway, from which Robert and Charlie had emerged, opened on one side into a modest overlook that spilled grand, curving staircases down each side of the Great Hall, which was swirling below in colors, music, and celebration. This upper floor, however, was devoted to the solemn business of running the kingdom, and it was now almost deserted.

Robert draped his arm around his son's shoulder and introduced him to two councilors who were headed for the Great Hall. The two men shook Charlie's hand vigorously and disappeared down one of the staircases, leaving the hallway quiet and still. Charlie had washed after the tournament and donned the clean grey shirt he was to wear at the ceremony that night.

On each extremity of the corridor, tall oaken doors showed wide, austere faces. Both were closed and locked tight.

"Have you seen Tergiver since he left today?" Robert asked.

"He didn't want to talk to anyone. It'll take him a while to accept what happened."

Robert's office was a hundred paces to the right of the stairs, in the eastern wing. He unlocked the modest door, and they entered the small, dark, windowless room that sat in the heart of the building. He lit a bright row of red candles that were arranged against the inside wall between two bookcases, and then he and his son sat down across from each other at the desk.

Robert's eyes gleamed subtly. "I suppose this means that you will soon be off to sail the world? Well, you know I will miss you. Let us spend the next few days together, for after that time you will have to attend your duty." He paused, then said, "You are all I have left, Charlie, and you make me so proud ... your mother ..." His face wavered under his white hair, and he smiled, knowing he would not be able to finish the sentence, and that he didn't have to.

Charlie rose and wrapped an arm around his father's shoulders.

The old man cleared his throat and said, "Well, we have a few hours before everything begins in earnest. I should spend some time speaking with these emissaries that have come from so far to enjoy our festivities." Then his expression changed slightly, and he pulled Charlie gently to one side so he could see his face better in the light. "I wanted to tell you though, now, before you go away, that everything I have, son, you should consider yours. Whenever you decide to return from your service, I would have you consider all of our land and riches your own, to manage as you please. Study well on your journeys, for when you return I will be even older, and you will be the more capable of us."

Charlie stood humbled, affected by his father's generosity and tenderness.

Then Robert smiled deeply at him and said, "Here are the keys to this office and to my quarters downstairs if you wish to have a place to rest or get away from the crowd later. I, unfortunately, cannot share in that luxury." He put his hand on the back of Charlie's head and said, "I love you, son. Today you have made me very proud." Then he walked to the door and pulled it against the lock, leaving it cracked behind him.

Charlie sat against the wall of his father's chamber for some time, watching the long row of candles burn with high flames. He pondered what he might do when one day he returned to take control of the family's land, and he knew immediately the first act he would perform. Even before he sailed away, he would ask that the small number of acres worked by Tergiver and his father Jerrand be increased and given them to own permanently. He would ask that they be freed from all tributes or percentages owed to Robert's house.

He had been staring absently at the candles, lost in his imagination, in which he gave Tergiver the good news and made him forget about not making the King's Guard. When he came to himself, still staring in the direction of the candles, he noticed something odd about them.

The flames seemed to be pulled upwards toward the ceiling with more force than could be attributed to the fire itself. This puzzled him, and he watched longer, contemplating the flames and briefly forgetting everything else in that semi-darkness. He moved curiously to the door, closed it, and knelt down. He felt a slight but steady flow of air sliding under the tiny space between the door and the rug below it. Then he opened the door and walked into the hallway.

It was now completely silent. Save the figures in the paintings, there was no one in sight. As far as he could see, all the other doors were closed. He returned to the office and closed the door softly, feeling the gentle and almost imperceptible inward pull as the latch clicked.

Charlie's curiosity grew greater with every moment. He pulled the brightest candle from the row and held it high over his head.

He saw no holes in the ornate ceiling, and the stone wall looked solid. After a moment, however, he noticed a spot at the top of the inside wall, where it joined the ceiling. There the shadows from the candle bent oddly. He pulled the chair from his father's desk and set it against a tall bookshelf. Soon he was sitting on top of it, smiling and satisfied. He had solved the mystery.

Between the ceiling and the grey stone wall was a tiny open crevice that ran horizontally for a space, hidden from view. Charlie held his candle to it and watched as the wisps of smoke fled quickly into the cracks. He lifted his eyes to see inside the space, but the tiny corridor was dark. He smiled wide, having never before considered why the castle didn't fill up with the smoke from so many torches. Then, as he lowered the candle and prepared to climb off the cabinet to go find Tergiver, he heard a faint noise through the crack, and it froze him in place. An airy swish of wind had drifted across the hollow beyond the crevice, but it had been punctuated clearly. Someone was whispering.

It was against Charlie's nature to spy; he held it to be dishonest, but he was enthralled with the sound and the mystery of voices in this dark place. He strained his ear hard against the crack, and discovered that he could understand each word perfectly. There were two distinct voices sending low whispers cleanly across the hollow channel, their words echoing and bending around corners, yet remaining intact.

"We see him weakening, do we not?" said the first voice.

Charlie strained with all his energy and sought hard against the darkness to be as silent and still as he could.

The second voice was hoarse and anxious, "Yes, he is folding too easily — we see his eyes and thoughts bending to places they should not go. His people will lose faith in him and they will not follow any longer. He is dangerous and blind! What to do? What to do?"

"He is hiding something, and when Borleaf steps down officially he may do something unpredictable that makes everything we've worked for irrelevant."

"Yes, he may! You must act!" The second voice paused and added cautiously, "To strike soon would increase our hope of saving the kingdom and ensure the stability of …"

The first voiced laughed in deep breaths that rushed through the space. Then it replied coolly, "Do not forget to whom you speak. You dare sell me the hopes of credulous peasants? Hope and stability indeed! You may lie to everyone else, but understand me: if you are equivocal with me again, if you lie to me or forget that I am your master in all things, I will know, and I will kill you before the next moon rises."

There was a long space of silence. Charlie had begun to sweat heavily, yet he dared not move to wipe his forehead. His heart thumped so hard in his chest that he feared it, more than his breathing, might give him away.

The second voice became obsequious and timid, whispering, "Forgive me, please." There was another silence, and the second voice collected itself and spoke again, "What shall we do then? Command me. What should I do?"

Charlie's eyes widened and his hands shook. His muscles were cramping from his awkward position on the cabinet, but he held fast.

"You will draw him out to the pavilion tonight, late, after everyone has gone to bed. There you will wait. We shall come to him in red, and he shall see before he dies that he is killed by his own men."

"Yes, I know how, I can do it! You will be pleased!" whispered the second voice in an excited, servile tone.

"Do you still believe you can take his place?" said the first.

"Only by your leave, of course, and with your guidance, I know never to act in this matter without your direction." Then the voice asked carefully, "Then tonight you will finally reveal yourself to me? You know I have waited so long."

The second whisperer and Charlie waited eagerly for the answer, but none came. It became clear to Charlie that he was alone with the second voice, and he felt a surge of pressure, as if he must speak to it, being the only one present, or flee. He left his perch with as little noise and movement as he could manage, forgetting the burning candle on the top of the bookshelf. He dropped to the floor and blew out the rest of the candles with shallow breaths. Then he nosed hesitantly out into the deserted hallway, then ran as hard as he could, beset and terrified by the many sets of painted eyes that watched his every step.

The dirt road that ran through the East Gate was long and continued for many miles until it reached the town of Eastport, which sat opposite Talus on the Silver Channel. Just outside the wall, however, it served as the lower boundary of a cemetery that lay dormant in the late afternoon sun. The cemetery stepped upward to the height of the castle cliff in wide, terraced levels cut deep into the escarpment that defined the city's northern edge. The lower levels contained straight rows of stubby headstones, and the middle levels were dotted with memorials and monuments. At the very top, a row of majestic granite statues stood proudly on the northern plain, overlooking the levels below.

Above, an armada of sharp clouds drifted toward the sunset, each one growing a darker shade of orange the farther it sailed.

In a wide, rocky ditch that ran down between the wall and the cemetery, Tergiver stood defiant in his filthy fighting clothes like a beaten slave before the house of his master. He had been there since he had left the tournament field, picking up large rocks and clods of dirt and hurling them with all of his diminished might to burst and split against the high East Wall. He was sitting with his arms hanging at his sides, gathering strength to begin again, when he spotted a familiar figure running toward him from the East Gate. He grasped another rock and stood up. Then he sent it crashing against the wall in demonstration, hoping to make his mood clear.

Charlie staggered toward him, his blue eyes wide and filled with alarm. Tergiver did not look at him, but raised another stone as Charlie caught his desperate, heaving breath. He threw it hard at the wall and turned his back to Charlie, "I don't want to talk about it; I'll see you tonight!"

"Tergiver!" said Charlie, his voice sounding constricted, "Listen to me! I think someone is going to murder Herrick."

Tergiver turned quickly, "What?"

Charlie began to ramble in his fright, gesturing with shaking arms. "I was in my father's chamber, I heard voices, they said to lure him out, and they would wear their red cloaks so he would know; they said that with Borleaf gone he will be able to do whatever he wants, that he would kill him, but then, he didn't know who he was, they hadn't met …"

Tergiver took him firmly by the shoulders and held him still. "Tell me slowly, and calm down." Charlie collapsed to the ground and sat on his knees. His nerves prevented him from speaking for a few minutes. When he finally did, Tergiver sat opposite him and listened carefully; he had forgotten his own grief in trying to settle his friend. Charlie started slowly, omitting the details of his discussion with Robert, and told his tale as best he could. When he was finished, Tergiver stood up and paced silently.

Charlie spoke more calmly than he had until that point, "We should go to someone in The Guard right away and warn them that he is in danger, right?"

Tergiver thought for a moment and then said, ignoring Charlie's question, "You are sure no one saw or heard you? No one knows you heard anything?"

"No one knows; I couldn't find my father and I didn't know what to do, so I came looking for you."

"Well, we cannot go to The Guard; that is for sure. You said yourself that his own men were doing this, didn't you?"

Charlie looked like he was too tired or nervous to think.

"What do you think would happen if we walked up to the conspirators and told them we knew of the plot? You said you didn't see them, and they whispered so you couldn't recognize their voices, which you probably wouldn't have known anyway."

"I know some of them. We should at least tell my father, or Marscion, no — the king! We should tell him, he will know what to do; my father says he is very wise." He spoke decisively, knowing his decision was unsound.

Tergiver answered quickly and passionately, hoping to persuade Charlie with careful inflections and smartly placed looks. "No, we can't tell anyone. Think! If we tell the king, or even Herrick himself, surely there will be some commotion made and the thing will get called off — if anyone believes us. Then where are we? Yes, we will have postponed the murder, for now, but do you think they will never carry it out? Do you think they won't be angry with us for having stalled them? Because of that, don't you think they would include us in any future plans? Do you understand this?" He grew more energetic as his mind churned the problem and looked for the best solution.

Charlie offered weakly, "We should at least write a note, it can be anonymous. We have to do something; we can't just let it go, Tergi — I can't."

Tergiver stopped pacing and knelt down quickly in front of Charlie, "Listen, a note is no-good because you don't even know if anyone will find it, or worse, who will see you drop it — think, Charlie! You just might deliver it personally into the hands of the assassin! No, this is what we will do...." Tergiver's eyes flashed as if he had received a great epiphany, and then he leaned forward slowly, still dirty and stained from the tournament, and conferred his new idea to Charlie with an ardent passion.

"We know where and when they plan to do it, we know who they plan to kill, and how many will be present, right? Charlie, what do you think would happen to me if I saved the life of Herrick, the new chief of the guard, and killed a pair of traitors in the act? This is my second chance! The killers won't know I'm there and the worst I can do is stick a few arrows in them from the shadows. They will never expect it! You and I will be heroes, Charlie; think of it! You know there's no other way. We've gone through every alternative. Maybe this was supposed to happen! If we had been together in the castle celebrating you would have never found out about this!" Tergiver stood quickly, and though he was visibly worn, his eyes shone with new hope.

Charlie had no mental strength left to combat Tergiver's persistence or to come up with a better approach. He reluctantly agreed to the plan, which Tergiver reviewed carefully, always stopping to make sure that Charlie was not wavering.

"Let's meet tonight; you know the shed that's just over the wall in the Pine Wood — the one with the well?"

"Of course," Charlie replied.

"Meet me behind the shed after the ceremony ends tonight. We should split up at the party and see if we notice anyone acting strange. But no matter what, do not mention this to anyone; you have to promise! Remember what we talked about; it is very important that we do it this way. I should clean up. Let's go."

Tergiver pulled Charlie to his feet. The sun began to fall in the west, pursued by the wide trail of steep orange clouds, and the air began to chill harshly as the two friends returned through the gate. Tergiver strode ready, with purpose and hope, while Charlie plodded along coldly, hounded by dread.

6

Exchanges

The evening banquet began after sunset in the same hall where Borleaf had been honored the night before. The royal family sat high upon the dais, on which was hung a felt tapestry of bright purple, embroidered with a gold kite. King Wiston's crimson robe drooped from the sides of his high seat and spread before him on the floor. The queen's eyes flickered around the room as usual, and one could find her clapping at random.

Agatha sat slouched in her seat, pulling distractedly at the folds of her long white dress so that it rose just above her thin, pale ankles. She sat as a portrait of melancholy, observing nothing, yet drawing everything in the room into herself. The king leaned toward her and whispered kindly in her ear, after which she sat straighter and more dignified, although anyone who knew her could have seen that it was a façade. Even so, the hundreds of lighted candles and the four great fires seemed to burn brighter as she did.

The king had said to her, "My daughter, this night is not for you or me; it is for these men who would give their lives for us. Honor them; be the Princess Agatha that will give them hope and strength in times of pain and trouble. Also be patient; I have not forgotten the matter we spoke of earlier today."

Agatha could only think of the secret ship he had prepared at Tholepin Bay. She had drawn herself up in the strength of her indignation, and this might have made her appear horrible and bitter had sadness not tempered her large blue eyes.

Below the dais, hundreds of people conversed and drank. There were long tables piled high with sweet-smelling meats, ripe apples, grapes, cheeses and every food the kingdom produced. The air was hearty and warm, and all of the thirty-two new soldiers were present and uncloaked, enjoying the company of their families, and mixing with their new brothers in the king's service. Stacks of wine barrels covered the walls, and all night, servants went back and forth from the kitchens like hurried bees.

Near the barrels, Robert, Borleaf, and Marscion stood discussing the tournament, various details of dealings with foreign kingdoms, and their drinks, which they were eager to keep full. After a while, Charlie joined them. Robert pulled him in close with a hand on the back of his neck and bragged with enthusiastic gestures.

Across the room, opposite the great, frosted oval windows, Baelin stood speaking with two guards, Anson and Loren. Anson was exaggerating an adventure of his while the others laughed incredulously. Baelin looked to Agatha on occasion, and when he did his face turned grim. Then he would scan the room, searching for signs of Herrick. Finding none, he would glance back to Agatha as if he demanded to know where she had hidden his captain.

On the dais, the king received his subjects in a long, unceasing line, meeting each one of them with a genial embrace and sincere welcome.

From the high timbers in the ceiling, long ribbons of maroon, purple, yellow, and green hung above the brightly decorated guests that animated the floor below with dancing and revelry. Agatha stared up at the ribbons absently, considering which color she preferred, when a familiar shade of red attracted her attention to the door.

Herrick stepped into the room slowly, a man bemused and deaf to every sound but those in his own thoughts. His eyes went directly to the dais where they were met, not by the princess, but by the king. He wandered forward aimlessly, in noticeable contrast to his usually quick and calculating manner. Baelin watched him with great concern, careful to note any silent orders or meaningful nods. There were none. Many old supporters and fellow guardsmen congratulated Herrick and slapped him on the back, declaring their loyalty and service to him. However, Herrick acknowledged no one and paced through the crowd as if he were alone in the wide room. Then, as if by doing so he might gain more time to gather his thoughts, he moved to the end of the king's waiting line and stood with his chin rested on his thumb. He did not look at Agatha, but only by force of great restraint.

Tergiver had been pacing the room, studying every look, word, and gesture he could capture, and when he found nothing truly intriguing in the jokes, toasts, and gossip, he wrapped them in mystery in his head. He counted the number of colored ribbons on the ceiling, hoping they might hide a clue; he silently analyzed the positions of each Guard Member in the room, and he made careful conversation with many of them. Despite his growing fatigue, he guarded his intentions skillfully from those with whom he spoke. His spirit was light and compensated for his weakening body during this undertaking, which he considered to be not only his one chance at redemption, but a great adventure in itself. He even had the courage to approach Baelin, to sound him under the pretense of apologizing if his manner had been rude earlier in the day at the saber table.

He met Charlie briefly and asked with a casual air, "We're meeting later, just the two of us, right?" Then he put his hand on Charlie's shoulder, as if to hold him to his promise not to speak to anyone. Charlie nodded. Then Tergiver said, in a voice that Charlie could hardly hear, though it looked plainly spoken, "Keep looking; I've got nothing so far."

Two of their peers walked up to them and one took Tergiver by the arm. Peter, the new guardsman, looked on him confidently and said, "I've got to tell you, when they called our names together today I was scared to death. I thought I was going to go out hard; I sure was lucky to get by you."

Tergiver responded stolidly, looking into one of the fires, "If we meet again, I'll make sure you aren't disappointed."

Charlie's face reeled at these words as Peter and the other young man walked away to find friendlier conversation. Tergiver said, "He was gloating, and I meant what I said."

The royal waiting line wound around the south side of the room and stretched long under the oval windows. Under the frosting glass, soft white rays mixed with the smoke of the fires to create a shifting column of moonlight that shone from the high windows down to the floor. Tergiver noticed Herrick near the front of the king's line, and he left Charlie to walk past him and join the end of the line himself. Tergiver had nothing to say, but he committed to think of something before the time came, knowing it would disappoint his father if he ignored a chance to speak with a king.

Soon Herrick came before King Wiston in the noise of the crowd and bowed on one knee.

Agatha rose from her seat as if it could hold her no longer, and left to join Marscion, Borleaf, and Robert by the wine barrels. As she crossed the busy room, a wide path spread for her. The smoke from the fires wavered in her secret uncertainty, and everyone present, foreigners and citizens alike, beheld her like a sullen goddess treading among them.

The king took Herrick's head in his hands and said, "Rise. I can tell you have considered my proposal; it is visible and heavy on you."

Herrick looked forward into King Wiston's chest with a strange difficulty.

The king continued, "I now give you leave to speak to her about this, but only tonight. If you choose, you may deliver the proposal we have discussed. My blessing rests on one condition; you must make her understand that the arrangement cannot be altered or undone, that it will be immediate and final, but that it will have my most sincere approval and support. However, if you see any regret, if she wavers for even a moment, then I charge you to forget yourself and to be cruel and firm. If my daughter's sentiments prove to be lukewarm, you must freeze them with unmistakable finality. Can you do this?"

Herrick's eyes had been glossed and struggling under his sandy brow when the king had begun to speak to him, but as he listened, they cleared and brightened. Herrick stood bemused, like a prisoner newly released, and answered, "Yes, I can, and I accept. You are a remarkable king worthy of my every allegiance, and I will serve you mightily as long as my life lasts, no matter her feelings or answer."

Everything in Herrick's periphery seemed luminous and blurred. In that moment he was consumed by a new perspective that had been bestowed on him by the incalculable generosity and understanding of the king. He would have renounced every achievement he had ever claimed or planned to claim, and count as nothing all the ambition that defined him, simply to serve such a man.

King Wiston removed a ring from his finger and placed it in Herrick's hand, closing his fist over both. "Take this as a sign of my approval and good faith, should you need it. Then return it to me immediately. When you have spoken to Agatha, apprise me of the outcome, and then, if she accepts, all three of us will discuss what to do next."

Herrick placed the ring in an inside pocket of his cloak and bowed to the king. Then he stood peacefully, reviewing the course he had fixed in his mind. As he stepped down from the dais he was filled with serene contentment for the first time in his life. He saw his future glowing before him like an unexpected harbor on a tiresome black sea.

Agatha stood across the room in a pathetic state. Her face was sunken and disconsolate, and she hovered near Marscion, who comforted her with wise words. As Herrick crossed the room to meet her, she turned her head toward the wall with great pain in her face. Marscion reproached him with a look of spiteful disapproval.

Robert and Borleaf had left them moments earlier, and now Borleaf stood before the king. He came forward to the end of the dais, dismissed the receiving line with a kind wave, and shouted, "Now! We have waited long enough. Let us honor our new soldiers and the future heroes of Murmilan!"

The crowd gave a booming approval, lifting their glasses and voices high. Herrick receded backwards to the platform, and Agatha, taking a different path around the room, regained her seat beside the king. Two servants pulled ropes that hung on pulleys below the oval windows, and the frosty panes creaked open slowly, swinging outward into the night, allowing the moonlight to beam resplendent in a wide silver circle on the floor.

The king rose and walked down to the circle, where he stood in the pale column of light. He carried with him a polished, intricate sword. Its black blade was emblazoned with golden symbols and insignias, and the hilt was jeweled with emeralds and diamonds. Then the princess arose from her seat and lightly descended the steps of the dais to join the king in the ethereal circle. Her skin matched the hue of the sovereign moon, and she stood as a fairy in its light. Above her head, a few sparse, curious snowflakes circled and hovered about the open windows before venturing into the warm air, where they twisted once and vanished. The room grew silent in awe, and a chill wind entered to bestow a serious and noble air on the proceedings. The ceremony had begun.

Herrick stood beside Borleaf and spoke in an exalted tone, "Tergiver from Northford, come, and be honored."

Tergiver stepped forward and bowed before the two men. Borleaf draped a royal-blue cloak around his shoulders. On the left shoulder, a lone kite was stitched in silver. Only guardsmen carried the full crest of Murmilan on their cloaks. Tergiver stood straight and Borleaf connected the silver clasp around his neck. Then Tergiver entered the aerie circle and knelt on one knee before the two figures that appeared as living sculptures of nobility and divinity in the soft light. He stayed silent and kept his head low as the king raised the heavy sword high and rested the flat of it on his right shoulder. The rest of the room seemed miles away, and the hot fires and candles dissolved into blue and grey in his periphery. The world was silent, slow-moving, and majestic. The king raised the sword, and Tergiver felt a light kiss on his forehead that sent a warm rush into his fingers and toes. Raising his eyes, he saw the unearthly princess offering a slender, pale hand to raise him to his feet. He took it, and as he stood, she said in a soft, translucent voice, "Rise, noble Mure, and serve Murmilan well all of your days."

He bowed low and walked out of the circle as a new man, forgetting for a long space every concern he had brought with him to the banquet.

So began the induction of the new soldiers. Each young man

was cloaked according to the service he had chosen; blue cloaks were given to those in the naval forces, and green to those in the army. Each man knelt before the king, and each took the hand of his princess, who raised him with kind words. Agatha moved elegantly and spoke with a presence none of the soldiers ever forgot. Only once did she waver, when a nervous blonde boy took her hand awkwardly and uneasily as he rose, and walked quickly out of the circle. He had pressed a tiny scrap of paper into her hand and had not let go until she clasped it. She shifted it to her other hand, unobserved by anyone, and received the next soldier.

After the first twenty-eight cloaks had been presented, the last four men received dark red ones with full green crests on the shoulders. Servants pulled the ropes to close the oval windows, and the fires regained their spirit of warmth and merriment. The king closed the ceremony with a brief speech, after which the crowd gave solemn oaths that ended in cheers and a return to high spirits. Then music started again from a small band near one of the fires.

As the night wore on, Agatha was beset by admirers and well-wishers. During the ceremony she had seemed to grow supernatural in the eyes of the onlookers, and now they all sought to be near her and hear her voice. The number and constancy of these visitations exhausted her, and she struggled to keep her eyes from Herrick and to choke down the image of her father's ship, sheathed in that harbor like a threat, only days away from setting off to fetch her an appropriate husband. Deep in these concerns, she forgot about the note, which she had secretly tucked beneath the cushions of her chair when she sat down.

The noise of the room gradually declined, and after two more hours, the number of remaining guests had diminished by half. The moon shone higher and smaller above the windows, and Herrick was still roaming about the room, gathering courage for the most difficult and marvelous task he had ever undertaken.

Tergiver ran quietly through the Pine Wood, staying close to the high trunks that cast a pattern of long, woven shadows in the slanting moonlight. He reached a woodshed, which was hidden at the edge of a small clearing that also contained a well. His breath bellowed out from his face in white puffs as he slowed, turned the corner, and called softly into the darkness, "Charlie?"

He heard a timid voice come from behind the woodshed, near the mossy well, "Here."

"Come out into the light, I want to show you something."

The noise of slow rustling pine needles crept nearer until Charlie crawled forth from the darkness and said, "I don't like this, Tergiver." His teeth were on the verge of chattering and he was wrapped tightly in a blanket. His blue cloak hung out from under it at his waist. "Let's go back and just tell somebody; this is not for us to do."

"Stop talking like that!" Tergiver hissed under his breath, "We've already discussed it. We must do it this way or not at all. You do want to help, don't you? What did you find out tonight?"

Charlie sighed and his eyes seemed to roll upward into his head. "I couldn't find out anything! I just stood before everyone, my father, the councilors, my friends, and just lied. I pretended it was the excitement of the night that made me act strange, but my insides were burning, Tergi. I felt like more of a foul villain than any I ever heard whispering in secret."

Tergiver stood before his friend, incredulous and condescending. "What are you talking about? Someone's life depends on your ability to act — and all you can do is think of yourself! Did you do anything or did I work alone tonight?"

Charlie sniffed slightly, trying to conceal his face in the shadows.

Then he offered, "Let me go back and tell Herrick myself. I won't tell anyone that you knew anything about —"

"No!" Tergiver interrupted, "We have an understanding! Everyone knows you wouldn't keep something like this from me —" He broke off suddenly and leaned down into Charlie's face, "Did you tell anyone else? Did you tell your father?"

Charlie turned his head to the side and whispered, "No. I didn't ... tell him. That is why I feel so awful. I stood right before his face, and — did you see anything tonight, Tergi?"

Tergiver rubbed his eyes and turned his head to the side, "No. Who can tell what is going on with those people? I've always been able to read faces, but these ... they don't make any sense. I can't begin to put it together, but something is definitely happening." Tergiver yawned wide and then shook his head in frustration. Charlie was still staring ahead, crippled by his self-loathing.

"Listen, Charlie," said Tergiver, "we just have to act. It's simple. We will figure it all out later. Everything is going to work out, alright? We will both have much greater stories to tell our fathers once this night is over. Here, look — this is what I wanted to show you." Tergiver pulled his bow out of the sling on his shoulder and set it on the ground. Then he removed five sharp arrows carved from Black Ironwood and stained mahogany. The feathers were a deep red, and the arrowheads were sharp and green.

"Where did you get those?" demanded Charlie.

"When a quarter of The Guard is drunk at the banquet, it isn't hard to grab a few arrows from the stock on the way out. Now we'll see who shows who their own colors!" Tergiver held them tight in triumph as if he had already succeeded.

"Did anyone see you? Do you realize how much trouble we could be in? Tergiver, let's just go back and get this over with! Come on, first we're lying, and now stealing!"

Tergiver pulled Charlie roughly to his feet and pushed him hard against the shed, producing an ominous thud that seemed to echo from the corners of the short wood. "You are going to stay here until I get back! I will not have you killing us both before we can save Herrick. Sometimes you have to do things you don't want to do; you have to be a man and take chances. Now straighten up and stop being a child; I am not going to let you ruin this!"

Just then there was a sharp movement of leaves deep within the trees. The two fell silent. They held still for a minute until Tergiver turned his head toward the noise slowly, then rushed suddenly to the spot from where it had come, causing a large animal to dart away through the trees. When he returned, Charlie was still half in the shadows, showing wide eyes.

"See, it was just an animal — a dog or something. Stay here. Just wait for me. You have your sword with you, right?"

"Yes," said Charlie, nodding to the hilt that was sticking out from beneath his pack, which lay on the ground.

"You have nothing to be afraid of. You could come with me...."

"No," answered Charlie meekly.

"Alright." Tergiver began to string his bow, pulling it tight, "If I don't see anything I'll just come back here; but if I succeed, I will send someone back to get you, I promise, so stay here."

Charlie glanced up expectantly, waiting to hear what he should do if Tergiver failed.

Tergiver finished stringing his bow, stood up, plucked it once, and said, "I am going to the back of the castle to wait. I can hide in the shrubs of the garden on the east side, but if the moonlight keeps up, I might have to hide in that guard post at the top of the lawn. If everything is as you said, it should be empty tonight." Tergiver arranged the quiver over his shoulder and plunged into the wood, making little sound as he ran toward the rear of the castle.

7

The power of a note

More than half of the candles had burned down to stumps, and many of them were out. The four fires no longer blazed high in the banquet hall, but nibbled contentedly on the last of the remaining logs. The queen was drunk and snoring in her chair, and the king was standing in a large group of councilors and generals, laughing and telling stories. Borleaf and Marscion were still at the barrels drinking heavily together, and Robert had gone to bed. Agatha, having spoken with the last of the people in her line, sat tiredly on her hands until she remembered the note given to her during the ceremony.

She removed it from the space between the cushion and the side of the chair where she had hidden it, and stood up to stretch her back. She looked at Herrick and Baelin across the room. Baelin appeared to be repressing anger or disagreement, and Herrick's hands were open as if to console him. Their eyes flashed toward her, and Agatha turned away and rushed out the door into the Great Hall. She walked eagerly across the floor to the other side, fleeing the expectations and the hurt that had smothered her in the banquet room.

She walked under the high vaulted ceilings and stole toward the open mouth of a quiet, rising corridor on the east side of the hall. There torches burned at long intervals, and the space was empty. She passed the two marble guardians at the entrance and walked up the sloping corridor a few steps. Passing the first torch on her left, she stopped and leaned back against the wall. Then she lifted the note in her left hand and unfolded it tiredly with her right. She was weary of praise and compliments, and she considered simply dropping the paper on the chance that it was just another fawning sentiment. Yet the face of the boy who gave it to her had not been one of admiration, and the memory of it stirred an eager curiosity in her as she held the note under the torch light. The words undulated in the firelight and struck out at her like a snake. Her shoulders hit the wall behind her as she read:

> They are going to kill Herrick tonight
> — I don't know who. Please help.

She gasped and held her hand to her mouth. Then she remembered every line on the young blonde's face; she remembered how his hand had shaken, and how he, unlike the others, had not fought to suppress a growing smile as he stood. She moved her hand to her eyes and then to her head, and back, with panicked uncertainty. The weight of Marscion's words, and her dread of telling Herrick about the ship had ground her spirits into a dull ache all evening, but this threat stirred her despair afresh and kindled it with fear and anger. Would they make her decision for her — like this? Who but her father and Herrick knew of her feelings, and who would dare such a thing? She was still worn from the long ceremony, and this anger drew greedily from her remaining strength, leaving her eyes weak and shining pitifully. Hearing a noise, she brought herself under control again as best she could.

There was a voice from the hall, at the entrance of the corridor. It spoke her name with a light touch of hesitation, "Agatha?"

She turned to find Herrick standing awkwardly under the stone arch that opened onto the Great Hall. He had a curious spark in his eyes, and she had never seen him so unsure of himself. To Agatha, who feared for his life, this strange vulnerability appeared dangerous and frightening. Herrick's face was fully illuminated by the torch, while half of Agatha remained in the shadow of the dark hallway.

The sensation of being alone with Herrick was no longer sweet, but awful and paralyzing. The note seemed to pick at her hands with eager paper fingers, and she deliberated, saying absently, "You haven't used my name in days."

She started toward him, confused and apprehensive, and Herrick looked down, examining the floor and taking deep breaths. Agatha's fears rummaged through her mind violently. If she told Herrick about the threat he would surely stay, as he was terribly brave, but they would kill him nonetheless. If she sent him away cruelly, he might not ever return. Lost in this silent dilemma, she tried not to look at him. Then she suddenly imagined herself dressed in black, weeping, and clinging to his coffin as thick red arms lowered it into the ground and away from her forever. Her stomach quavered under this image, and she decided at once that the only solution was to order his departure.

Herrick looked up after exhaling another deep breath and said, "I have been so unkind to you lately, and I am truly sorry for it, but it has not been without reason. There are ..." He fumbled with his thoughts for a moment, and then reached into his cloak as if to make sure he had not lost something.

As he gathered his words, Agatha saw Baelin and Anson appear behind him at a distance, watching them from the hall and trying unsuccessfully to look as if they were not. Marscion's words echoed in her mind, *"Things often go poorly for young men who court the daughters of royalty."*

"I would like to talk to you, well, I should say that I can finally talk to you openly about …" and in this next pause, Herrick gave a little smile, as if he could not believe how difficult, or how wonderful his words were.

Agatha's fear overcame her, and she looked down on Herrick with hurt, pleading eyes and said, "You have to leave; you have to go right now."

This broke through Herrick's line of thought, and he stood straighter, with boyish eyes desperate for a second chance. "Just let me talk to you. Please, I at least deserve …"

As he put his hand into his cloak again, Agatha reached out as if to push him away; then she retracted her hand, and her eyes flicked over his shoulder to the men now advancing from behind. She whispered desperately, "I want you to leave. I want you out of Murmilan, if only for tonight. Return tomorrow if you wish." Her eyes began to shine as she added, "For me, please go."

Herrick's brow became stern and he righted himself in a rigid, soldierly stature. He remembered the king's condition that he had only this night to propose. Baelin's warnings collected themselves in a rush and presented this desperate Agatha as proof. Herrick understood that King Wiston must have given her the same speech, and this was her cowardly way of answering — to simply cast him away. Herrick stood firm, unwilling to leave until he had at least completed, for good or ill, his part of the difficult order given to him by King Wiston.

While this quiet contempt nested in Herrick, an idea occurred to Agatha, and the finality of the thought drained her heart and made her chest feel cold. Her lips shook slightly as she calmed herself, and said, "There is a ship, *The Dolphin*, in the royal anchorage at Tholepin Bay. Two days from now it sails to find a —" She choked on the next word, but to Herrick it sounded like emphasis, "suitable prince for me."

The power of a note

Herrick retreated a step. His dauntless posture cracked under the blow, but he regained it quickly. He puffed himself up with a callous air, unwilling to give the cruel girl the pleasure of enjoying the last game she would ever play with him. He let go of the ring in his pocket and pulled his hand from the cloak definitively, as if it were he that withdrew the unspoken proposal.

Agatha glanced repeatedly from Herrick to the guards behind him. Herrick's face was set hard, hating her, and she felt that each word she spoke emptied her chest of breath, which she would never draw again, leaving her to suffocate, hollow and alone. Yet she continued on, feeling that harsh looks from Herrick's living face were better than calm ones from his corpse. "I want you to sail to Talus and bring my friend Sophia back here tomorrow morning. If I cannot go on the journey to choose for myself, she can go for me. I trust her. You can find her at her father's inn, *The Gil* ..."

"I know where to find her." Herrick interrupted her viciously, with measured words. "However, while I assure you there is nothing I would rather do than leave this castle and your presence tonight and forever, I still have a duty to protect it, and that duty I will keep."

Agatha stood firm, while hot streams pooled and burned behind her eyes, which appeared weak under the strain of holding them back. She closed them and concentrated on keeping her composure. This produced an air of peremptory authority as she said, "Herrick, I command you to go and you must do it! Leave anyone here in your place, but do not stay yourself. Leave now, take the ship and do not come back until tomorrow when you have found my friend." She was faint and might have collapsed, but she feared falling and killing him should he catch her, and stay. Instead, she stepped away, giving one more curious instruction, "I also command you not to communicate this to anyone in any way, and to take with you only those you trust with your life."

Baelin and Anson had come close, and Borleaf had joined them, tottering sideways and leaning hard on Anson.

Agatha pleaded in a desperate whisper, "Leave now! Please!"

Herrick turned his back coldly on the princess and hailed his guards in a loud voice. "Baelin, Anson." They approached and saluted Herrick, whose return to strict form comforted them. Anson struggled to shift the drunken Borleaf, who was mumbling verses from an old song. Herrick commanded sharply, "Go quietly and take three horses from the stables. Take care to go unseen, and speak to no one. Do this after you put Borleaf to bed." Then his tone was crisp with bitterness, "Then meet me outside the West Gate. We will ride to Tholepin Bay in this cold night to undertake a short sea voyage, which is very dear to the heart of her royal highness, your most noble and honest princess."

Agatha had retreated into a world of misery and nausea, pretending strength by propping against the wall and looking away from Herrick. Her mind fought against alternating visions of swords driving through him, and of finding his body lying dead on the floor of the hall. Her anger grew in these images, and she began to color thoughts of her father in wicked, dizzy shades.

She did not hear Anson when he nodded to Herrick and replied, "Sir," or Borleaf when he raised his arm in a drunken salute and slurred, "Aye, Captain," she only saw Baelin as he stepped forward in protest, cast a sharp stare at her, and said, "Sir, someone must command tonight and Borleaf is not fit. Leave me to run the watch in your place."

Baelin spoke with an air of understanding, and his eyes, when not pointed accusingly at Agatha, were drawn in genuine sympathy for his captain. He alone of the guards had known of Herrick's intention that night in the hallway.

Borleaf, on hearing his name, lifted himself off Anson's shoulder and said with difficulty, "Let me go out there, it is a lovely, fine night for it. I used to sail on a ship."

Herrick looked beyond the men to make sure no one had heard Borleaf, then he said, "Thank you, Baelin. You will manage our absence; Anson, take Borleaf, get him sober, and meet me as I ordered. Let no one see you and answer no questions. Borleaf, sir, you may come with us, but please keep quiet."

Anson and Borleaf went back into the hall, leaving Herrick, Baelin, and Agatha standing under the waving torchlight. Herrick stood as if he wanted desperately to turn and address Agatha, but instead he held his back to her and said in a voice she could hear clearly, "Baelin, you were right about her. I will never again be so foolish, and I will never again be so humiliated." Then Herrick turned, avoiding Agatha's face, and marched away into the darkness of the corridor and out of sight.

As he disappeared, Agatha sank against the wall, overcome at last by dizzying despair, until she rested on the floor. She rolled her head to the side to look at Baelin with watery, languishing eyes.

Against his instincts, Baelin knelt compassionately. He turned his head toward the empty hallway, then looked back at her and said, "I'm glad you finally let him go."

Agatha, seemingly struggling to remain conscious, said under her breath, "You knew he should go too?"

Baelin looked at her with a curious expression. "Yes. I wish this had happened sooner. I wish you had been more honest with him."

She did not seem to have heard him, but spoke weakly, "If you know too, then you can tell them what happened here, what I did, and that I promise to leave him alone; tell them I said I promise." She drew a breath and finished, "Then will he be safe?" Baelin moved closer to her, and his eyes narrowed in concern. Agatha leaned forward feebly, her eyes half closed, and offered him the scrap of paper, speaking through tears that were now falling unrestrained. "See Baelin, I knew too. Did I save him?"

Baelin started to his feet and stared at the words on the paper, holding them at arms length as if they were a poison. Then he knelt again, closer to Agatha, and asked, "Where did you get this? Are you sure it is real?"

Her head hung low over her shoulders and she whispered through a mess of curls that covered her face, "It was real to the boy who gave it to me."

Baelin gently lifted Agatha to her feet, and she clung to his arm. He said, "If this is true, then yes, you may have saved him. Tonight I will rearrange the watch so that I may wait in Herrick's chamber. There I will test this note and anyone who tries to fulfill it." Agatha held tighter to him and pulled herself to a stand, then she wiped her eyes and tried to compose herself. It was then that Baelin suddenly understood exactly what she had done, and why. He felt a swell of admiration and compassion that moved him to say, "Princess, I misjudged you, and I ask your forgiveness."

An hour later, Agatha entered the hall and stood abruptly in front of her father, who was helping the queen out of her chair and having some difficulty, as he never allowed anyone to help him with that particular task. The room was by now mostly empty, as only a few scattered councilors and guests remained. King Wiston could tell by his daughter's eyes that she was careworn and angry, and in his face Agatha found a mix of both pity and relief. The king began to speak softly, as if he immediately understood her troubles, "Herrick and I spoke tonight...."

Agatha eyes were gleaming and incendiary. She exploded before he could continue, "I know what you were going to do! You had everything ready! I know about the ship ... I know ... everything!" It was only out of her newfound fear that she did not make a greater scene or hit him with her fists. She had never believed that her father was the kind of man who dealt with threats in such a callous and wicked way; but now she saw him as a simple king, as power-hungry, frightened, and predictable as any other. At the mention of the ship, King Wiston's expression had accused him of planning everything that tortured Agatha's imagination, and he denied none of it.

The king decided that Herrick must have found Agatha unwilling to give up her throne or leave the kingdom, and that her present display was the result of the horror she felt at the idea. He remained silent, hoping that his daughter, though she was offended at having her capricious feelings exposed in this way, might nonetheless come to understand the power and consequences of her affections.

Contempt raged in Agatha's stomach as she imagined her father ordering Herrick's execution in one breath and commanding the ship ready with the next. Then her face softened as with a revelation, but her eyes resembled her father's at the height of their fury, shining in the firelight like blown glass. The king closed his eyes to gather a reply, but before he could begin, Agatha drew all of her emotion into an imperious, scornful composure and said, "You are no better than any other king, whatever you pretend. Know that this will not end as you wish it to, and know that you have forever lost your daughter's love."

8

A shot hits its target

Tergiver stole in darkness to the edge of the Pine Wood and knelt. Before him rose the wide east side of the castle. Slices of balconies, corbels, and windows jutted into the light from sharp black shadows. The moon had crept higher and brighter still, drenching the sky and the city floor in silver pallor. Tergiver evaluated every window and balcony above him, and then he bolted from the woods, gliding like a shade across the grounds before disappearing into another stretch of black.

As Tergiver crept against the stone, the noise of the high, punching waterfall grew louder until it washed away all other sounds. He reached the back of the castle and snuck along a low hedge that stopped just before the east arcaded walk. The walk was covered by a stone roof that began at the wooden doors and ran down and at an angle to the pavilion at the bottom of the lawn. There it joined the other arcade, which climbed up the far end of the lawn to the west side of the castle.

Tergiver took a deep breath. His eyes were wide open. He crept through an arch into the walkway and paused to listen. Hearing nothing but the water, he stuck his head out of the shadow and scanned the lawn. The shadow sculptures were terrible in the moonlight. Their edges drew out like wet knives on the clean, clipped turf. Each of them now looked as if they had been designed by wicked men to commemorate unspeakable acts. He saw no one in either of the walkways, nor on the high west stairs that climbed the precipice to the wall.

Tergiver hid for a few minutes in one of the many consistent, curving shadows. There he had a decent view of the pavilion and the pool before it, but everything was empty.

His spirits began to drop. The moon waited high over the castle like his only supporter, waiting for his next move and offering light for the path, but in every dark place lingered a doubt. One seemed to question whether Charlie had heard anything at all, another suggested that he was not strong enough to succeed, and another said he might die in the attempt. Tergiver was impatient and anxious. Finding no one on the pavilion, he looked up to the wooden guard post at the top of the lawn. It too was empty.

He told himself desperately that as long as he had not already missed the attempt, there was still a chance to avoid telling his father that he too had failed at the castle. He reminded himself of what he had said to Charlie — that everything might have happened for a reason — and he tried to muster patience and vigilance.

He decided to make for the guard post and then wait in the shadow that ran along the crease between the lawn and the back wall. From the post he would have a clear view of both walks, the pavilion, the pool, and both the East and West Wall stairs. He would be unseen and within a long bowshot. Only the sculptures made him uneasy, still jutting irregularly and scrambling low black lines in ugly rites on the wet grass. The smell of the falls drifted up to him on a light wind, and the icy, moist air raised bumps on his arms.

He sprang from the cover of the walk and sprinted into the nearest shadow that would lead him along the wall to the guard post. He reached the post easily and found it less impressive than he had expected. It consisted of no more than a simple wooden stand with three sides, open at the back. However, its humble condition proved suitable to his task. As Tergiver crawled into the cover of the three short sides, he found a sizable knothole from which he could view the pavilion without being seen. He saw clearly the slick floor that ran almost level with the water, and the thorny vines that wrapped jealously around the pavilion, which was glimmering with thick layers of mist.

After a half hour of watching and waiting, freezing cross-legged and peering through the hole, his body began to collapse once again. He found himself leaning hard on the post too often and he decided to retreat to the castle wall to watch from the shadow. He reached it by crawling and leaned back with his bow and an arrow on his lap. The cliff spread wide and high before him, shining black with silver streaks. Mesmerized by the water in his sleepy state, he followed it to the very top and noticed something curious. There was a speck of a man on horseback standing near the cliff's edge, looking down on the castle and the city. Tergiver leaned back against the wall and pondered who it might be, but before he made his first guess, he was asleep.

Herrick, Anson, and Borleaf had left the city. Herrick met the two men just outside the West Gate and they had not questioned him, finding him in a powerful temper. The men were silent as their horses climbed the western escarpment with lumbering strides, jerking and snorting in the cold air as the castle dropped away on their right.

At the top, the ground leveled into a high, rocky plain that overlooked the castle and the city far below. Herrick ordered the horses stopped and gave the name and location of the ship, the details of their errand, and then he ordered the men to go ahead of him. Then he rode to the edge of the waterfall and looked down on the scene below.

Herrick gazed on the long rows of spotted torches that lit the obscure city wall, and he watched as the bright moon extinguished the far ones in its light. He was angry that Agatha had already known about the ship, and that she would humiliate him by sending him away on it to fetch her ambassador. He was angry that he had been so willing to rework his disposition, duty, and every ambition only to be made a fool by a girl who did not have the courage or courtesy to be honest with him. He looked down and imagined Agatha in the banquet hall, carousing, laughing at him, and hanging affectionately from the arm of her next prize.

There was no one in sight on the brightly lit castle grounds. Before turning away, Herrick said, "coward," in a loud voice that was drowned by the moving water and dumped over the falls. Then he pulled his horse away with a jerk and charged toward Tholepin Bay.

Anson met him with a wide smile in front of the ship. "You should have seen the crew! They certainly weren't expecting us. Borleaf and I climbed on board to wake them, and though there are only five, they were ready to fight us both to the death until they saw who we were." Anson stopped, seeing that his story was not bettering Herrick's mood. Then he said in a more even voice, "I apologize, sir. The ship is exactly as you said it would be. Captain Sunger and his crew are awake and informed. The ship is prepared and we can depart as soon as you give the order."

Herrick climbed the wooden platform to the deck.

Anson had sailed in his hometown of Eastport, and once on board, he immediately fell in line with the crew, unwinding ropes and listening intently to the ship's rough, aged captain, whose leathery face was thrust forward between hunched, blue-cloaked shoulders.

Herrick crossed the deck and stood next to Borleaf, who was leaning over the port side with a sickly face. They stood for a long moment until Borleaf looked at him through his thick eyebrows and said, "Go ahead, chief, give the order. Let's get out of here for a while."

Herrick made a sign to the ship's captain, and the broad canvas sail struggled up into the night, catching the cold breeze and snapping tight. *The Dolphin* jerked forward, and within minutes of the captain's first cries it had cleared the bay and tacked eastward into the North Sea. It would follow the rough northern coast of Murmilan for several hours before turning southward into the Silver Channel.

Borleaf nodded once to Herrick, and lay down on a bench, where he drifted into unconsciousness.

Tergiver awoke with a sudden start. He was cold, shivering, and disoriented. His heart thumped so hard against his chest that it hurt. He found his hands to be numbed and slow. He gathered his thoughts and remembered why he was at the top of the lawn. His pounding heart subsided as he rubbed his hands together, working a slight sensation back into them. He began to feel ashamed and stupid as he stared down at the bow on his lap, and thought, Charlie sure has a great imagination.

He wondered how long he had slept as his eyes readjusted to the light. The moon was still bright, though more westward than it had been earlier. Looking forward — Tergiver's heart began to thump into his throat. A lone figure stood on the pavilion with its hands behind its back, staring straight ahead into the falls. Tergiver strained his eyes, trying to force them to wake and focus more quickly, but he could only see that the figure was a man with moonlight reflecting brilliantly in the water behind his head. Tergiver scrambled harder against the wall to avoid being seen, for the shadow had moved, leaving his leg exposed on the lawn as he slept. Fear constricted his neck, and his arms shook as he tried to steady himself. He repressed a sudden urge to cry out, "Herrick!" fearing that the shadows might be hiding other figures like himself, which would not show themselves if he acted too early. As his eyes began to sharpen their focus on the image before the falls, Tergiver's skin grew even colder, and he heaved a shallow breath as the hairs rose on his arms and head. The light reflected and shimmered, not in the water before the man, but in his crown.

The king's robe was a dark, muted crimson against the silver falls. Tergiver scanned the lawn, barking desperately, "No, No, No!" He fumbled for an arrow and rose to his knees, dropping it several times, tearing his eyes away from the falls repeatedly. The king seemed to be deep in thought, but at peace, looking up at the falls as if he had never seen their like before. Tergiver heard a loud snap from the doors of the west arcade and cried out. He saw the figure of a man descending quickly to the pavilion below, blinking in and out of the curved shadows cast by the columns of the walk. Tergiver finally pulled an arrow onto the string and measured his shot, but his hand shook and the arrow jumped a few feet away on the lawn. The assailant was closer, and now stood in a dark patch at the end of the walk, pointing an accusing finger and moving his head threateningly.

The rumbling falls drowned out their voices in the same way it covered Tergiver's panicked shouts. He scrambled frantically on his knees and elbows for another arrow. "Be calm, be calm, be calm!" he said, as another arrow slipped through his numb fingers. He glanced down the slope and saw the figure of the king with his arms outstretched, still facing the water. The second man lunged for him. Tergiver picked up the arrow, held it fast against the string, and measured his shot. The second man had grabbed the king from behind and raised him high in the air by the throat. The king thrashed, kicking and choking in the powerful grip of his enemy. Tergiver let the arrow fly with a zip, and for a moment he felt paralyzed, hearing only the long whistle of its feathers against the rush of water and foam.

It struck the attacker between the shoulder blades, and Tergiver knew it had gone deep. The king fell crumpled to the pavilion floor. The crown rolled sideways for a few feet and settled on the ground.

Tergiver picked up another arrow and ran down the steep lawn, taking long, bungling steps, still yelling out in disbelief and terror. He let his second shot fly, and it caught the man in the neck as he reeled sideways, trying to grasp the first arrow in his back. Then, when he was halfway down the hill, just past the last set of pointed sculptures, Tergiver saw his king, whom he had bravely saved, stand, pick up the crown, and slowly turn his gaze, whereby he offered the moonlight a monstrous face, painted a deep red, unfamiliar, slick, and smiling.

Tergiver's feet buckled under him and he slipped on the wet grass. The face beheld him with an odious curiosity.

Then the figure let the king's robe fall away. It wore all black, and its hair was tied fast behind its head and covered. Tergiver could not move, and his struggling, straining breaths drew little air.

The red face looked at the crown, then dropped it on the body before his feet and watched it roll off and away, circling round and around and clinking to a stop in a pool of black blood that was spreading across the cold marble. With a large booted foot, the figure rolled the dead man toward Tergiver and bowed humbly for his approval. On the pavilion, King Wiston lay dead.

The world seemed to go silent.

Then the face changed. Its obscure eyes glowered at Tergiver in the darkness, making him feel deplorable and insignificant. Then it heaved the king into the pool with a heavy kick, where the body floated, a bobbing mass punctuated by the single arrow that stuck out of its back. The arrow drifted back toward him, toward the pavilion, then descended under it slowly, bending against the stone, until finally it was dragged down and out of sight by the current.

Tergiver began to regain control of his limbs, and crawling upward and exposed on the lawn, he turned to find another arrow. He looked quickly over his shoulder and saw the black figure standing tall at the edge of the pool, where it considered him once more, then stepped backwards into the water and disappeared with a soft splash.

Tergiver gained his feet, but his periphery was growing black. On the pavilion, the king's crimson robe lay in a puddle of black, in the middle of which sat the glistening crown of Murmilan.

9

Disquieting sounds from the pine wood

The Dolphin jumped easily through the pearl-tipped waves of the North Sea, guided by a strong westerly wind and an able crew. The moon was still full and high, and the men could only see a tiny band of stars in the far north. They kept their bearings by staying within sight of the coast. Herrick leaned over the starboard railing and stared ahead into the narrow mouths of the numerous, curving fiords of the kingdom's northern shore. The crests of the waves raced like a hoard of white flames seeking shelter in the dim cliffs. The fiords passed quickly as the ship sped on, and the rocky Murmillian forest appeared, its high pines swaying together in the sharp, cold air.

Borleaf had awoken and staggered across the deck to join Herrick. He studied him with a fatherly kindness, then looked down to watch the ship smashing through the small whitecaps. After a moment, he turned to Herrick and said, "I'm not sure what happened back there, my head isn't the clearest, but …" Herrick did not respond, and it made Borleaf stare back down into the water. "Well, I think you are going to be the finest chief The Guard ever had, but, just so you know, if things had gone another way, I would have gladly served for a few more years." Borleaf left him, having given all the comfort he knew how to give, and crossed the deck again to have a drink with Anson.

Herrick turned his head to the east and saw the snowy peaks of the Brumal Mountains rising over the bow, pasty and surreal in the moonlight, partially covered by a shimmering, diaphanous blanket drawn across the top of the range. He left the railing and moved to the foremost bulwark on the ship, where he stood and gazed forward in search of the first sign of the channel.

In favorable winds, *The Dolphin* could sail to Talus in a few hours, and this wind was exceptional. The mountains loomed larger in front of the ship, and the northeastern coast of Murmilan gave way to the wide channel that ran southward. Captain Sunger shouted his orders in a clear rhythm and the boom swung hard to the port side, slowing the ship as the sail relaxed and flapped before drawing tight again and dragging the ship tilting into the channel.

Within a few minutes, they saw the high peak of Allocausus smoking visibly in the moonlight. At the bottom of its steep southern foothills, the port city of Talus slept quietly. Talus was split in two by a deep river that emptied into a bay where it met the eastern side of the channel. Vestiges of tall city walls were scattered about its borders, crumbled, dilapidated, and low, the ornaments of a long peace.

Captain Sunger docked the ship at the nearest open anchorage. The crew lowered the royal flag on Herrick's command and stowed all identifiable markings below.

Herrick gazed for a long time at the ancient city in the dark, where only a few windows still flickered with firelight, barely illuminating the hard-packed roads that ran quietly between them. He stared longest, however, at the quiet, smoking peak, and the curious stone tower that rose up before it on a hill just outside the city's northernmost border. The tower reared up unevenly against the snowy background, as if it had grown naturally out of a pile of stones long ago. Now it stood like an unwanted visitor, unsightly, colorless, and ignored. Herrick was the last to descend below the deck for the night. Anson was granted his request to sleep above board.

Charlie's face was ice cold. It had been hours since Tergiver had disappeared into the wood, and the noises had returned. He guessed that the shifting pads on the straw were simply those of roaming dogs or raccoons, but the ambiguous darkness magnified the sound, drawing them in the image of huge, hideous beasts in his imagination. He had moved from the lighted clearing where he and Tergiver had parted, and crept to the dark side of the woodshed. There he shivered and gripped his sword, scanning the thick darkness and trying not to pick at the long scrape that was itching from his wrist to his elbow. He had run through Tergiver's arguments repeatedly in his head, trying to convince himself that, despite his feelings, keeping the truth from his father had been the right thing to do.

Now it was hours later, Tergiver was gone, he was alone, and he had still not convinced himself. Only Tergiver knew where he was, he was catching a chill, and there was something moving in the trees before him. He felt hunted, and the only faces he could imagine on the sounds before him were those of his father, of Herrick, and everyone — including Tergiver — whom he had deceived that evening.

He felt as if he deserved to have this creature emerge from the woods and consume him in punishment for his turn to schemes and deceit. Charlie flung his sword into the moonlit clearing and lay back, unguarded in the darkness, with the resolve that he would wait for Tergiver, and no matter what had happened, tell him the truth. Then he would go to his father and admit everything.

Not long after his resolution, there came a sound from the other side of the clearing. It was something, or someone, pacing back and forth heavily and taking little care to hide the noise. Charlie came out from behind the woodshed and peered as deep as he could across the clearing and into the trees.

At first, there was only the tramping sound of feet on straw, then he heard a choke and a muffled cry. He stood straighter, frigid and terrified, blowing white, ghostly breaths into the dark. The sound paced for a long time, during which Charlie reinforced his resolution. His nerves had grown weaker since he had first allowed Tergiver's arguments to convince him, but now his mind was clearing, and his fear resolved into courage. He would make his confession and face his punishment, even if it were to be doled out to him by a wild beast or a vengeful ghost.

He went boldly into the harsh, chalky light and spoke into the wood. "Come out from there." The pacing stopped, but he could still hear the choking and groaning. "Do you need help?"

The steps came toward him, shifting pine straw under heavy, dragging feet. Then the sound was a shape, and it approached the clearing, passing under the thin moonbeams that shot through the trees, and Charlie saw that it was a man hunched forward in pain. It reached the edge of the clearing and hovered just outside the patch of light. Then it stumbled forward reluctantly, the most pitiable figure Charlie had ever seen. It was Tergiver.

Tergiver's face was contorted and he was having trouble breathing.

Charlie rushed to him and searched him desperately. "Are you hurt? What happened?"

Tergiver did not answer. His hands shook uncontrollably and he could not speak.

Charlie waited a moment, comforting his friend in silence until it seemed that he could breathe easier, and then he asked softly, "What did you see?"

Tergiver began to make an answer but his face screwed itself up again into an expression of suffering and torment. Charlie moved him to sit down but he would not.

"Tergi, please, what happened? Did you see them? Is Herrick alright?"

After a long while, Tergiver was able to speak. He opened his mouth again, agonizing over the words, "n-not Herrick, I … the king is killed!" Then Tergiver began to cry between stifling, difficult breaths, and he did not speak again for several minutes.

Charlie felt as if the beast from the wood had approached him from behind and swallowed him whole. Everything seemed to go black and he felt the king's sword still resting heavy on his shoulder from that evening. Charlie had been prepared for any punishment that he might personally have to face, but he was not prepared to be punished so heavily by the consequences of his inaction, and they enveloped him in remorse. His body began to droop and weaken, and he fell to one knee. His mind, however, remained fixed in his recent resolution. He looked up at Tergiver, who was still standing and staring at the ground with unmoving eyes. "We are going to go from here, and we are going to wake my father. We were wrong to hide our part, and now we have to report it no matter what happens to us."

Tergiver's eyes opened to their full width as he looked down at Charlie in horror. He stooped and jerked Charlie up off the ground, and spat out, "No one! You tell n-no one or you kill us both!"

Charlie shoved himself away angrily and said, "We've obviously done enough and I won't lie to anyone else!" Tergiver stepped forward as Charlie continued, "I even lied to you, Tergi. I gave a note to the princess tonight — even though you said —"

Tergiver charged forward in fury and knocked Charlie backwards several feet. Then he dropped to his knees in a paroxysm of rage and despair, slamming his fists into the dirt and cutting his shin on the sword that lay in the clearing.

Charlie stood up, bleeding from his nose, and took the stand he had been preparing for all night. "I decided, even before you came back, that we were wrong. Taking this chance was stupid and dishonest, and I don't care if you won't come with me — run away if you want — but I am going to my father like I should have in the first place! People stronger than us could have stopped this from happening."

As Charlie spoke, Tergiver's wet eyes grew dark and harsh around the edges. In the shadows at the edge of the clearing, Charlie looked to him as the red face had looked: sinister, disappointed, and ashamed of his stupidity and cowardice.

Charlie stepped forward once more with a humble authority and asked, "What exactly did you see, Tergiver? Tell me or at least come with me and tell my father. It's plain that you saw it happen. If you need more time, that's alright. But if we run or if we do nothing, the people who did this will never pay for it." Charlie reached out his hand softly, "Come with me."

Tergiver tried to speak but he only choked on the cold air. He trembled as he slowly gained his wobbling feet, the cold sword hanging from his hand. Charlie stood with his arm outstretched until all of the blood had left it and he could hold it up no longer. Tergiver's eyes had frozen hard in place, distant, fearful, and he could only manage, "No ... Charlie ... don't ..." which he uttered with an agonized, sick face, as if they were the last words he would ever speak.

Charlie did not plead again, nor did he reconsider. Instead, he looked on Tergiver with compassion, and spoke with all his courage. "We did our best, Tergi, but now we have to go and take responsibility for the mistakes we made. I don't blame you for any of this, and I hope you change your mind." He turned, sad but determined, leaving Tergiver standing like a rigid corpse in the bright clearing.

As he entered the trees, Charlie thought he heard the rush of his friend catching up to join him, but before he could turn around he felt the freezing blade of his own sword sliding stiffly through his back. As he fell, Charlie felt Tergiver's face sobbing against his neck — shaking and wet with hot tears, and he heard, as from a growing distance, the terrible sound of his friend weeping and convulsing in the darkness.

10

RED MORNING

Twilight crept upon the deck of *The Dolphin* to find Anson cradled in a web of netting that hung from the mast. He yawned a long, wide yawn and opened his eyes. The ship rocked gently from side to side, and the smell of raw fish drifted across the air from the fishing boats next to it. A few stars still sparkled, but the moon was gone. As the light began to wash the blackness out of the sky, the charcoal outlines surrounding the ship resolved themselves into the crisp forms of buildings, boats, and trees.

Anson sat up, swinging the makeshift hammock. He yawned again and pushed his blankets aside. He found Herrick below, staring northward off the stern, looking again at the curious, cylindrical tower that seemed to lean forward over the northern half of Talus. Anson dropped to his feet heavily and then picked them up in quick, alternating steps, grimacing from the pain of his blood working itself back through his legs. Then, as he joined Herrick, his eyes followed the river northeastward. Four hundred yards up the river, a wide stone bridge connected the city's two halves. Just past the bridge, the river emerged from a great, hilly forest with intermingled treetops that had accumulated caps of snow, mimicking the mountainous ridge that cascaded down the northern horizon. Anson rubbed his hands together and asked, "Sir, what is that tower there?"

Herrick answered him with icy breath, "Wake Borleaf."

Anson nodded and went below. Within a minute, the three men were walking down the dock among the silent fishing vessels that rocked gently in the current.

A few blocks inland, near the great bridge, stood *The Gilded Gosling*, a modest, three-story inn. It was beset with close rows of thick-branched elms, which provided shade and privacy to the rooms on the upper floors. A wide, railed porch ran across the face of the inn, which was open and welcoming. On it sat two weathered rocking chairs and a long, swinging bench that hung from two chains in the ceiling.

As the men approached the porch, Borleaf remarked, "Look Anson, there are two of your kind." Two boys were sleeping heavily on the hanging bench. A thick blanket had been placed neatly over them. Herrick saw lights burning in the inn, and when their boots made the first clunks on the cold wooden steps, the boys awoke and sat up, yawning like puppies.

The three entered the inn, and the warmth from a large fire met them at the door. There was no one on the main level, but they heard movement from below. There was a sign in the shape of a finger, on which was painted the word "Tavern" in blue and white. It pointed down a set of wide, open stairs.

They descended to the lower floor, which was divided into five sections, four of which had tables still piled with chairs and beset by rows of tall booths stained in dark cherry. The tables were of thick, hard oak and had innumerable scratches and gouges that showed their age. The kitchen, which made up the last section and consisted of a narrow portion against the far wall, was a large wooden box with one door. It had a long, horizontal window that opened onto the largest section of tables. Along the upper edges of this cellar tavern were thin strips of windows at ground level, through which the growing morning light was creeping and pushing the orange firelight back into the hearth.

There was a noise from the kitchen as the men approached the window. Inside the enclosure, a large man with thick eyebrows and a beard called out in a nasal voice from a side of pork he was slicing, "Still got a few minutes before dawn; I'll help you then." He did not look up but went about his business, cutting the meat with determination.

Anson smiled at Borleaf, finding the man funny, but Herrick walked forward and put his hands on the ledge of the window, "We are looking for the proprietor of this place, or his daughter, Sophia."

The man still did not look up, as if it were a point of pride not to allow any disruptions to his chore. He cut another slice and complained, "I'm never going to be ready if I have to open up this place by myself! Where's my help? I'm not taking down chairs too!"

Herrick ignored him and repeated his statement.

The cook grumbled as he stacked another piece of ham against a table on the far wall of the kitchen. Then he turned his back to them and muttered impatiently, "OK, just hold on a minute and I can take care of that for you, and if you see two boys around here tell 'em they're late!"

They turned around to the sound of scrambling footsteps and saw the two boys rumbling down the stairs. Seeing the strangers, the boys sped to a table near the fireplace and pulled the chairs down from it. One of them, freckled with dark, bushy hair, sniffled and yawned, then said, "You can sit here, sirs; we apologize for being late."

The other boy went to the far side of the tavern to begin taking down the other chairs.

The group walked to the table and sat down, unfastening their weapons and laying them with soft clangs against the floor at their feet. The bushy haired boy began to work nearby. Borleaf looked over to him and said, "You boys must be quite hardy to sleep out in a cold like that. What is your name?"

He approached the table and said, "We didn't mean to, sir, we were up late and must have fallen asleep. My name is Henry."

Borleaf nodded in approval and said, "Henry, would you tell us when the proprietor or his daughter are awake and able to speak to us?"

Henry noticed their cloaks and the long swords they had set by their feet. He was accustomed to seeing soldiers in the tavern, but he found these men peculiar. "Yes, sir. Would you like something to drink?"

They answered yes, and Henry went back to the kitchen where he was met with a cry of dismay from the cook, who claimed that he still had a few more minutes to prepare before taking any orders.

While Henry waited for the drinks, he went to help the other boy with the chairs. "Those soldiers want to talk to your father, or Sophie. They seem really friendly, at least the bald one. They have huge swords too, and their cloaks look fancy." Henry seemed to be excited. "They don't look like the normal soldiers we get through here."

The other boy looked over at them and asked, "Those patches on their shoulders, what are they?"

Henry yawned, and then shrugged blithely as if he had never been less interested in anything. He mumbled, "I don't know," and walked back to the kitchen, annoying his friend.

The boys had finished with the chairs by the time the drinks were ready. They carried them to the table where Henry's friend looked over the men with some reverence, then spoke, "Welcome, sirs. My name is Manchester. Are you looking for my father?"

Herrick responded, "Yes, but we would like most to speak with your sister. Is she here?"

Manchester stood half a head taller than Henry, and he had long drooping bangs cut just above his eyebrows. He replied in a respectful tone, "Sophia is here. I'll go find her for you. My father is on a trip to the southern farms. He won't be back until tonight."

"Thank you, Manchester," said Herrick. Both boys left the table running and climbed the stairs with a thunderous clamor. The men heard their stomps rumbling across the ceiling, and then fainter, as they climbed to another floor, then back down. Finally, they heard the door slam as the boys rushed outside.

After the quiet calm of the morning returned, Anson leaned forward curiously, noticing the cook hanging out of his window to watch them. When the cook saw that he was caught, he looked the other way quickly, then down as if he had lost something on the floor, and then he disappeared back into his box.

One by one, sailors, merchants, and travelers trickled down the stairs to find places among the tables. The light seemed to grow with the chatter and noise until both filled the room with a clamoring haze.

The stomping returned as the boys ran back down the stairs, each carrying a small armful of logs for the fire. Manchester slowed himself and walked to the table, breathing heavy, "She's coming," he said, and then, after depositing the wood on a stack in the corner, he began making rounds to the other customers. Henry had poked his head around the bottom corner of the stairs for a moment to stare in awe at the three men before coming down and tossing his logs into the stack. Then he rushed to the kitchen to help with the cooking.

Anson twisted around in his chair to see the tall, slender form of Sophia easing down the stairs and carrying a massive bulk of firewood in her arms. She was Agatha's age and her face was pale with sharp, pretty features. Her hair was long, tied back in a rich, wheat-colored tail that hung past her shoulders. She wore a common brown dress, and to Anson, she seemed graceful even as she dumped the logs on the floor beside the neat woodpile.

Sophia smiled wide and brushed her arms with her hands, then walked up behind Borleaf and gave him a warm hug around the neck. "Hello, Borleaf; I didn't expect to see you so soon!"

He smiled warmly, reaching his thick arm above his shoulder to pat her on the back, and replied, "How are you, Sophie?"

She sat down at the table, opposite Anson and Borleaf, and said with a sly, knowing look, "Well hello, Herrick. I thought this was the last day of the festival. I wanted to come but I had to be here because my Father is away. Was it moved this year?"

Herrick looked at her as if all the light had been drained out of his eyes, leaving them black and numb. "Your friend the princess has sent us to ask you to join a party that sails to the Northern Kingdoms in two days."

Sophia marked the depression in his tone and asked, "Is everything alright? I was just at the castle this summer and Agatha didn't mention any travels. Where is she going?"

Borleaf and Anson looked away — Anson to the fire, though he stole several glances at Sophia first, and Borleaf to the other side of the room.

Herrick answered in a repulsed, formal tone, "Apparently, she wishes to be married, and this voyage is to find a suitable prince; she will not be going, and she asks that you take the trip as her representative."

Sophia stared at Herrick for a moment, then said plainly, "But why would she send you? I don't understand."

Borleaf said to Anson, "Let's go have a talk with some of these fishermen — see if we can get a read on the weather today." Anson agreed and the two men were away.

Herrick's stomach burned. He was embarrassed that everyone seemed to know his shame, and Sophie's polite, girlish concern made it worse. He answered roughly, "You may ask her why when we return; she may answer you better than she answered me."

She looked at him with sympathy and companionship until she realized that he would have neither. Then she said, "Let me tell my brother I am leaving; then I will get my things. I'll have Cramwell cook you some breakfast before we go." Then she rose, said a few words to the cook, and led her brother into an empty section.

Borleaf and Anson returned, sat down, and said, "Take a look out the windows; this doesn't look good at all. One of the old fishermen said his knee felt like it was on fire, and he says it never fails to measure the strength of a coming storm." Anson laughed to himself, and when pressed, said, "Oh, it's just that my uncle used to say the same thing, but it wasn't about his knee." Borleaf laughed and shook his head sideways, taking a long drink from his cup. The windows were bright pink, and the sky had turned cloudy and red as the sun drew nearer to rising. There was grumbling about a short day on the channel, and the fishermen argued about how or whether the fish might react to the storm.

Henry joined Manchester in the vacant section after Sophia went upstairs. Then he looked across the room at the soldiers and said, "How did you know who they were? And why did you keep looking at that one sword? He saw you staring."

"Lots of my father's books are about other kingdoms and customs. You'd know if you would ever read any of them. But he also used to tell me stories about his trips to Murmilan, about the king, and that kind of thing. He told me a lot about their castle and their guards and stuff. That's how I recognized the crests and what they meant. I had guessed at the names from talking to Sophie, but I didn't say because I've never met them before."

Henry looked astonished. "Your father talked with a real king in person! I thought he just traveled around here!"

Manchester shrugged, "I don't know where he goes. He did travel farther before I was born, though. Sophie used to go with him, and I guess that's how she met her friends at Mure Castle. That's why Sophie goes across the channel all the time."

Henry continued to stand amazed, and Manchester pretended not to notice.

"As for the sword, it just reminds me of something I've seen or read about before, I don't know; it's probably nothing."

"You never told me any of that stuff about your father or Sophie! I thought she went over to buy supplies for the inn, or to — I don't know. She always comes back with supplies and things."

"I tell you all kinds of things, but you don't care; you always pretend to die of boredom."

Henry grinned in concession; he did enjoy that joke in particular.

A few rough voices called to the boys to refill their mugs, and somewhere in the back of the kitchen Cramwell was crying out for help as if he were drowning in orders that would be the end of him.

After a short breakfast of ham and toast, Herrick, Anson, Borleaf, and Sophia walked back to the ship under an ominous, yet beautiful pink sky. Sophia carried a worn leather bag across her shoulders.

The captain collected his crew, who were making conversation in the fishing vessels that sat high against the docks, reflecting orange in the windblown water below. Soon, *The Dolphin* had raised its sails and let the river's strong current push it into the channel. There it would spend the next few hours fighting the wind, climbing northward in wide, angular tacks under the huge shadow of Allocausus, which spat its dark smoke into the air to meet the fiery morning clouds.

Mure Castle had been sleeping within a bowl of fog. Gears and pulleys squealed to life as its city gates were raised under a glowing sky that layered streaks of pink and red over the castle. Crowds and lines of carts streamed once again into the half-shrouded city, ready to begin the last day of parades, markets, and ceremony.

A few dim lights began to appear in the blackened windows of the castle and in those of the market buildings against the West Wall. There was an air of excitement as the city began to chatter and move in the early stillness. Yet it was still quiet enough that everyone on and within the walls of Murmilan that morning heard the long shrieks of a woman who had gone to draw water from the lake.

It was as if the entire city stopped breathing. Even the crows were silent as the woman's lone, screaming voice soared in all directions through the fog. Men and women rushed through the haze to find her. One scream piled on top of another until the guards arrived to settle the scene. There they found the familiar face and form of King Wiston, waterlogged and twisted backwards on itself on the muddy bank. There were two dark ironwood arrows in his bloodless body, and the guards had to chase away a pair of ravens that picked at his face.

Inside the castle, Marscion was turning heavily, disturbed by a horrible dream. In it he saw a young boy with a crown on his head, looking out through the iron bars of a prison. Nearby, a hooded, grisly ax-man split wood on a high platform in front of a cheering crowd. Marscion jerked with each knock of the wood until he awoke in a sweat.

"Marscion, sir, please wake up." The muffled voice came from the other side of his chamber door. Then it knocked again.

Marscion rose with a dull headache and cursed himself for drinking so much the night before. As he turned the latch, he looked down and saw that he had slept in his clothes. He snatched a thick robe from a hook to cover himself before opening the door. Then he yawned wide and rubbed his face with the inside of the robe. He pulled the door open, still wiping his eyes.

On the other side was a lower guard named Loren, who looked shaken. "It is still rather early in the day is it not, Loren?" said Marscion, stifling another yawn.

Loren was wide-awake and his eyes moved back and forth nervously. Marscion noticed this and assumed his normal, authoritative posture.

"Sir," said Loren, "Baelin commanded me to your chamber to tell you what has befallen us, and to ask you to speak to her highness the princess regarding it."

Marscion repeated curiously, "Befallen us? What has happened, Loren?"

"Sir," he said, "someone has murdered King Wiston. We think, well, we suspect, sir, that someone in The Guard has done it."

Marscion was awake instantly. "What?" Then he asked contemptuously, "Where is Herrick?"

Loren looked at his feet. His eyes showed a mix of disbelief and confusion, and he answered, as if he could not believe it, "We don't know, sir, no one has seen Borleaf either. We fear the worst, and we have parties searching for their bodies as well. The king, sir, they found him in the lake." Loren's teeth began to clench. "His crown was left on the pavilion … stuck fast in blood."

Marscion stared at Loren, hard and blank, then said, "Why is The Guard suspect?"

"Because, sir, the arrows in — that killed the king, were ours."

"And Herrick cannot be found?"

"Correct, sir, nor Borleaf."

Marscion paused in heavy thought. "I don't think we will find him, Loren. In fact, I think he will only show himself when he is ready. I have warned against him from the beginning. When was the king found?"

"At sunrise, sir, just after the gates were opened."

"Close them and let no one leave. The princess doesn't know?"

"No, sir."

"Can you tell me anything else? Did you, or anyone else, see or find anything more that I can tell her?"

"Not yet, sir."

"Thank you, Loren. I will dress and then go to her."

Marscion stood before Agatha's chamber, and after a short wait, he heard her yell weakly that the door was unlocked. He opened it and stood in the doorway, taking notice of the room. Papers were strewn across the green carpet, and plants and candles had been knocked over and scattered against the walls. The princess sat at the desk before the window with her head down, between her elbows. The warm morning colors brightened the wood in the room and made the carpet glow with an orange hue. Agatha had stacked several books on the desk to shade her face from the incoming light. She looked up, exhausted. Her tangled hair hung down in a mess over her struggling red eyes. She had not slept all night.

Marscion walked to her gently and knelt down beside the desk. "Has anyone spoken to you this morning?"

She looked up and stared at the books that covered the light, "No."

"I only ask because your door was not latched, and — your chamber is …"

"What do you want, Marscion?" She said helplessly, restraining tears.

"I need you to prepare yourself for the worst news, princess."

Agatha's face stretched wide in a silent agony that preceded the cries she buried in her hands.

Marscion sat quietly beside her, curious and patient, and when she looked up, wiping her nose, she cried, sniffling, "Who? Who did it?"

Marscion looked on her strangely and asked, "How can you know, Agatha, if no one has spoken to you this morning?"

She repeated in a weak, exasperated voice, "Who did it Marscion? Just tell me."

He lowered his head and said, "We don't know yet, but we think it was ... this will be difficult for you to ..."

"Tell me!" she shrieked, biting her lip and closing her eyes.

"We think ... we think it was Herrick." He turned his head away solemnly to avoid her face.

In her mind, a thousand possibilities battled one another, but none prevailed. She decided that she had misunderstood. "What do you mean?"

Marscion hesitated, nodding his head up and down slightly as he drew a breath and answered, "Agatha, they found your father this morning, killed by arrows from the King's Guard. Now, no one can find Herrick. We ... I ... fear that he has run away."

Agatha swallowed and looked pale as if she were bleeding from a deep wound. Her mouth hung open slightly and her eyes looked on Marscion with a painful glaze.

Marscion looked down at the floor and said, "I don't know what you thought I was talking about, but I'm sorry."

Agatha struggled to understand the situation. Herrick, her love, had not been killed as she had feared. Instead, he was reborn in the shape of a villain who had murdered her father. She could not speak for several minutes, but then, as if a thought had occurred to her that might repeal the entire situation and bring both men back, she said, "But no, Marscion, I sent him away — he wasn't here! Herrick could not have done anything! I made sure he was gone!"

Marscion's eyes grew wide and he spoke with an urgent, careful voice, "Do not do that, Agatha! You do not know what trouble your words may cause you!"

"But it's true!" she urged, trying to find hope in her own words.

Marscion only grew more stern, "Ask yourself what this implies — that you, the sole heiress, commanded the heads of The Guard away from the castle on the night your father was to be killed! Now, I don't believe you had anything to do with this, but trust me, if you speak like that to anyone else you might succeed in getting yourself hanged!" Marscion mastered his emotions and continued. "There is also the simpler matter of lying for him. Do not dishonor your father by making up stories to protect his murderer. We know you loved Herrick, and if I ever urged you to stay away from him, understand that it would benefit you most to disassociate yourself from him now in every way."

Agatha grew weaker in the defeat and her nose turned down in a bitter, sorrowful expression, "I am not lying. I swear, I did send him away; and I would not dishonor my father."

Marscion continued to gaze on her with critical eyes in a gentle face, and said, "I beg you, Agatha, say no more of your part in this, or I promise you will most likely hang. Think of your mother, think of the people, and think of what Herrick has done to you. Most of all, Agatha, think about what you say. I know you are blameless, but I am not the only one who overheard the last thing you said to your father."

Agatha walked down a broad stone hallway near the top of the castle. Marscion stayed close to comfort her. As they neared the throne room, they saw into it through the wide, arched doorway, which was washed out and pink in the strong morning light. Marscion removed his hand from Agatha's shoulder as they approached the entrance.

Angry and inconsolable voices rumbled loudly inside the room, but one by one, as they noticed the princess standing in the doorway, they fell silent. No one moved, and all stared at her, still, quiet, and reverent — all except Baelin, who watched her brokenly, fighting the suspicion that she had tricked him the night before by orchestrating a pathetic scene. But it was he alone who was not moved to compassion as that devastated girl stepped unsurely into the room with wide, pitiful eyes, walked in the abject gloom to her seat beside the empty throne, put her face and hands slowly into her lap, and wept.

11

Unwelcome

Herrick sat alone in the lower quarters of *The Dolphin* as it rounded the northeastern horn of Murmilan and leaned westward toward Tholepin Bay. His eyes were open and angry against the weak, blinking strips of light that shone between the boards above his head. He gripped the table before him as if manacles held him fast to it. For Herrick, the minutes flitted by with cruel speed as each lurch of the ship threw him forward in time to meet again the face of that heartless princess. Chilly water poured in thin threads from the seams above and sloshed in alternate corners of the dark hold with every roll and plunge of the ship. Rats fled noisily and blind across his boots, side to side, avoiding the water. One tugged on Herrick's cloak, hanging above the flood with scrambling feet. It caught hold of the fabric and began to climb. Herrick sat as a granite statue under the salty drops, thinking on Agatha, and he shook the creature violently from his cloak.

Above board, Captain Sunger and his crew fought an arduous, repetitive battle with the wind, swinging the boom left and coursing along an angular northwestern path, then back to the right, riding a southwestern tack back toward the coast. The ship spent the long morning hours fighting its way westward under a blanket of strangled pink clouds that were lit deeply by the red sun that hid within them. The mainsail whipped in the wind and slung cold sea spray into the faces of the crew as they pulled the wet ropes. Anson and Sophia had joined them, working tirelessly with faces wet and chapped with the slapping salt spray. Everyone slipped and sloshed with waterlogged boots through the tilting sheets of water that continually flooded the deck.

As the morning ended and afternoon began, the waves lifted and dropped the ship with greater force. The clouds darkened, lost their color, and hung in the sky like a thick woolen shroud, brushed by severe winds. Borleaf worked steadily on the port side, his huge arms pumping endless volumes of water from the bilge below. After another hour, they had worked their way past the winding, windy fiords off the coast and arrived at Tholepin Bay. It was astir of fishing ships turning in early to secure their boats against the weather. The captain and crew were relieved as the ship drew into the calmer waters of the bay.

Herrick emerged pensively from below as if he expected to see Agatha holding hands with an executioner and waiting for him at the edge of the royal docks. He found everyone on board soaked through, weary, and glowing pale from the wind and the satisfaction of the accomplished journey. The captain was known well in Tholepin Bay, and he hailed the other ships, which passed by with busy crews and wide, canvas sails tanned by the sun.

The royal docks sat high on the far end of the bay, and they reached it easily. Borleaf joined Herrick, who was staring at the docks with an odd, changed expression. Something was wrong. A few marine birds sat huddled on the pilings, staring westward, and a few crabs crawled slowly across the worn planks of the near docks. Apart from the swaying of ships, this was the only motion at the anchorage. "Where are all the dockhands?" asked Borleaf.

Captain Sunger cursed the dockhands furiously under his breath before apologizing formally to the honorable officials he carried on board. "Sirs," he growled, "I seen plenty of lazy hands in my day, but never not one to be found. After I get the horn from below and call them out, they'll wish they never woke up this morning to hear any sound — I guarantee that."

Anson and Sophia joined them at the rail, and the captain went below the deck to fetch his horn. *The Dolphin* banged against the dock repeatedly, waiting to be tied.

Captain Sunger returned and growled at his crew to descend immediately and secure the ship before she damaged her hull. One sailor reached the dock before Herrick recalled the order hastily and commanded them to draw all external ropes back into the ship. A crowd of blue-cloaked sailors had erupted from one of the harbor buildings, and they were stampeding down the long docks to meet the ship with unmistakable hostility. The mob shone as bright sparks of blue between the pallid greys of the sky and the water.

Sophia looked at Borleaf inquisitively and understood that he knew no more than she.

"Sophie, go down below for the moment, but if you feel the ship start to move, come back up to help sail us out of here. Something is wrong."

Reluctantly, she turned and disappeared below the decks as the first of the sailors reached the ship.

The men below looked at each other, hearts and lungs pumping hard in the cold. They beheld the ship and its crew like warriors or ghosts come from a fable. They were visibly nervous, but their anger propelled them to yell quickly and passionately, "Drop your ropes and prepare to be boarded! Now! Where is your captain?"

Herrick watched in disbelief. The long morning hours of reflecting on Agatha's rejection still colored his emotions, and to him, these were her personal agents. He left them without answer and began to pace up and down against the railing. Without a word, he prevented Captain Sunger from approaching the rail, and encouraged him to remain out of sight.

When Herrick turned, one of the sailors saw the silver crest on his shoulder and yelled, "That's him! That's him!"

Borleaf roared down in his deep, commanding voice, and by his sudden sense of presence, they knew him too. "Do you realize who it is you address? Answer, sailor!"

The foremost man was shaking; he widened his stance and answer bitterly, "We were speaking to Herrick, the traitor and murderer who stole this ship, and now to you, who it seems has joined him, sir." The sailor's tone was respectful against his will.

Herrick flew to the railing and picked up a coil of heavy rope, which he hurled down on the man, who leapt back and drew his sword as if he had been attacked. "Let one of you come aboard and explain yourselves, for you show a great disrespect for two of your king's highest servants."

At these words, the sailors began to curse Herrick and Borleaf, shaking their drawn swords. The leader of their group ordered the men on the ship to cast down all the ropes and surrender their weapons.

Borleaf's voice boomed once more, commanding one of them to explain the charge, but the sailors were outraged as if they had been mocked. While Herrick and Borleaf studied the mob, Anson noticed that one of them had taken the end of the rope Herrick had dropped and was slowly wrapping it around a piling to hold the ship in place. Herrick saw it too and ordered the Captain Sunger to raise the sails and start away immediately.

The sails popped into place and the ship lurched forward, tugging against the pier and injuring the sailor whose arm was caught in the taught rope. Borleaf hacked through the rope with two strong strokes and the ship was free, gliding quickly away from the docks under the heavy wind. The sailors on the dock raced away, climbing and crawling aboard other royal ships. Before any of them could give chase, however, *The Dolphin* slipped out of the bay and began its flight back to the east under a straining sail that threatened to drive the front of the ship below the piling waves.

Behind them in the west, the thunder growled under darkened clouds, and the wind soon threatened the mouth of the bay with such a menace that every ship that started out in pursuit of *The Dolphin* soon turned and fled back to the docks.

Herrick and Borleaf went below and closed the hatch. Borleaf was rigid and formidable as if he were entering into battle, while Herrick's emotions were cooling into bitter resolutions. They sat on opposite sides of the table and Borleaf spoke first, resuming the authority that he had cast off two nights before, "Can you explain any of this Herrick? Tell me everything you know, right now."

From the moment he had heaved the rope overboard in anger, Herrick's breaths had become more steady and his manner more calm. Now there was no inflection in his voice, and his breaths were regular, low, and firm. "Just before the ceremony, King Wiston spoke to me privately. He said he was grateful for my noble efforts to avoid his daughter. He said he trusted me and found me honorable. Then he grew sad and oddly reflective. He told me that love was the most cruel when one had to endure its face every day without escape. He said love could be a great destroyer of persons, and that duty and propriety were often its chief weapons."

Borleaf looked keenly at Herrick and asked, "Did he tell you why he said that?"

Herrick laughed a short, bitter laugh and said, "I couldn't make sense of it. It sounds like something Baelin would say." The two men sat in the tilting room for a few minutes, listening to the water beating against the ship, and the loud straining and creaking of the boards. Then Herrick answered directly, "No, he did not explain the statement further, but last night you said that you would have put off retirement for a few years. What did you mean?"

Borleaf leaned back, watching Herrick avoid the rest of his story, but he considered it a fair question. "King Wiston said something rather puzzling to me the afternoon of the tournament. He said, 'If for any reason Herrick decided to leave his post at the guard with my blessing, would you remain for a few more years?' I assured him that I would serve for as long as I lived, and then I asked if he would explain the situation to me. King Wiston said only that you were to make a choice that night after the ceremony, and that I might know by your happiness whether you had decided to leave. Therefore, although I had no details, your misery was plain, and it was all I could say. Now I have answered. Tell me what the king said to you."

The white of Herrick's eyes shone bright on his dark face as he spoke with sharp notes of resentment. "He asked me some questions about Agatha, and what I might do if traditions were not as they are —" Herrick grimaced, as if the shame were a nail twisting into his side. "It doesn't matter what he said, Borleaf; it all comes to this, he acted as if he were taking a great stand to spite the cruelty of love and politics — he gave me leave to propose marriage to Agatha on the condition that if she agreed, she would forfeit her ascendancy and I would give up my rank and place in the guard. He said we could live under a pension in the palace of Ordon in the Northern Kingdoms of the queen's cousin.

"He said the throne of Murmilan could be given to one of the members of the royal line of Ordon. He didn't say who, only that they would have returned to Murmilan immediately to secure their place as the kingdom's heir. This very ship was to be among those that brought him to Murmilan, had Agatha accepted."

Borleaf was speechless. The wind whistled across the open cracks in the boards above. Herrick turned the burning inside his heart into a terrible smile and said, "But it was all a joke, my friend — a test for Agatha, perhaps."

"You should have seen her. She wasted no time but cast me out of her sight as fast as I could speak her name. Baelin was right. She was playing with me, and the king simply tested her. I grow ill thinking of how she trembled, knowing what I was going to say — so afraid of it that … Borleaf, I don't ever wish to speak of this, or of her again. I can only assume that she, or the king, or both, would now have me put away, and so I will flee for my life."

Borleaf leaned forward and raised himself on his huge, hairy forearms. His voice was soft, but intent and peremptory, "I have known King Wiston for more than thirty years, and you are wrong to question his honor, especially in matters such as this. I cannot speak for Agatha. Though I love her like my own, she is spoiled, headstrong, and immature. I can only assure you that if you were to be 'put away' by the king, I would have received the order to do it, and you would not be sitting here."

Borleaf sat back down but his eyes kept their intensity, "Have you forgotten that they called us murderers and thieves, and worse, traitors? Have you forgotten that I was accused alongside you? Whatever is happening back there is greater than your feelings, Herrick. I have never known you to allow your emotions to inhibit your reason. Do not start now."

Herrick covered his face with his hands and then brought them down with a crash on the table. The calm resolution with which he had begun the conversation was gone. He struggled to regain his composure, and as he closed his eyes, he seemed to drift for a moment into a state of surprised disbelief. When he opened them, he recovered. He gathered a deep, determined breath and said, "Let us take shelter in the fiords. There we can moor the ship among the trees and move inland until we can discover why anyone would chase us."

A few minutes later, Borleaf and Herrick climbed into the bright, drizzling rain and ordered the captain to halt the ship near the coast. The boom swung straight and the sail flapped violently in the wind. They rode high-pitched waves, up and down, just off a smooth section of grassy coast that preceded by a mile the first of the fiords that wound intricate channels into the northern coastline. Then, despite their protestations and oaths of loyalty, Captain Sunger and his five crewmen obeyed Herrick's command and parted with their ship. They settled into the high swells in a tiny rowboat, in which they worked their way to shore, carrying enough food for the long hike back to Tholepin Bay.

The Dolphin was sailed by the remaining four. Sophia held the tiller while Anson shouted orders that he, Borleaf, and Herrick followed.

After a few short minutes they steered the ship into the first narrow fiord. The wind did not abate between the high rocks and trees, but instead, trapped in narrow paths, it blew stronger and more sporadically.

Once in the channels, Herrick directed the ship as it glided in and out of the maze of water and rock. After scraping the walls several times, they reached a tight spot before a little bay that was surrounded by high pines. The wind swirled out of the bay in great gusts, and they had to retreat and come at it again with full force, dropping both sails and turning the tiller so that the ship rotated and faced outward. This caused the port side of the ship to smash against the rocky bank, and several boards cracked and bowed just above the waterline. Anson and Herrick climbed carefully to the shore and tied the ropes to nearby trees.

Sophia and Borleaf climbed off as well, and all stood on the shore watching *The Dolphin* roll from side to side, rising on gentle grey waves in the high wind, and ramming the rocks on either side of her makeshift anchorage.

The group sat among thick burgundy pines whose tops swayed with heavy swishes above them. It began to drizzle, and the ground was as cold and wet as the decks had been.

Sophia said, "Can any of you tell me what just happened or why we are here?"

Borleaf looked up tiredly and answered, "We hope to find out. We know as much as you." Anson lay on his back, resting in the misty air and listening to the thunder in the west. Herrick was deep in thought, rubbing his forehead with his hand.

"I mean no offense to you three," said Sophia, "but I think I have a better chance of making it to the castle without you."

Herrick answered, "You are free to go. We trust you."

She hugged Borleaf, gave him a worried smile, and then ran light and fast into the trees.

Anson shook his head and followed her with his eyes until she had disappeared, "I should have gone with her — you know, to keep her safe."

Borleaf looked at him with an incredulous, amused expression and said, "You would only get in her way, my boy."

Then Anson looked to Herrick and said, "We are in Northford, in the high plains above the castle, are we not?"

Herrick nodded yes, and then removed his cloak and ordered the others to do the same. "Let's look in the ship to see if we can find more modest clothes. There are a few settlements a mile or so inland; we should be able to find our way into one of them without too much trouble. The ship's mast is well below the treetops so it should be hidden, and I don't think there will be much of a naval search made for us today — they know we won't go out to sea under this sky."

The rain began as they climbed back aboard the ship. It came first in sporadic, heavy thumps on the wood, and then it erupted into a full downpour, pelting the trees with icy drops and freezing the men's backs as they descended the ship and began the hike into Northford.

12

Too many advisers

The storm reached the city of Murmilan by late afternoon and sent its inhabitants scurrying for shelter. The city gates were closed tight, and the King's Guard was busy enforcing order on a wet and angry crowd, which, despite many conjectures, was still unable to find out what had happened. The witnesses and the body had been taken away immediately, and only rumor was left. Aside from the constant hum of the rain, The Great Hall sat empty and quiet, devoid of the noisy, chattering crowd of dignitaries and guests that should have been there on the third day of the festival. All had been relegated to their quarters for the remainder of the day.

It was soon ordered that the princess and the queen be escorted by two members of the guard wherever they went. Agatha had withdrawn into herself and spoken little since appearing in the throne room that morning. She had been overwhelmed by the venomous disputes between the council and the guard, and their explicit descriptions of her father's body, which some councilors had used in hopes of shocking their opponents into submission. Marscion had been the only one to speak on her behalf, and she left him to broker peace between the two sides. She walked wearily up the sloping stone hallway toward her chamber, and commanded the guards to leave her alone to sleep.

Agatha entered, closed the strong door behind her, and walked, tottering with a heavy head to collapse on her bed. She listened to the rain thudding against the panes of her windows, and she drew a silk pillow over her head and closed her weary eyes tight. Her white dress shone bright in the pale light of the windows. From close behind her, she heard a soft, cautious voice say, "Agatha." She raised her head slowly from the pillow and listened. The voice came again, "Agatha."

Around the room, long rows of candles flickered and cast thin shadows on the walls. A small fire burned in the chamber's hearth.

Turning onto her side, Agatha looked toward the window and found Sophia bedraggled in wrinkled, damp clothes. Agatha righted herself quickly, and Sophia sat down next to her on the bed. They embraced, and Agatha cried for several minutes.

Sophia consoled her friend, but she was still confused, and asked as they parted, "What is going on here?"

The princess sat upright and wiped her eyes and nose. Then she took on a look of hope and said, "Sophie, did he come to get you? Is he alright?"

Sophia looked as if she did not understand, and shifted back a few feet on the bed to get a better view of Agatha. "Yes, Herrick came and got me, but that was before your father's soldiers chased us out of the harbor. We had to hide in Northford; it took me forever to get here and even longer to get through the gates. I almost didn't make it into the castle. I was stopped by the guards and sent away twice before I took some of our old shortcuts to get up here."

There was a long pause in which Agatha looked blankly and pitifully at Sophia, as if she could not hear her. The fire hissed and a log cracked and fell into the ash. "My father was killed. It happened last night and they think Herrick did it — but he was with you right? It wasn't him; I told them it couldn't be."

Sophia froze in place for several seconds, and Agatha went quiet. Then, for the next few minutes, Sophia prodded Agatha gently, to uncover what she knew, but Agatha offered little and always returned to the same subject. "So where is Herrick now? Is he safe?"

Sophia had ignored the question several times and she became angry. "I've already told you he is safe for the moment — considering that your people are still chasing him. Doesn't your father's death move you more than news of a man you apparently dismissed? He left me with the impression that you no longer cared for him at all. Have you thought of anything else? Think of this, Agatha — who will rule now that your father is gone? It's not going to be Herrick."

The princess stared down at the green carpet, tracing its intricate patterns with her eyes. Sophia repeated the question louder and with more emphasis. Agatha flopped her hands at her sides and said, "You of all people could not understand."

Sophia's face reddened at the insult. She had never really been in love with anyone, having worked steadily most of her life running *The Gosling* for her father while he attended his other duties in Talus. Sophia turned her thoughts to the late king, whom she had loved like an uncle, and she too began to cry.

Agatha made a weak, but sincere attempt to comfort her and apologize for her unkind words, "I guess the council can take care of things for a while. Marscion was doing a lot to help stop the fighting between everyone today. They wanted to disband the guard permanently and find some other way to protect the castle, but I think they will listen to him in the end."

"You have to tell them to let Borleaf and Herrick return if you know they haven't done anything wrong. They should listen to you above everyone else now, except for your mother, of course."

"I can't," replied Agatha. "They know about me and Herrick,

and they say I am just defending him. Even Baelin won't speak to me anymore — and he was there when I sent Herrick away. Instead he just looks at me with hatred. He must think I made Herrick leave so my father would be unprotected."

"Who is Baelin?"

"He has spoken for the guard in Herrick's absence, being the next highest in rank. You wouldn't know him," said Agatha, "he was a lieutenant on the walls until recently and he doesn't like to come to the castle. I don't think he likes people very much. He makes me feel horrible about myself sometimes."

There was a short knock on the door, and Sophia whispered quickly, "Say nothing of how I came here!" She finished the sentence as Marscion let himself into the room.

Sophia could tell by his eyes that he was disturbed to find the princess in another's company without his knowledge. She felt the force of his driving gaze and straightened herself.

"How did you come here without my being alerted? The castle has been secured, or so we thought, for the safety of her highness and the queen."

Sophia gave a weary, confused look and said nothing.

Then Marscion recognized her. "Of course. You are Agatha's young friend from across the channel. It has been a little while since you last joined us at Mure Castle, has it not? Well, at least you have come in time to comfort your friend. However, I would ask you to leave us for a moment while we discuss certain items pressing to our kingdom."

Sophia was anxious about moving from her spot and looked to Agatha, who was listening eagerly to Marscion as if she would agree with anything he said, as long as he said it kindly.

As Sophia began to rise reluctantly, Agatha said softly, "No, let her stay. She is like a sister to me and I tell her everything anyway."

"I do not mean to offend you, young lady," said Marscion, nodding politely to Sophia, "but it is a terrible policy and one I would advise our princess to cease immediately. Nonetheless," he said, turning back to Agatha, "if you wish it so today, then so be it. We have news of the assassins."

Marscion casually noted Sophia's appearance and asked, "Which way did you come to the castle, by chance?"

Sophia knew he was testing her, but she remained calm. "I came alone for the last day of the festival, but I waited outside in the rain this morning trying to get in the East Gate. Is that what you mean?" She was thankful that the rain had washed the salt out of her clothes or Marscion would have smelled it.

His suspicion dropped as suddenly as it had come, and he turned back to Agatha. "Princess," he said solemnly, "we have news that the murderer and his crew sailed the stolen ship back into the harbor at Tholepin Bay where they mocked a group of sailors before fleeing into the North Sea. With the weather as it was we were unable to pursue them. However, we do have a report of who was on the ship. It was, with certainty, Borleaf, Herrick, Anson, and the ship's crew, who were obviously taken by some pretense or threat, for their captain did not show himself. There may have been others below, but no one else from the guard is missing."

Agatha listened like a child, waiting for Marscion to tell her how to act next.

Receiving no response from Agatha, Marscion turned to Sophia and said, "You must understand that as the result of your hearing this information you must remain in this castle until further notice. It is for our own security. Do you understand?"

Sophia was fascinated by Marscion's account of their landing at Tholepin Bay and she would have promised anything to hear more. She wanted to ask questions, to sound Marscion for more information, but she feared that Agatha, being sad and weakened, might miss her subtlety and let something slip.

Marscion leaned forward in his chair and spoke in a voice that was soft and gravelly, "We think we know why they were trying to land at Tholepin Bay. One of our councilors has a son who is missing. We all knew him, and he is not the type to run away. He was one of the thirty-two — a sailor. He disappeared last night after the ceremony. We think the three rogues might have wanted to offer this boy in trade. We don't know for certain yet, because they fled under the threat of our brave naval officers."

Sophia rolled her eyes against her will and asked, "How are you so sure they did anything? How did they get off the docks if the ship was truly stolen? And why wasn't a missing royal ship and crew reported to you until after they came back?"

The rain continued to pound on the windows in waves, rushing across its surface and receding in steady sheets. Marscion's suspicion returned fully and his stare made Sophia sink away from him.

He spoke low and carefully, as if each word moved a part of her face into the light in order to inspect it better. "Perhaps you have some information that might lead us to a different conclusion? It does appear that you have a decided interest in the subject. So tell me again, in what ways is our case flawed? I've already said that the crew must have left under a pretense, which would account for their cooperation, yet you seem to think otherwise. Tell me about it."

Sophia had slipped. She concentrated on quieting her nerves and producing an apologetic countenance. Then she lied calmly, "I am sorry, sir. I only heard of these things about ten minutes ago and I am still trying to work them out for myself. It's only that Borleaf was such a good friend to me, and I just can't imagine that he could be a part of this. I was looking forward to seeing him again, and now, instead —" Sophia ended her lie with a pause and a bemused, hopeless expression.

"Borleaf has been a surprise to all of us. Now, Agatha, we still have several interrogations left, and at least one of them, I think, should be particularly helpful. So do not worry. Soon we will find out exactly what happened, and we will catch and punish everyone who played a part in this. Now let us go to your mother; she has been calling for you."

13

Incompatible deceits

Borleaf had developed a dangerous fever under the pouring canopy of the forest, and his breath became thinner as he, Herrick, and Anson walked across the broad pools created by the rainfall. Before them, in the south, the rainy haze between the trees was lighter. They climbed a small hill to find themselves at the edge of the wood.

At their feet was a square acre of dying stalks, under which hundreds of tiny rivulets rumbled through muddy furrows. The forest cradled the right side of the field, but to the left of it, through the browning, crumpling stalks they saw the worn, patched roof of a tiny house. Thin puffs of smoke squeezed themselves upward out of a cobblestone chimney and were immediately separated and beaten down by the rain.

"We'll stop here," said Herrick. "This house is near enough to the castle that if any searches were made this morning they would have already passed by. Borleaf, we should get you out of this rain."

Borleaf coughed and took Anson's elbow to keep his balance. The three moved along the edge of the wood, careful not to trample the farmer's field. They found a mule tied to the back of the house and shivering in the rain. It started backwards, frightened at their sudden appearance. Anson lagged behind the others, removed the brown cloak he had taken from the ship, and placed it across the animal's back. Then he jogged forward to catch up.

The outside of the house was poor and dilapidated. It had only one dirty window near the door, which opened southward onto a field of dead grass. Herrick stood in the mud before the doorway and knocked. The rain slid off the roof in thick sheets, slapping the pools that lay all around the house.

Two dogs began barking inside and a man's face appeared framed in the short window. His eyes were suspicious and frightened, yet he soured his face into a look of anger that he hoped would appear menacing. His hair was short against his head and grey above his ears. "What do you want!" he demanded.

"We are travelers caught in this storm, we would be obliged if we could stop here for a while."

Borleaf began to cough heavily, but repressed it as if he were embarrassed.

The man shouted back against his window, "Everyone has their problems; I've got mine, you've got yours. We all do our best."

Anson looked at Herrick and mumbled, "He'll do it for a few coins; I know this type."

Herrick's eyebrows were set in a menacing frame on his forehead as he stepped away to let Anson speak. In less than a day, Herrick had been rejected by the highest family in his kingdom, which he had begun to love; then, at the harbor, he had been rejected by his fellow brothers in the king's service. Now, he was rejected by this rude peasant, for whom he cared nothing.

Anson took notice of Borleaf's shivering and spoke loudly, "We can perhaps help you, sir, we have only a few coins but we would gladly trade them for a small meal and a place by your fire."

The door opened a little. The man was taller than they had expected. He had stooped to look through the window. He stood in the doorway, beating back the two roan hounds at his feet and said,

"How much can you help me, kind sir?" Anson stood in the rain and counted out six golden coins that shone wet. The man's eyes glinted at them and he said, "Come in, please, let us get you three out of the cold and wet. No one should be out in this weather; come, come."

He took the coins from Anson and disappeared into the other room of the house. The three men stood in front of the fire, which was modest, but warm enough to dry their faces and hands. Piles of old logs leaned against the wall on each side of the fireplace and caused the entire house to smell like sap and rotting wood. In the corner of the main room there was a wooden bucket catching loud water drops from the ceiling. The two dogs huddled against the wet men, shoving their noses under the strangers' hands and wagging heavy tails. Soon the dogs were wet and the house smelled worse. The peasant returned from the other room with a lamp and a loaf of bread. He placed both on the table, which sat in the middle of the room with two chairs. He took Anson by the shoulder and led him to one of them, and they both sat.

Anson heard the coins moving in the man's pocket as if they wanted attention.

"So, traveler," said the man, "my name is Jerrand. Here, have some bread, for all of you are drenched, and if I may say, you look weary and hungry as well. It is lucky you came here to get out of the rain. I wasn't even here an hour ago. You are lucky indeed — lucky that I was here and able to help."

Anson replied, "We certainly thank you for your hospitality; you are very generous." He took the piece of bread, tore it in two, and offered the pieces to Herrick and Borleaf, who were still sitting by the fire with the dogs.

Jerrand's face turned back to the other room in dismay, but righted itself again into a flattering expression when he addressed Anson. "So, where are you traveling to and what are your names?

Moreover, do you know where you are now? Do you know who owns this piece of land? A councilor! His name is Robert and he is a very powerful and influential man. Have you heard of him? He is my good friend too. I speak with him every so often, I do. He has shaken my hand countless times."

Herrick looked into the fire, and his mouth turned up into a slight grin. Anson could get any information he wanted from a man like this, and he was sure to tell an entertaining story as he did it. Herrick let the fire warm his body and he put aside the questions about his own fate to listen to Anson work. He heard a subtle accent in Anson's next reply. Borleaf noticed too, and raised an eye at Herrick in a smile that made them both forget, momentarily, the weight of their problems.

Anson started naturally, "Oh, my brother and uncle and I were on a hike from Linnesen over to Tholepin Bay to help our father cut wood for the winter. We don't have any horses, being poor, and here we get caught in this downpour that soaked us through. It is lucky indeed that we should have pooled our monthly wages for food and brought along the money we did, for we were lucky to find you here in your fine house — we've only one room for the six of us back home."

Jerrand, spurred on by this compliment and feeling superior on account of Anson's seeming simplicity, replied, "Well, it was good fortune for both of us." Anson had begun to win him over, but at the end of Jerrand's reply, his face sank again.

Anson noticed it and said, "For a man in such good fortune as yourself, what with this house and a fire and good roof against the rain, you still seem troubled. Is it anything we might help you with as we are so obliged?"

Jerrand's face lost its hope with a devastating sense of finality as he stared away into the back room. He suddenly became strange, as if a different man now sat at the table. He was again the angry, suspicious face at the window. They had misunderstood his greed as stupidity. He said, "You didn't tell me your name, and I asked you. I told you mine."

"Oh, I forgot, my apologies, sir. I am Stephen, this here is my brother Randall, and the big fellow is my uncle Sal, short for Sally, but he doesn't like to be called that, right, Uncle Sally?" Borleaf feigned irritation and Anson laughed, entreating Jerrand to join in the joke and put away his suspicion.

He didn't. Jerrand asked more questions, which Anson answered as if there were no other truth in the world. Anson told him that his father had injured his left hand in a fishing net the previous spring, leaving him unable to cut wood for the winter. He said their work as carpenters had kept them away from Tholepin Bay until now, but they were eager to get home and help their father.

Anson told his story with such nuance and sincerity that at last Jerrand leaned back in his chair in defeat. He had lost his composure and felt that his chance of extracting more money from the men was gone.

"You see," he said solemnly, "not only do I speak with Robert the councilor, but I am also visited by the King's Guard themselves, and we are in a terrible, terrible time. It makes men unsure of themselves and too suspicious. It makes them not know what to do, and so I apologize if I have been too inhospitable."

Borleaf and Herrick turned quickly to study the man's face, which was drooping to the table. Anson did not flinch, but replied carefully, "The King's Guards? I thought they couldn't ever leave the castle." He knew this was untrue, and he had erroneously pluralized 'Guard' to emphasize his unfamiliarity. "And what do you mean by 'terrible time,' Jerrand? Has something happened?"

Jerrand looked up with a palling face as if the words were too gravid to utter. He lowered his voice to a whisper and said, "I should not be telling you this, because they told me not to say anything to anyone. But this morning, two of the king's guardsmen came to my door and told me that," and here anger contorted his whisper, turning it coarse and hard, "the king was found murdered this morning."

The two men by the fire started loudly in unison, sending the dogs scrambling into the far room. "No!" said Borleaf, raising himself up to his full height over the table in an imposing silhouette against the window.

Herrick closed his eyes painfully against the fire that shone bright and deep on his face. Then he turned to Jerrand and asked, "Who did it?"

Jerrand's hands trembled with anger and he raised his voice, "It was his own men, the dirty Red Guard and their new henchman leader! May he die and rot!"

Anson was rattled and broke from his act. "Herrick?" he said incredulously.

Herrick responded by standing up and looking at him in an unexpected and mistimed reaction. Then, as if to cover, he stepped over to the table and commanded Jerrand to repeat what he had said.

Jerrand shrank away from the imposing posture of the two men and said, "They told me that Herrick and the old chief are missing, and the villains may have kidnapped Councilor Robert's son too."

"But is there any proof against him?" Anson replied. "We thought he loved his king, at least that's what people said in our town." Jerrand's suspicion returned. He suddenly became frightened by the men in his house. He noted their offense at the accusations, but he continued anyway, motivated by his own grievance against the Guard, "They said the king was stuck full of arrows shot by his own men! I knew something like this was going to happen. That lot has always been full of cheats and scoundrels, abusing their power and showing favoritism! They should have been disbanded years ago, then this wouldn't have happened!"

The eyes of the three glowed with anger at the insolence of the peasant. Herrick wanted to rip the ungrateful limbs from his body. Borleaf spoke in short breaths, attempting to ease the tension, yet he struggled. His fever made him dizzy and his head was burning hot. "Why would the King's Guard come to this house, Jerrand, and what is your problem with them? The way you speak it sounds as if they have done you some great personal wrong."

"You sure are smart for a carpenter from Linnesen," Jerrand replied. "They came this morning to take my son from me, who was sick and asleep. He went to compete in their so-called tournament some days ago, but they sent him home so humiliated and cheated that he would not even speak to his own father! He just slept in his bed all morning, feverish and sweating. I don't know what they did to him down there but I know it wasn't fair. They are never fair."

Jerrand jerked his head from side to side as he spoke and raised his hands accusingly, pointing at the three men before him as if they were at fault. This only encouraged their anger, which they barely suppressed. They were still in shock over King Wiston's murder, and Herrick felt buried and humiliated under the allegations.

"I've seen some of the hogs they let into the King's Army. They have something against my family! My son Tergiver is the best swordsman and fighter in this kingdom, but he never had a fair chance at that — that fixed sham they call a tournament. It's all a show, just a pretense for the favorites, not for the rest of us."

Herrick and Borleaf had heard this every year from disappointed parents, and it took the edge off their anger by placing them again in a familiar situation. Borleaf said, as if by rote, "I'm sure your son was brave and fought well, however —"

Jerrand smashed his fist against the table, "You should have seen him when they ripped him from his bed this morning! He did not look brave or well then! He looked like a yellow rock hung around some criminal's neck at the bottom of the lake! And still they took him away! He was so ill he could not even say good-bye to his father — and you want more proof? I heard one of the guards say that Herrick voted against him! Doesn't that prove something? Maybe that pig saw how good, how honest my boy Tergiver is; maybe —"

"Please!" said Anson, hoping to intercede before Herrick took the man by the throat. "Did they say anything else about the guard itself? Did those two actually believe the charges against Herrick?"

"I don't know," said Jerrand. "To me they are all snakes in the same pit. What do I care how they bite one another?"

"Did they tell you why they took your son?" asked Anson.

"No, but their weapons were drawn and I fear I will never see him again. He is all I have." With this, Jerrand's anger began to release itself into the grief that had initiated it. His eyes watered and he said, as he opened the door of the house, letting his dogs scramble out into the rain, "You may stay here tonight; stay as long as you like." Then he stalked out into the downpour, and they saw no more of him.

14

Tergiver's charge

Tergiver knelt on both knees, leaning forward so that his forehead rested against the straw-laden floor. High above, a single barred window peeked in at him and shed raindrops down in trickles on the stone. From behind, two voluminous torches burned and cracked at the iron-battened door that creaked on its hinges as it opened. Tergiver's head swam in the light and his mind was weak with fever and disorientation. During the few hours he had slept at his father's house, his body had plunged into a dizzy state of black, exhausted sleep, and he had been dragged out of his bed only half-aware. His mind now dreamed in and out of a painful consciousness that only gradually returned as a voice behind him spoke. He did not know exactly where he was, but he began to understand that he was awake, and that his nightmare had followed him out of the maze of guilty dreams. His heart ached hot in his chest and a place deep behind his eyes began to burn. His throat was stiff and knotted, and his blood had rushed to his head, making him even more dizzy.

The voice behind him was mournful. It was crying. "You know I love him too, Tergiver, this is a bad … no, the worst of dreams … the most horrible …"

Tergiver could not place the voice. It could have been his conscience; it could have been Charlie himself — it spoke with the same inflection. He closed his eyes tightly and heard something shifting the straw behind him, drawing nearer, torturing him in a weepy voice, "Where is Charlie? You are his best friend. You loved him; tell me where he is."

Tergiver's back heaved in dry sobs that stuck in his throat. He imagined Charlie with his hand outstretched, dueling in the firelight, and then lying dead in his lap.

"We know you were with him last night. He told me he was going to meet with you." The voice grew closer to his ear as the figure knelt down beside him, "Where is my son, Tergiver? Tell me we have not lost him." Robert laid his head across Tergiver's back and began to sob.

Tergiver shut his eyes as hard as he could. Still he heard Charlie's voice echoing in Robert's, creeping out to the corners of the cell and dripping back, wet with rain. *Tell him where I am Tergi — your best friend — tell him where you put me. Remember where we used to play when we were kids?* Tergiver released the breath he had been holding involuntarily, and shuddered.

Robert stood after a few minutes and said, "How did we come to this, Tergiver?"

Tergiver's knees had been pressed into the stone for so long that they sent sharp pains up through his legs. He leaned harder on them to punish himself. He had forced his plan onto Charlie, afraid of failing, and now he had killed the two noblest people he had ever met. The walls of the room seemed to close in and touch him on every side. The stone floor was wet around his face, and his forehead was beginning to bruise.

Robert stood near the door of the cell and said, "Marscion is on his way here. He knows … we both know your situation, and you will hear what must be done."

Tergiver was comforted by the thought of confession and

punishment. He found that all he wanted to do was to clear his conscience, no matter the cost. He was caught, and he finally understood one of Robert's sayings — that taking responsibility was often the best way to cease one's own suffering. He tried to lift his head. He took the deepest breath he could but found that he could not yet speak. He felt that if he could only give a detailed admission of what he had done, he could go to the gallows in peace.

Yet some subtle fear held his words in his throat. The most he could manage was to raise his shoulders and head away from the floor and sit up on his knees, still hunched forward. He found that he could not yet look at Robert; he could not look on Charlie's face again, even in its older form.

A heavy latch squealed on its hinges and fell hard against the other side of the thick door. Tergiver heard another set of steps and a robe shifting on the floor, and he knew it must be Marscion. Now he also knelt before the judgment of King Wiston's representative.

The low whisper joined Robert's, and together they stirred the memories in Tergiver's mind. He saw again the king's crimson robe falling to the marble floor, his arrow speeding toward the king's neck, and the ironwood shaft failing below the pavilion like the mast of a slow-sinking ship with feathered flags. These images pulsed in succession against the inside of Tergiver's eyelids. He remembered the horrid red face that condemned him as it rejoiced in its own work; he felt the wet slope of the hill as he fell back against it, and he watched the blood pooling out again in clean circles on the marble. As Robert's voice drew nearer to him, Tergiver leaned forward again, almost to the floor, and he heard behind him the ruffling and unfolding of the blanket in which he had wrapped Charlie's body before lowering it into the broken well by the woodshed, and cutting the rope.

The hushed talking stopped and Tergiver awaited his sentence, holding his breath to keep from crying out when it was pronounced. Then, without a word to precede it, he felt across his shoulders a heavy weight, like an iron yoke, pressing him hard to the ground. But it was soft. It flowed over his shoulders and careened in folds to the floor. Tergiver opened his eyes and saw through his blurred vision, bloody folds spilling from his shoulders and pooling about him, deep and red on the cell floor. The air expired in his lungs and he struggled to breathe.

Then Robert's voice spoke again, moving from behind him and lowering itself to his face, "Charlie always told me that if anything happened to him, you would be the one to rescue him."

Tergiver caught a shallow gasp of air with an audible sucking sound.

"Tergiver, right now we do not know who in the Guard conspired with Herrick. We can trust no one. But you — you grew up in my house, I know that you are as intelligent and determined as any other, and you were very popular in the tournament … despite the result. Councilor Marscion has agreed to this arrangement, but if you are to gain his confidence, you must show greater resolve than you demonstrate now. Charlie and I both need you to be strong for this." Here Robert's voice began to waver, "I know that if anyone cared for my son it was you. Please use all the power we now give you to bring him back and to find and punish the king's murderers. Please, Tergiver. I know you, and I know there is nothing you cannot do if you try. You are stubborn and brave and … our only hope. Stand up now to your new duty. Do this for Charlie." Robert's hand rested on Tergiver's left shoulder with the weight of a fallen tree.

Tergiver's eyes burned and his mind choked with confusion. With all his strength, he lifted his head in the swirling darkness that encircled him, and he saw, creeping out from under Robert's trembling hand, on his own red shoulder, the golden crest of Murmilan. Blackness soon engulfed it as Tergiver lost his sight, then the sound of his breathing, and then consciousness.

An hour later Marscion walked down a steep hallway hung with paintings of warriors, weapons, and battles. He entered a set of wooden double-doors and stepped into the antechamber of Mure Castle's armory. Seven councilmen stood chatting with an air of importance, and the twenty-five highest ranked guard members were gathered in clumps, discussing their situation in grave tones.

Agatha stood next to the councilmen, staring with empty eyes at the array of eager cloaks moving before her. This was a place into which she was forbidden to bring Sophia.

The high walls were dressed with spears and swords, and along the wall above the entrance lay rows of tricolored shields: green, black, and red. Upon seeing Marscion, another councilor with a peppered, grey beard raised his voice above the noise of conversation, "Let us begin." The members of the Guard arranged themselves in a line, and the council members took up a similar formation.

Agatha stood next to Marscion, facing the two lines. There was a brief silence. Baelin stood at the forefront of the guards, hiding his emotion. His dark hair was cut clean and neatly parted. He understood that in the mind of the councilors, his close affiliation with Herrick would be a point of suspicion, and because of this, he was determined to remain silent and obedient until he had gathered enough proof to accuse the princess. He knew the other guards respected him, and he had discovered early that morning that his influence was powerful enough to sour the attitudes of the entire lot. With these things in mind, he fell in line and waited.

Marscion stood before them in his white council robe and began, "As some of you already know, Herrick's ship was last seen at the docks in Tholepin Bay. The weather is not safe enough for any ship to risk a prolonged search, but we expect him to show himself again. We believe, however, that he has not gone far. We were all aghast to learn of his crime, and even more so to learn that Borleaf stood beside him on the deck — not a prisoner as we had surmised, but as a partner."

The guardsmen grumbled in anger, and their reaction was met with stern, reproachful glances from the council members who stood opposite them. Baelin said nothing. The councilors began to fling accusations at the guards, who returned their enmity and suspicion in force. Baelin only glared at Agatha, noting that she had nothing to say, no reaction, and no inclination to place blame.

Agatha stared into the drab tile floor, wishing for a curtain of numbness that might hide and comfort her. Throughout the disruption she avoided Baelin's eyes and only rarely looked up.

Baelin held up his hand to silence the guards. They responded by tightening their line and staring forward, angry and silent. Then, as the noise of the satisfied councilors died away, he spoke. "We will know soon who is responsible for this. Until then, we of the guard should do our duty and show strength and respect as we are bound. By this everyone will know that we are honorable, and that we had nothing to gain by this crime." The guards stifled their emotion obediently, and waited quietly for Marscion to appoint Baelin their new leader.

Marscion stepped aside as a short, bald councilor took the floor and announced eagerly, "By the privilege of our noble Murmillian tradition, long kept by the honor of its Royal Family and upheld by its citizens, the council, with full consent of the queen, has appointed a new chief of the guard." Then his tone grew less formal as he spoke, almost to himself, "I wouldn't have dreamed yesterday that we would be doing this again today, especially under these circumstances."

Marscion thanked him, and the councilor stepped back into the front of his line. Then Marscion looked at Baelin and said, "The Representative of the Guard understands and submits to this process?"

Baelin struggled against himself. He did not care for processes and ceremony, nor did he believe this one was necessary. He wanted desperately to draw his sword and hold it to every throat in the room until he could force enough information from them to clear his noble captain and expose the princess. Instead, he responded to Marscion with a tone of strained resolution. "The guard does so submit."

The bald councilor stepped forward again, carrying a large black sword that was gilded at its handle with intricate silver lines interwoven with deep green paints. The blade itself was black, with the inlaid shape of a long talon emerging from the hilt in green. He presented it to Marscion, who presented it to Agatha. The guard waited for Baelin to step forward.

Instead, Marscion went to the door and opened it. Robert came in first, followed by a sickly and pale young man with short-cropped hair, who wore a red cloak similar to their own, with one side of it folded up over his left shoulder. This showed the black underside of the cloak and covered the emblem. Many recognized him from the tournament as the one who had challenged Baelin at the sword table. He glanced at them hesitantly and stood close to Robert.

Marscion spoke, "Princess, will you, on behalf of our most noble family of protectors, bestow the sword upon the new chief of," he paused to change the word, "the Queen's Guard?"

Agatha walked to Tergiver, who knelt, and then accepted the sword on one knee. Marscion unfolded the shoulder to display the golden crest. Baelin was the only guard who was not shocked and furious, and he turned a sharp eye on them, commanding them to remain dutiful and quiet. Marscion raised Tergiver to his feet and then addressed the gathering, "If there is anyone unwilling to honor the choice of his Queen's Council and her Royal Decree, let him step forward and resign himself immediately."

The guards watched for Baelin's example. Marscion scrutinized Baelin intensely, then added, "Baelin will become your new captain. He will answer only to the new chief."

Baelin noted how this appointment suddenly eased the anger and unease of his fellow guardsmen. Because of this he stood firm and obedient, and nodded in deference to the new chief.

"Then," said Marscion, "it is done. Tergiver of Northford, we charge you with the safekeeping of the Royal Family of Murmilan and the protection of this city. Serve it well all of your days. Baelin of Murmilan, we charge you with the oversight of the Queen's Guard and the protection of this city."

Where normally there would have been celebration and a cheer, there was only uncomfortable silence. Tergiver looked as if he were struggling to stay on his feet. At first, it was clear to all that he was terrified by the responsibility. However, his fear did not culminate in rash words, awkward acts, or even a reluctance to speak. To the contrary, his fear seemed to disappear entirely in his first order, which, by its end, had won him the absolute confidence of the council. Although they would only later admit it, with this first order, he also gained the respect of the Guard.

Once he had regained consciousness on the floor of the cell, the cloak about Tergiver began to stir a change in him. Again, he began to convince himself that he had been spared punishment for some purpose. The same denial of pain and consequence that had led to his original mistakes was redoubled in his mind. He told himself that he did not know conclusively whether Herrick had been the figure at the waterfall that night. He reminded himself that he had not acted alone, and that he had not acted in malice. He focused on everything but his own actions, and after a half an hour, he felt that his role, though fatal and tragic, had been brought about by fate to bring him to this point of power, from which he had the perspective and insight to find the real assassins and restore Murmilan to its former security.

However, he had to wrestle with himself twice as hard to believe these lies now. He knew he was not a hero, and he would have gladly gone to the gallows that morning.

He began to repress a new, crawling resentment of the fact that he had been denied this escape of conscience, and he ceased lying to himself outright. Without allowing himself to distort his thoughts further, he stood up and acknowledged with a quiet understanding that his punishment was to be much greater than a simple confession and death. He would be forced to serve under the man whose son he had killed, whose familiar face would daily remind him of his crime. He would serve as the one charged with the responsibility of finding the man whose bloody hand he had held in murder, and worse, it fell on him to carry out these duties in the agony of silence, without a single release by word of confession.

Tergiver stepped forward, frightened, yet resolute in his determination to face the new life set before him, and he gave the following order: "Men of the guard, my first order as your chief is this: let every man in this service turn his cloak." As he spoke he unclasped the chain at his neck and turned his red cloak inside out. It hung on his back like a black void set with one mangled mess of golden threads on his right shoulder. He began quietly, checking Marscion's face as if he sought approval or direction, but as he spoke, his voice and confidence adjusted to the ostensible influence his words commanded, and near the end of his speech, his humble passion had raised the hairs on the arms of several guardsmen. "Let us do this in mourning of our great king, and let us look on our sleeves and remember that until we find the traitors and murderers who have robbed us of such a man, we will not be whole. Let us hold the old colors close against our backs, and let us remember that it was one of our own, one close to our hearts, who betrayed us. And let us strive for the day on which our crests, and our honor, may be restored."

The men shifted their cloaks eagerly in submission to the honorable order, and without realizing it, in submission to Tergiver. Until that moment, the guardsmen had felt helpless. This small and simple act empowered each man and affected a physical change in him. Only Baelin was hesitant, following cautiously in the motions, and his cloak sat black upon his shoulders like a gloomy, purple-eyed raven. Yet this was true for no one more than it was true for Tergiver, who accused himself bitterly with every word, condemning himself in a lifelong sentence that hung painfully by the golden clasp around his neck.

The sound of running footsteps in the hallway echoed against the closed doors. Robert turned the latch, and a breathless young guard entered. He looked first to Baelin, then to Marscion, then back to Baelin, and said, "Sir, a man from Northford just came to the castle and said the men we seek may be lodging in his house right now — sir."

The young guard was large and red faced, and his complexion grew redder as Baelin sternly directed him toward Tergiver and said, "Peter, you should address the new chief."

Despite his attitude at the cloaking ceremony, the new burden on Tergiver's conscience produced a gentle response. "Thank you, Peter," he said to the young man who now stood horrified in front of him. "Baelin, take Peter and two others, and identify the men in Northford. If they are the ones we seek, send the fastest among you back to the top of the cliff — directly above the West Wall — and give us a signal. We will have twenty men ready to reinforce you."

Despite his anger and suspicion, Baelin respected duty and authority foremost. He obeyed Tergiver's orders immediately and without question, setting an example that the other guards would follow henceforward. He bowed slightly, said, "Sir," turned and called Jason and Loren to follow him, and hurried away.

Tergiver ordered another guard to take nineteen others and wait atop the cliff for a signal from Baelin. Agatha slipped away into the hall, unescorted and feeling numb.

After the councilors had finished congratulating Tergiver, Marscion led him to Borleaf's old chamber, which he had ordered cleaned out and prepared for its new occupant. He had refused Tergiver's request to live in the cell in which he had been given his post, telling Tergiver that one must always accept opportunity on its terms. He left Tergiver with a pat on the back and the words, "You did well to follow my suggestion about the cloaks; and you delivered it well. I hope you can see the effect it had on the men. You look exhausted; it might benefit you to sleep."

As the door closed, Tergiver dropped to his knees on the crimson carpet and sent the black sword glancing away from his side with a crash, losing al pretenses of strength and poise.

That afternoon, men and women throughout the castle raised a quick hand to silence their companions, and all stopped to listen with horror, as the castle's very walls seemed to wail for the loss of its king. Servants worked harder and tried to ignore it, those who were alone in the corridors hurried to find the company of others, and visitors locked their doors and thought of the people to whom they would relay their frightful experience whenever they returned home.

Between the thick stone walls of Borleaf's old chamber, the new chief of the Queen's Guard finally fell asleep, crumpled on the carpet, and the castle fell quiet.

15

Flight

Herrick and Borleaf stood at the same time. It had been one hour since Jerrand had left. The light shone brighter through the single window of the dirty house, and they walked outside to find the land wet and dripping under an odd green sky. Anson was running toward them through the broad acres of sopping hay grass that lay before the house. He had followed Jerrand for a while and then stopped to keep watch over the area. Had Borleaf not been sick, the three men would have fled the house immediately, but they decided the warmth of the fire was worth the risk. Now Herrick saw Anson waving his arms in a sign of retreat. Herrick and Borleaf scrambled to the back of the house and waited out of sight.

The spots of living grass on which Anson ran were a spectacular green, and the mud in front of the house was a dark, soggy brown. The peculiar light in the sky made every color rich and deep, but in the west, the sky was ghastly and black. Anson met them and barked, "Four horses riding hard up the western slope and coming this way."

Herrick turned his head and asked, "Were they ours?"

"I don't think so," said Anson. "Do you know of any service that wears black cloaks?"

Herrick's face turned down in a wry grin, "Not in this kingdom."

Borleaf looked at him curiously, and Herrick asked, "Are you well enough to run? If you choose, you may stay here and say we kept you hostage."

Borleaf started toward the wood, pulling Herrick with him, "The man who sold us to the castle will tell a different story, and those sailors on the dock knew I was no hostage. No matter what I do now I will appear guilty — you know that."

Herrick pulled away and soon the three were at the edge of the cornfield and the woods. He answered, "Trust me Borleaf; leaving now is the only chance we have to prove our innocence."

Just then, four horses appeared at the edge of the field. One man sat high on a black horse and shouted in a powerful voice, "Stop now and surrender yourselves by order of the queen!"

The three plunged into the woods and ran toward the ship. Baelin had recognized them easily, but he turned to the other three and asked, "Can any of you confirm with certainty that these are our men?" They each answered that they were not sure, so Baelin ordered them into the thick woods. The horses struggled through trees and brush for about fifty yards, each animal moving much slower than the men fleeing on foot. Baelin stopped the party near a tight clump of trees and said, "Peter, ride back and send word that we have pursued the men into these woods, and that we believe them to be the traitors. Tell the men to join us but to leave their horses at the edge of the wood."

Peter nodded and turned his horse with great difficulty before working his way back out of the trees.

Baelin ordered Jason and Loren off their horses, which they tied to low branches. Then they ran, three chasing three. Baelin asked the others as they slipped through the trunks, "Do you believe Borleaf or Herrick would ever do anything like this?"

They both answered quickly and unequivocally. Loren said "No, sir," because he believed, as Baelin did, in the sovereignty of authority and the trust between a captain and his men, which neither of the accused had ever broken, to his knowledge.

Jason said, "No, sir," because he was in awe of authority and he had worshiped not only Herrick and Borleaf, but Baelin as well. To him, whatever Baelin believed was the truth.

Baelin shouted the names of Herrick and Borleaf but received no answer. They were approaching a clearing where the green sky shone more fiercely through the trees, and he called out once again.

From another clearing to their left, Herrick called back, "Baelin? Who else is with you?"

"Friends," he answered.

They rushed to find Herrick and Anson each carrying one of Borleaf's massive arms on their shoulders. Then Baelin saw their ship rocking damaged against the stones in high winds. He shouted to Herrick in a confused tone, "I don't know what's happening, sir! But there are twenty men on their way here to arrest you."

Herrick looked over his shoulder and said, "Borleaf is sick and needs help, can you do anything for him?"

Baelin gestured to Jason and Loren, who entered the clearing with him and took Borleaf from the two struggling men. They proceeded to carry him toward the ship. "He won't get well in the dungeons, Herrick." They hauled Borleaf on board, and then Anson, Herrick, Baelin, and Loren worked to ready the ship to sail. Anson was disheartened by the reversed cloaks. Jason stood watch in the clearing.

Baelin said to Herrick, while unwinding a rope in the wind, "I have been treading on glass since you left last night. Something is going on back there but I have not yet figured it out. I suspect ... well, all I know is that it will not be long before I am accused as well. So I am coming with you." Then he turned to Loren and yelled against the swirling wind, "Tell them I was taken, that we fought. I will leave you my sword as proof that I was disarmed."

Loren said, "Yes, sir," and held out his right arm willingly, adding, "Before you go, cut my arm so they will not think we let you go without a fight. We are not cowards."

Herrick answered quickly, "They would never believe the story, especially if they already suspect Baelin." Then he turned to Baelin as he stretched a rope across the deck and said, "This plan would only leave these men in suspicion and danger. Leave your cloak in this clearing, then order Loren and Jason to split up and roam far from this spot. They will return to the horses after a while, claiming that you ordered them to split up — which will be true and therefore easier for them to say. Then, if the search leads back here, the rest of the party may draw their own conclusions."

They freed the ship from the rocks, and Borleaf leaned weakly on the tiller. Anson shouted that they must leave immediately. The others saw that the sky terrified him.

Baelin and Loren climbed down from the ship and stood on the bank where Jason met them. Baelin ordered Jason and Loren into the woods, commanding them to be true to each other and to watch for his return. "I promise we will come back. Be watchful, and know that we had no part in the king's murder. Now go quickly — I hear voices!"

Jason and Loren made quick bows of allegiance and sprinted in opposite directions, deep into the woods, drawing the oncoming men away with their calls.

Baelin unclasped the chain at his neck and let his cloak fall to the ground, red side up. Then he climbed aboard *The Dolphin*, which creaked and lumbered away in the strong wind. The ship swam uneasily, weighed down by a mass of water in the bilge, and tacked unsteadily from rudder damage it had sustained from the rocks in the shallow anchorage.

Herrick gathered their cloaks from the place they had hid them, and passed them back to Borleaf and Anson, securing his own across his shoulders. "To keep warm," he added, after Borleaf gave him another curious look. As the wind grew stronger and the ship began to move faster toward the open sea, Herrick stood at the railing, feeling the king's ring securely in his pocket. He took it out and held it over the splashing water below, which reflected the dangerous sky with a luminous green. He deliberated on his fate, mulling over a score of ironies that had brought him to this point. He thought of Agatha and cursed her, and he imagined Marscion parading about the castle, full of pathetic self-importance. Finally, he mused over King Wiston's kind words to him the night before, which had seemed so sweet and sincere. Now they sat black and dead, holding hands with Agatha's serpentine form, which still constricted his heart. He gripped the ring tightly in his fist, and then, instead of dropping it, he secured it with a piece of rope inside his clothes, and turned back to his work with an awful and determined expression.

Anson's heart pounded with the first pulse of lightning that flashed bright out of the black west. The sails were full and high and the ship was still gaining speed through the narrow channels. Borleaf had moved to the pump where he worked in his fever, watching the unceasing gallons pour heavily off the windward side of the ship only to blow back against it. Tying the sails in place, Herrick and Baelin began jettisoning everything unattached to the deck. Borleaf had pumped as much as he could in his weakened state, and he called out to Herrick in exhaustion.

The ship was near the mouth of the sea when Herrick stooped to him with his grim face. "Yes, Borleaf?"

With labored breaths, Borleaf said, "When we first came out of the woods this morning, you said that the house would have already been searched, being so close to the castle. Searched for what reason,

Herrick? Everyone seemed to know we were on this ship, and at that time we didn't even know what had happened."

Herrick looked at him kindly and answered, "Sir, let us review our theories in detail once we are safe, not now. The important thing is that I guessed correctly. Let me help you up; we need you."

"Alright, but first get me a draught of that whiskey we saw below board — unless Baelin's thrown that over the side too."

The Dolphin cleared the fiords and emerged into the most violent sea any of them had ever seen. The west was a wall of darkness cracked by lightning. Vigorous winds bent the mast forward, straining the sails and causing the deck to buckle.

Anson crashed to the deck with a sudden kick of the waves, and slid into the bulwarks, injuring his shoulder. The ship was rocked and battered as it fled northeastward in the chaotic gale. The black sky at their backs consumed the green sky in front of them with inexorable haste, bringing with it driving rain and hail. Off the Murmillian coast, they saw several high pines bowing and cracking in half. The men suffered under heavy hail, which pummeled the ship and stung their faces.

The sails held fast, however, and the wind rushed them toward the northern skirts of the Brumal Mountains, where rocky shores awaited them under the high, snowy crags.

Borleaf strained to hold himself against the dipping and bucking mast, and Anson had wrapped a rope around his waist to keep him from sliding overboard. Herrick and Baelin held tightly to the bulwarks. The ship swerved and followed a windblown path before the storm, riding the steep waves downward and jumping in the air as they heaved her up from below. One-hundred yards off the rocky coast of the Brumal Mountains, darkness overtook them.

Anson yelled frantically into the wind for the others to lower the sail. Baelin and Herrick fought to gain their footing, stumbling and sliding perilously across the watery deck. Baelin reached the boom, but the ropes were unmovable, drawn tight by the force of the straining sails. The noise of the wind increased, and the men could no longer hear each other over the gale. Lightning struck the sea around them and flashed white across their terrified faces. After a high lurch, the wind drove the entire ship downward between two waves and submerged it to the foremast. The winds continued to bully the sails forward until both the mast and foremast snapped, catapulting the front of the ship high above the waves and throwing the men into the air. Borleaf landed on an iron ring and was injured badly. The ship careened heavily under the weight of the masts, which were still attached by ropes and sinking quickly into the freezing sea.

The men were thirty yards away from the rocky shore when *The Dolphin* capsized. Baelin swam after Borleaf and Herrick swam after Anson, both of whom were struggling to keep their heads above the raging swells that carried them fast toward the jagged shore.

Borleaf slipped below the surface.

Baelin swallowed a mouth-full of salt water, and choked as he swam for Borleaf. Under the great, cold sea, he was unable to see Herrick and Anson struggling together in the high waves that foamed and broke madly, heaving man and wreckage into the rocky shore.

No other ships dared give chase that day. Four days later, a high-masted brig, *The Heron*, found the wreckage. From its decks, the searchers saw among the boards and debris scattered about the shore, the weather-beaten body of a large man partially covering a mound of grey sand, in which he had buried another. Next to it were two rough piles of sand and wood, marked with stones. As the icy wind blew a cloud of powdery snow off the steep rock bank that hung over the shore, the dirty red cloak of the exposed man flapped listlessly. Then, as the searchers lowered a dinghy from *The Heron* and rowed silently into the blue waters, snow began to fall.

Part Two:
Agatha

16

In name only

The sun burned cold and aloof behind a washed-out haze of clouds. Freezing mist lacquered the black cliff with frost, and the waterfall slid weakly over dramatic bulges of ice that threatened to break and smash the frozen silver pool far below. Steep winds piled snowdrifts high against Mure Castle, and servants spent hours each day clearing doorways and paths with loud, scraping shovels. The market was busy inside broad, smoky buildings that reeked with the smell of animals whose cries and groans rose up to the high West Gate.

King Wiston had been in the ground little more than a month, and across the Murmillian countryside, villages and farms remained still and pensive, like rows of quiet old men wrapped in white lap blankets, smoking tall pipes, lost in mournful thoughts.

Agatha tilted her forehead against the icy windowpane of her mother's chamber and looked outward. The Pine Wood stood in deep, colorful contrast to the stark sky and earth around it. The trees remained thick and strong, even under the breaking weight of snow on their branches.

Two days after the king's murder, the queen had risen from her bed to attend the funeral, where she made a point of telling everyone, with great certainty, that her king was simply playing a trick on his poor wife, and that he would return soon. She had smiled nervously and put her hand in front of her face, as if she knew everyone was having a good laugh at her expense. Her shaking fingers and desperate eyes, however, belied her light gestures and words, and even those who had often been intolerant of her took pity. Her mouth had been turned upwards in a ghastly twist as she had descended the hills of the cemetery and climbed into a carriage to travel back through the East Gate. She had immediately taken to her bed, and she had not left it since.

Agatha and Sophia watched the queen's steady decline. She slept through the daylight, waking at sporadic intervals and only for short periods. She ate very little. The servants gossiped and made quiet bets on how long she would live. The queen was withering in the dark.

Sophia sat by the bed, watching her in the dim light. "She looks peaceful today. I hope she is having happy dreams."

Agatha pulled her head away from the window and walked across the room, where she sat heavily on the bed and looked up at the ceiling with pouting eyes, "I wish she would wake up. No one ever told me what I'm supposed to do." A knock came through the door and Agatha sighed audibly in affected defeat, pleading under her breath to Sophia, "Please, no more. I don't want any more of these gifts, or sympathy, or some blanket that someone's mother knitted for me, or visitors from wherever — please, just make them leave me alone." She put her wrist across her forehead in a weak attempt to gain sympathy, and said, "I am so wearied."

Sophia stared at Agatha blankly for a second, suppressing a laugh, and then she stood up and walked eagerly to the door. She opened it as Agatha hung her head and ran her right hand over the back of her neck, shoving her curls into her face. "Hello, Loren. Come in."

Loren bowed quickly and entered after making a brief smile at Sophia, who returned it amply. He took a deep, silent breath. "The council humbly requests the audience of the queen. They say they have deliberated long and now need her endorsement before taking action on a measure they have prepared."

Sophia stepped aside to expose Agatha, who sat across the bed, still and silent as if she had not been listening. Behind her, one of the fires burned low and orange, and Sophia thought she saw a glimmer of tears shining on the princess's face.

Agatha looked up from the bed and replied evenly, "Tell them the queen will be there shortly. Thank you."

Loren bowed, nodded to Sophia with another smile, and left. Sophia walked softly to the other side of the bed where Agatha sat, and pulled a chair from the corner.

Agatha looked up at her and said, "My father was always there to do this kind of thing. I wish he was here now or at least that my mother wasn't a …" She left off the rest of the sentence as if her father were still present and ready to reprimand her for disrespect. Instead of finishing her complaint, she gently shook the queen, who mumbled something quietly through parched lips, and lifted her eyelids halfway to look out on Agatha from another world. Agatha leaned forward and touched her mother's arm, saying in a quiet, urgent tone, "The council needs you to help them with something; you have to get up, alright?"

Queen Rose did not move, but produced a weak, toothy smile and replied, "You always were the smart one. I wish it had been you instead." She closed her eyes again and said woefully, "I miss you so much, Laura." Then she drifted away again into sleep.

Agatha shook her arm and said, "Wake up! What are you talking about you … crazy …" She bounced off her spot on the bed in anger and clenched her fists at her sides, lamenting her misfortune with teary eyes. "It is bad enough that I have not had one moment to myself since Father died, that I am constantly babied and coddled by peasant women I've never seen before, but now this? I am not the queen; I don't want to be, and I won't perform her responsibilities!" She leaned against the fireplace and raised her hand to her face. "It all weighs so heavily on me, Sophie."

Sophia responded casually, reacting neither to the princess's anger nor self-pity. "It has been over a month. I miss my family, Agatha. I miss them and it seems obvious that I am not doing much good here. You have asked for my advice and I have given it, but you are set in your opinions. It is certainly your right and privilege to do and think as you choose, but I think I would be more useful back home. My mother and Manchester shouldn't have to run the inn by themselves when my father is away; it's my responsibility."

Agatha turned to Sophia with pathetic desperation and said, "Then you understand! Just wait a little longer, until the snow starts to melt."

"That will be two months from now. That isn't waiting; it's staying."

"Well," replied Agatha with a grimace, "you would be the last to leave me I suppose." Then she turned her head back to the window.

Sophia's response was cold and even. "You would be much better off if you stopped blaming the dead for your unwillingness to grow up, Agatha."

Agatha inhaled deeply, trying to calm herself, but she felt pressed between two icy walls, the wintry window and her friend. Though she tried to answer regally, her words were still lachrymose and full of affectation, "You have never lost your father and the man you love both in —"

Sophia walked out of the chamber and closed the door.

Outside, the wind had ceased. Early that morning it had blown furiously and driven billowy drifts over the grey city walls in broad, arcing plumes. Heavy snow from the night before had buried the stone paths and ringed the pointed hats of the spires in white. Tergiver walked northward on the West Wall through a narrow path that had been cleared earlier. His hands were folded together behind his back under a thick, black, woolen cloak that wrapped around his body and hung to the heels of his boots. He walked with his head down, through the midst of guards that shoveled hard around him to clear the snow from the wall.

They each hailed him with a somber and respectful "Sir" as he passed, and nodded humbly to them in return. Their red cloaks, like Tergiver's, had been replaced permanently by rich black ones.

Tergiver, to his great consternation, had been celebrated as a hero for finding the wreckage of *The Dolphin*. The peasantry interpreted Herrick's flight as a sign of guilt, and when his ship was found in pieces, they created stories and rumors about Tergiver, the Guard's new prodigy. They told one another how he had conjured the storm to catch and punish the king's assassins, and that his loyalty had been so fierce that he had refused to accept any cloak but a black one in noble mourning for his king. They said Herrick had cheated him in the tournament because, even then, Tergiver had suspected his villainy.

While these tales had strengthened his popularity, it had been one real act that had endeared him to the hearts of the people more than anything else. The bodies of Borleaf and Anson had arrived at the castle under the duress of a hateful mob. Tergiver had climbed onto the cart with them, drawn his great black sword, and threatened anyone who touched them with death. The crowd had clamored riotously, but still he had held a firm, passionate, and terrifying guard that no one dared to test. Then, with a redoubtable voice that faltered a few times, as if in secret remorse, he persuaded the crowd that they should not allow the honor of Murmilan to be sullied further by spite, revenge, and hatred. He entreated them to mourn and make peace instead, and to remember the service and sacrifices these men had made to the king in the long years before their unfortunate turns. As he stood against the angry faces, unwilling to move and unafraid to die, Tergiver's seeming honor and courage spread powerfully among them. In the end, Anson and Borleaf were not only allowed a modest burial, but they were laid to rest inside the royal cemetery, isolated from their deceased brothers in the Guard by only a short distance. They gave Baelin a humble monument beside them. Only Herrick was left unhonored. Afterward, the council decided not to replace Baelin with another Captain of the Guard, leaving the burden to fall entirely on Tergiver's capable shoulders.

The compliments and distinctions fell like firebrands on Tergiver's conscience. He had acted impulsively again, out of shame and fear, and they worshiped him for it. After the event, epithets rang from the peasantry, such as "Tergiver the good" and "Tergiver the compassionate."

There had been no sign of Charlie's body in the wreckage. This gave Robert hope, which he shared with Tergiver whenever they met. Then Robert would prod him for details of a search that was not taking place, and each time, Tergiver saw Charlie in Robert's face, and felt sick at the image of him dropping slowly into the cold, shadowy well.

On many mornings, Tergiver had awoken to a knock on the door and found himself scrambling fearfully to shred a letter of confession he had drafted late the night before. This morning had been no different, and he walked along the wall with weary steps, listening to the snow squelch under his boots.

He considered all the good he could do as chief of the guard, and he realized that he had done none of it. He had not solved the mystery of Charlie's whisperers and he still did not know who had stared at him with that red face, from the pool of King Wiston's blood. All he had done was see four guards killed, and he had only buried two of them properly.

As he walked toward the rising bridge above the West Gate, he heard laughter. He looked up to see one of the guards laughing over the inside edge of the wall. Tergiver moved through the deep snow to the edge of the wall to observe. Below, a shabbily dressed man was coaxing his horse through a snowdrift, in which his cart was stuck fast. He brushed the snow lightly off his balding head and offered a conciliatory smile to the guard above, who promptly flipped another shovel-full over the wall, dousing the man again and laughing.

Tergiver started from his position like an arrow and cleared the distance between himself and the guard in a blink. Flying with outstretched arms over the piled snow, he caught the man's chin in a powerful hand before his heavy cloak could drift back to the ground. The mustached guard was clearly his elder, yet he stood terrified as Tergiver pushed his head backwards against the stone with a suffocating grip.

Tergiver's face was unforgiving and brutal, set coldly in the same stare with which he had threatened Baelin on the day of the tournament. He did not speak for a long moment; he only tightened his hand as the man cowered before him. Then he released it from the guard's face and held him pinned tightly to the wall with an elbow pressed into his chest. He commanded in a low, harsh, monotone, leaning close to the guard's face, "For the rest of the day, you are that man's servant. Tonight you will come to me and tell me his name, his wife's name, how many children he has, and the nicknames he gives his animals." Sweat and panic came over the guard as Tergiver continued, lifting his finger to point to the man. "You will push his cart out of the drift with your own hands, you will follow him with blessings from his queen, and when you have finished serving him, you will eat at the lowest seat at his table."

The guard's hands pressed on the frozen stone behind him and his brown eyes pleaded with Tergiver to be merciful, to allow him to simply apologize and avoid the embarrassment it would cause him to serve the peasant. However, he feared Tergiver much more than he feared the loss of his reputation. That day became the first of many in which this particular guard was found assisting peasants through the gates, as in time he came to enjoy their attention and appreciation. On this day, however, the still-fearful guard told the peasant that he arrived with blessings from his chief, and again Tergiver's renown grew.

Tergiver tramped back into the cleared path and turned up the slope that led to the bridge on the West Gate. There he stood against the high mesh that rose over the bridge, and rested his hands on the cold metal bars. He looked downward through them and saw the roof of the inn where he and Charlie had sat on a night that seemed years away. The row of oaks stood as skeletons against the dreary sky, and the roof was hidden under a layer of snow. To his right he heard the faint sound of laughter on the wind, and looking northward he saw children sliding down the long hill that ran up to the plain above the castle. He watched them for several minutes then turned his head back to the slanted roof. He remembered the words he said to Charlie as they had sat there, and he felt tiny pieces of ice forming in his eyelashes ... *and they would send me to find you."*

Six fires shouted across the council chamber, each striving to match the heat and voluminous din of twenty-three councilors engaged in boisterous debate. High windows dropped pale daylight into the oval room, though the long deliberations often outlasted it. Servants stoked the fires as the debate stumbled and briefly gave way to the voice of an enormous councilor with a broom-like beard. "Then we send emissaries to each of these kingdoms — politely. We bring them peace, but we let them know the sword hand remains strong."

"But still they may not care!" Another councilor responded quickly. He was a thin, older man with a brackish voice. "What if they do decide to test us? No amount of courtesy or diplomacy will help then! Marscion, what do you say?"

The councilors suddenly grew silent, and only the noise of the fires was audible before he answered, "With the approval of the queen, of course, we do both. Each of you has a valid suggestion, yet alone they are weak. We will send emissaries, though we might properly call them spies, to carry friendship in the left hand and the sword in the right. There are wise men in these kingdoms, and they would be wiser to understand our gesture. At the same time, we should levy greater taxes across the kingdom to pay for ships and weapons, for the time will soon come when we will need them. Yet there is another matter. Do not forget that we will also need to strengthen our existing army. We must expand and train new soldiers. Too many kingdoms lose good fighting men simply because they never prepared them for the day of battle."

There was a general muttering of approval and the large man retorted, "The better we tax our lands, the better we tax our enemies!" A few councilors laughed, while others frowned to make a point of their superiority. "Our king, while honorable, should have put more trust in us!" To support his statement, the man began to list his terrible ideas, which the king had prevented.

As the councilor continued to rant, Marscion listened and watched the reactions of certain councilors, and the reactions of the guards at the door. He noted the disgust on the face of Loren, the guard who had returned from his errand to Agatha, and he noted the expression of his partner, Jason, who stood awed and impressed by the simple grandeur of the deliberations.

Then, from the dimly lit hallway between Loren and Jason, Agatha emerged alone. She too was struck by the weight of the proceedings, but she was more frightened than impressed. As a little girl she had often danced in front of the fires, unaware of the arguing men around her. Now everything looked severe and threatening, and she felt that the dark-stained stairs leading up to the royal seat resembled those of the gallows. Marscion welcomed her and showed her to the royal seat without mentioning the queen. Though the council looked to her with respect, automatically imbuing her rank and function with wisdom, she sat troubled, as one on trial, dreading every question in the certainty that she would not know the answer. However, she discovered Marscion to be competent, comfortable, and reassuring. He relished in the particulars of debate, and led her patiently in every answer she needed to give. He acted not only as if the kingdom rested on his shoulders, but as if he had been born for the weight. Several times, he looked to Agatha to provide an answer of her own or to take this responsibility from him, but she was content to sit quietly, unsure of herself, and to nod in agreement with everything he suggested.

17

The wanderer

The city of Talus spread darkly under a ceiling of heavy charcoal clouds. Its northern half was black against the mountain, and both the old tower and forest were invisible in the freezing darkness.

Near the high bridge that spanned the river, a row of four ground-level windows were growing dimmer against the late night. The thin, icy panes were half covered by snow, and in the wide room beyond them, the cellar tavern at *The Gilded Gosling* was closing.

Henry carried an armful of plates to the kitchen and stacked them with a loud clink. Cramwell the cook met him at the window with a lift of his eyebrows and said with grim satisfaction, "No more orders. The kitchen's closed. I've poured water on the gridiron so it's too late." Henry, clearly having no new orders, did not acknowledge him, but walked back into the noise of voices, which steadily declined as groups of tired patrons pushed themselves away from the tables and lumbered up the stairs. Pipe smoke hovered along the low beams of the wooden ceiling directly above one booth as Henry watched three weathered fishermen rumble their glasses together for one last, drunken toast. He nodded to them humbly as they left, blew out their lamp, then gathered the dishes and carried them to the kitchen. His thick hair had shifted into a bunch on one side of his head, and his freckled face was dirty and tired. The plates he had set on the counter previously left no room for the new ones, and Cramwell was pretending not to notice.

Manchester passed Henry and entered the kitchen, where he pulled the plates from the counter and began to wash them.

Henry went to a table near the fireplace, and sank into a chair. There were still five occupied tables. After a short while, Manchester joined him, and they waited for the rest of the patrons to leave.

"Your mother says you got a letter from Sophie," said Henry. "Did you read it?"

"Not yet. I hope she's coming back soon."

"What do you think she's doing over there? It must be weird, with what happened and everything."

"I don't know," replied Manchester. "I like it better when she's here."

Henry nodded in agreement and counted the occupied tables again. Then he looked hard into the far corner of the section opposite the fire. "Is that man still here?"

"Yeah."

"Did his lamp burn out? We should at least fill it up for him if he's going to sit by himself."

"I think he blew it out," said Manchester. "Hey, remember that one who came in last week and got so drunk he started gnawing on the table?"

Henry laughed tiredly, "Or that table of fishermen who smelled so bad that your father offered them free rooms for the night if they would only bathe before eating?" He put his hand to his nose involuntarily and the boys laughed to themselves. Henry stretched his legs out before him on the smooth wooden floor.

Cramwell's voice shot out from the kitchen window, interrupting the conversation of the few remaining tables, "I could use some help!"

They laughed again and Manchester shook his head. "I washed all the dishes; there's nothing for him to do in there." Nevertheless, he got up and said, "I'll go see if that man is asleep and wake him up if he is. Cramwell will feel better if he sees us moving."

The four tables took Cramwell's yell as a sign to retire for the night, and they gathered their belongings and went up the stairs.

On seeing the tables clearing, both boys set about wiping them down and helping Cramwell with the dishes. As they were drying the last of them, Manchester made a face and said, "I forgot to wake that man, I'll be right back."

Cramwell raised his thick eyebrows and removed his apron quickly. He followed Manchester out the kitchen door as if it were his only chance to escape, and said, "Well, I'm done for the night." Then he added, "Yep, you boys can finish up here; alright," replying to his own announcements as he often did.

Henry responded anyway, and told Cramwell good night.

Manchester entered the row of high booths to find the shabby, bearded man staring into the table. The boys had not blown out the lamps in the rest of that section out of courtesy to him, yet his own table was shadowy and cold. His dark head hung forward with glazed eyes that sat worn and sad in his face. Manchester assumed he was drunk until he noticed that the man's glass was still full with the first drink he had brought that evening. With a polite voice, he interrupted the silence. "Sir, we are closing for the night."

The stranger looked up wearily, and his eyes moved from Manchester to one of the frozen windows behind his head. "Might I put off the night just a while longer? I will cause no trouble. Please." He was weathered and desperate, and it was clear that winter had been unmerciful to him. His grey cloak was tattered and worn thin, and it drooped unevenly from his shoulders as if it had been cut for a packhorse instead of a man.

Manchester could have sent him away with a simple, "I'm sorry," but he was moved by the deep and gentle lines in the man's eyes. He sat down in the booth across the table from him. This gesture comforted him, until Manchester asked, "Where are you from?" Manchester could tell that he was deliberating, pressing his answer back into his mind to hide it, so he added politely, "You don't have to tell me, I was just wondering. If you want, you can wait here until we put the chairs up and sweep."

As Manchester rose, the man began to speak feebly and cautiously, as if he were compelled to speak and be silent at once. "I ... I am not from anywhere now, I guess."

Manchester sat back down, enthralled by the pain in the man's voice. "I have this knot in my gut that turns harshly every ... I don't suppose you should understand any of it at your age. Still, for that reason ... perhaps it would be alright if you did listen."

He failed an attempt to smile at the boy across the table. His eyes were too sunken, and his hair and beard too unkempt to produce any expression apart from haggard wretchedness. He began again, "I've been living in your woods for, quite a while. But ..." He stopped.

He paused often and changed the direction of his words, which made them hard to follow. Manchester did not mind; he was exhausted from the workday and his body was content to sit still regardless of the man's speech.

"You should be happy in your youth," he continued, "before you have lost everything. I hope you never find yourself longing for that fire over there, or searching for those two friends of yours, only to realize that you are coming out of a dream to find the fire cold ash and your friends dead."

Manchester realized that he had been referring to Cramwell and Henry. He had never before thought of Cramwell as a friend.

Henry appeared around the corner and stood for a second. Then he disappeared and came back with a chair, which he set next to Manchester's side of the booth. He sat down curiously, as Manchester asked the man, "What happened to you?"

It was plain that he wanted to tell everything, but would not. "I ... once had friends, brothers, but we have been separated ... there was an accident, and ..."

"Are you a sailor?" Henry asked. Most of their patrons came from the docks, and Henry thought it a decent guess.

"No," he replied, "but it wouldn't have mattered. Even so, I am now the only one, and I am nothing."

The two boys sat exceedingly still. They did not know what to say or do, and they held their breath during the long pauses, unaware that they were doing so.

The man began to speak rhetorically, gazing at the low fire across the room. "What is the purpose of it all? You have a brother only to see him choke and breathe his last; you have a friend who falls deep in the ice, and you cannot get him out. You have a home, you have a country, but only for a moment, and then they are gone, life blames you, and you don't even know what you did wrong. In the end all you learn is that you were a coward."

He seemed to grow afraid of some thought or memory churning in his mind, and he said, "And then it comes. I hear it at night, I feel it near me, but I don't know why it follows, and I don't know what it wants. I don't even know what it is." His eyes moved toward the high windows as if he expected to see something peering through them. "It just waits for me, shifting in the dark, watching. That's why I came in here. I could not stand another night out there. It is not the cold."

Henry noticed the full glass, and the stranger saw him looking. "I have no money to pay for it, so I did not drink. I am sorry I deceived you." He moved his arms from where they had sat at his sides and pushed the drink toward Henry in a show of sincerity.

As he did, Henry noticed the polished pommel of a great sword hilt pushing its way up through the underside of the ripped cloak. The stranger leaned back and it disappeared again quietly.

Henry was fascinated. He had thought this man a crazy vagabond, or beggar, but he had never heard of a beggar who could not afford to drink when he still had something to sell. "Where do you live, sir?"

The addition of "sir" moved him perceptibly. His demeanor shifted slightly from that of a man humiliated by defeat to one suffering for a cause. Then he answered with a slight tone of acceptance and perseverance, as if he were preparing for a difficult assignment, "I live in the forest, for now. There are places I should go, off to the east yet, but the snow is still too great for any long travel, and I have to make some decisions here before I go." He drifted into his thoughts momentarily, but collected himself and said, "I have spoken too much already. I owe you my gratitude. I have not spoken to anyone for many weeks, and all burdens are heavier when they are borne alone."

Manchester was impressed by the man's discipline.

"I only ask that you do not tell anyone what I have told you. It is all of no real consequence of course, just one man's rambling, but I would feel better anyway."

Manchester could tell that he regretted something he had said, and he wondered if the stranger had accidentally told them something important, which they had missed. He did not linger on the subject, however, but spoke thoughtfully and to the point, "There are a few open rooms tonight. You should stay in one of them. We won't tell anyone."

"I would be taking advantage of you," he replied, "and I won't do that. You obviously have a kind heart, but I cannot steal a room from the owner of this place any more than I could steal a drink. But I thank you sincerely; you both have already done me a tremendous kindness."

Henry had been staring at the man's side, hoping to see the dirty, tattered cloak part again so he could have another look at the sword. Perhaps he had only imagined a sword, and he had to put his mind at ease.

Manchester replied, "The inn belongs to my family, and if you will help us stack the chairs and mop the floor, you can stay until tomorrow. That is my offer. What do you say to it?"

"I say you are uncommonly generous and well-spoken for a boy your age. Thank you. I will be away before dawn."

"That's included, if you still want it," said Manchester, nodding to the drink, "but only after we're done. My father says people shouldn't drink when they're working." The man managed to smile back at him. He could not remember the last time he had wanted to laugh.

Henry stood up eagerly and said, "Let me take your cloak and hang it up for you."

The man thought for a moment, then said, "Let me finish the rest of your work tonight. It will make me feel better about staying. Yes, you can hold this for me while I work. Thank you." The stranger looked again at the windows as if checking one more time for something, and Manchester's eyes followed, seeing nothing. Then he stood and pulled the cloak over his head. It was a horse covering.

Henry saw it first. There was a large sword at his side with a pale, tightly wrapped leather handle and subtle white stones embedded along the iron hilt. On the hilt was engraved the beginning of a curious symbol, which continued into full expression along the blade.

The symbol on the blade shone brightly, as if it had been covered for a long time and only recently revealed.

Manchester looked up at the man with wide eyes. The symbol was complete, and he remembered where he had seen the sword before, and in what book. The question had bothered him since the day Sophia had left for Murmilan.

"I don't know!" said Manchester in a whisper, as he and Henry sat in their beds. "But that was the same sword, I'm sure. I didn't recognize it before because the symbol was covered up. I remember wondering what was under the wrap. I wish Sophie were here. She would know what to do."

"Let's follow him!" said Henry, excitedly. "It will be like an adventure! We can get out of here for a while, and …" He stopped and looked disappointedly out the window, knowing it wouldn't happen. "Do you think I could go across the channel with Sophie the next time she goes? I've never been anywhere. I don't even know what is east of us, except trees."

"Do you think it was … no." Manchester started and concluded his thought without giving it full voice, bringing Henry back to the subject at hand.

"Remember how Sophie wrote that a boat had crashed, and how those guards all died?"

"You think he's a ghost?" Manchester looked incredulous, and Henry looked back, stale and annoyed.

"No, I don't — but what if there were other people on it that might have survived, like a crew or something?"

"He said he wasn't a sailor though, remember?" said Manchester.

"But he did say that it wouldn't have helped anyway, and now he has that sword. I think he was on the boat. Do you?"

"It was a ship Henry, not a boat," said Manchester with mock condescension. "We live fifty yards from the water." Manchester mouthed the word *ship* slowly, and Henry flung a pillow hard at his head.

"Next time I'm throwing one of your books — a heavy one."

Manchester laughed.

Then Henry said, with a voice that began to grow loud in the quiet room, "Let's write Sophie! Maybe she will know something."

"Alright, we'll do it. Just be quieter. We'll send it tomorrow morning." Henry went downstairs to find a lamp and some paper, and then he settled in a corner of the hall to write.

The stranger sat awake in a black room, staring out his window. He saw dark spots moving through the woods and halting in line with his window. He gripped the sword tightly at his side. Then he closed his tired eyes, and before drifting into uneasy sleep, he said, "I don't know what to do now. I wish you were here now to give me guidance. I feel like such a coward."

Had he stayed awake longer, he might have seen a glimpse of the form that had also watched Charlie one night from deep within the Pine Wood. In the corner of his window, in a small break in the ice that crept along its edges, there appeared behind the foggy glass a set of dull yellow eyes. Then they were gone as quickly as they had come.

18

The northford magistrate

The hallway outside Robert's office was busy. Councilors dipped their heads in and out of doorways, discussing the preparations for new decrees, the building of ships, and the training of soldiers. At the far west end of the hall, Marscion's office door stood open.

It was his custom to keep it that way as a show of welcome to any councilors who might need him. Being at the end of the castle and having large windows, the office also emitted a considerable amount of light into the hall, a subtle point that Marscion enjoyed. Most days, one could see him sitting at his desk, silhouetted against the bright windows and working vigorously.

Tergiver emerged into the middle of the hallway from the west staircase that rose from the Great Hall below. He did not look in the direction of Robert's chamber for fear of having to speak to him. He proceeded to Marscion's door, and seeing him thumbing through a stack of papers, knocked. Marscion wore a thick grey mantle over his white robe. Like the other councilors, he too had a long row of candles burning against his office wall. He also had a fireplace to the right of his desk. Tergiver had never been in this room before. Marscion stood and thanked him for coming, pushing his work aside. He pulled his chair around the desk to sit before the fireplace, and then he motioned for Tergiver to do the same.

Tergiver sat hesitantly, as he was inclined to stand in the presence of authority.

"The windows allow a good amount of light, but it gets rather drafty in here at times." Marscion glanced into Tergiver's eyes as if he were watching for a specific reaction. "Is everything going well with the Guard, Tergiver? You seem just as distraught as the day we appointed you, and yet, it has been over a month."

Tergiver glanced out the window and answered, "Things are well with the Guard, sir. We caught a few thieves trying to break into the market last night. Other than that, things have been quiet. Thank you for your concern, but I am well."

Marscion continued, poking at the fire with an iron brand, watching Tergiver from the corners of his eyes, "The respect you command in the men is uncanny, Tergiver. I wanted to tell you how proud I am of what you have done. I think each of us owes a great deal to Councilor Robert for bringing you to this position. Would you agree?"

Tergiver had thought of little in the past month except for the real debt he owed Robert, and the impossibility of its payment had driven him to become callous in self-defense. The subject was a fixture in his mind, always pressing, but always ignored. Marscion's question went unanswered.

Marscion had expected a comrade in Tergiver, one who might be thankful for guidance and receptive to ideas that would help him in his pursuits. Instead, he found the young man to be an indifferent, if intense, puzzle. Marscion's eyebrows were set hard on his face as he poked the fire again with the long iron and asked, "Have you spoken to your father lately? It has been a while, has it not? We all need guidance at times."

"I haven't."

"Well, neither have I." Marscion looked out the window and

paused. "Not since he returned to your home, that is. He appears to be very fond of you."

Tergiver did not answer. Jerrand had lodged at the castle the night after he reported Borleaf and the other guards. The next morning he had begged for money in compensation for his news, pleading with the guards who handled him to ask the new chief for a reward. Concern for his son had come well after this. Tergiver had not seen his father, nor had he revealed his new position to him. Instead, he had hid in his chamber and sent Jerrand away with several gold pieces and the words, "Tell him his son is safe, and tell him to please return to his home." Jerrand did as he was told, but not before he had extracted a few more coins for his trouble. Tergiver had written to him a few days later to give him the basic details, although instead of reading the letter aloud and recounting the experience in person, as was his habit, he had sent Loren to read it instead. In his letter, however, he forbade Jerrand to come to the castle. Though he loved his father, he knew that the elation and attention would have been too heavy a burden. This had been the first time in his life that he had not wanted to see his father, and it was yet another shame loaded upon his conscience.

Marscion spoke, as if to someone else, "I would have expected him to stay longer and help you through this new trial, as a father should. Do you agree?"

"I sent him away."

Marscion was quiet for a few minutes, listening to the fire and watching the councilors stepping in and out of their doorways. The light was growing in the room as the morning wore on, and he said, lowering his breath, "Is this position — your position in the Guard — is it what you wanted when all of this began?" He waited, curious, and blind to Tergiver's mind. Marscion could see Tergiver's eyes moving back and forth, examining the floor, and he gazed into them as if he hoped to see Tergiver's memories in those lifeless pools.

Tergiver swallowed and replied, "I was in the tournament; you saw me. All I wanted to do was make it into the Guard. It was all I ever wanted, sir." It was the first time he had spoken openly to anyone since his last conversation with Charlie. "My father was in the tournament a long time ago, but he didn't advance past the first day. They didn't offer him a position anywhere. So, this was sort of what we both have always wanted."

A large, gravel-throated councilor knocked on the doorframe and hailed Marscion, who offered to visit him when he was finished with his present business. Then Marscion asked the councilor to close the door.

Marscion and Tergiver sat alone in the room, quiet for several minutes. Then Marscion said softly, "I don't know why things happened as they did. I cannot begin to understand how everything fell like this. I don't know why you were chosen for this position, but I support you." He waited, but he received no response. "You have come so far, Tergiver, and I believe that —" here he checked Tergiver's face hesitantly, then continued, "that you want to do the right thing, and since we are both where we are, I think we can help each other to make this kingdom into what it should be. Do you understand?"

Tergiver stared at the floor. He did not understand. His mind had wandered off again into its cellars of guilt. He looked up dutifully and answered, "As you command me, you command the Guard. And I will do my best to carry out your orders, sir."

The corners of Marscion's mouth crept upward. The Guard had never reported to the council, but to the king. Queen Rose had not yet claimed ownership of the Guard, despite its name, and it was unlikely that she would.

Marscion had mistaken Tergiver's intentions. For all the young man's worship of the guard, he had never studied its organization. Robert and Marscion had given him his charge, and he had never questioned their authority over him. Now he felt as if he were simply renewing a vow he had already taken.

The warmth of the fire was hot on their knees as Marscion looked on Tergiver and said, "Do you remember the magistrate of your home town?"

"Yes, his name is Feyton."

"We have received word that he has been spreading lies about our recent decisions to protect our kingdom. You might know that he is only years away from taking a place here on the council. If we lose either of the two current councilors from Northford, he will take their place. Councilor Robert is in good health, but Councilor Jirrack is old." Here he stopped and changed his inflection, as if he were speaking to himself, "This magistrate is an enemy of the kingdom — of the people. It would be much better for everyone if it were he, instead of Councilor Jirrack, who was old and on his way out." Then he turned to Tergiver. "What do you suggest?" Marscion's eyes became thin as he watched and waited for the answer.

"Councilor Marscion, sir, I leave all of that business to your office. I am still learning what I must know to run the Guard, and I trust the council to handle political affairs. I don't think I would be very good at it, sir."

There was a marked disappointment in Marscion's face. He prodded the fire again and said, "You might benefit by an understanding of this man's position on your Guard. He has suggested repeatedly that the Guard be disbanded. He blames them for what happened to King Wiston, and in doing so he has convinced many of your impressionable countrymen; they mimic whatever he says as if his thoughts were theirs."

He waited to see if this reference had hit its mark, but if it had, Tergiver did not show it.

"Feyton is dangerous, and he is a criminal. He has been stealing from the town, your town, Tergiver, and I would like you and several of the men to visit him. Councilor Robert has returned home for a week and he has invited the man to dinner tonight on my suggestion. You will also be there. Beware of him, Tergiver. Do not trust him. Know that you are serving your kingdom well by watching him." Then Marscion stood up and set the iron poker against the wall. "I also think it will be good for you to go home, at least for a day. Perhaps when you return, your head will be clearer."

Tergiver sat still and quiet. This aggravated Marscion, who finished politely, despite his growing temper, "I will send instructions by this afternoon. Thank you, Tergiver. Please prop the door open when you leave."

Tergiver did as he was told and walked out of the bright room, looking forward into the shadowy hall. Robert's office hunched darkly among the others, and suddenly it seemed worse for being empty.

Later that afternoon, Tergiver walked through one of the royal stables. The horses watched him with huge eyes as they stood quietly in their stalls. The hay was cold on the ground and there was a chilly draft coming through the wide open door, where Loren and Jason appeared.

Loren greeted him. "Good afternoon, sir. Marscion sent us to accompany you to Northford. We are ready to leave at your command."

Jason had an eager look about him and he shifted his weight on his knees repeatedly. Tergiver answered, "Let us leave now." He walked past them and spoke briefly to a stable hand who led them outside to where he had prepared three horses — a Palomino for Loren, a chestnut for Jason, and for Tergiver, a dark bay.

They left the city by the East Gate, and their horses climbed the escarpment by a narrow trail at the western edge of the cemetery. They reached Robert's house after a short ride. Tergiver slowed his horse, and the others did the same. The windows in the upper floors were wide, and Tergiver thought they looked like Charlie's eyes watching him approach from afar. After pausing for a few moments, he proceeded to the front of the house.

Nine chimneys poured smoke into the wintry sky, and the boards of the house fit tightly together to keep the cold from creeping through to its warm insides. Tergiver tied his horse to a large hitch post at the doorway, and walked up familiar steps, feeling as if he were an old man, wandering like a stranger through a dream of his childhood. He paused at the high door as if he were not sure whether it would let him enter, and waited.

A large servant woman, having seen him through the window, opened the door quickly and said, "Master Tergiver, when have you ever done anything but rush straight in this house, right over my clean floor? Come in, come in, you are going to freeze out there in that cold!" She removed the grey woolen mantle he wore over his cloak, and folded it over her arm. Then she offered to do the same for the other two.

Jason had not seen her in the window and he stood stunned, wondering at how Tergiver had commanded the door to open simply by standing at its threshold. For the rest of the night he watched Tergiver with even greater interest and curiosity.

The floors were wide and waxed, and thick purple carpets softened the tramp of their boots. Colorful paintings and silver candelabras adorned Robert's rich house. The lively foyer transformed the pale light from outside into rays of warm purples and yellows that shone and reflected in the polished furnishings of every room.

Robert welcomed the guards in the name of the queen and the council, and then he embraced Tergiver as a son. Tergiver fought to keep tears from his face as he stood away from Robert and looked down the empty hall to Charlie's room.

"Come," said Robert, "you are the last guests of honor to arrive. We are ready to start."

Just then, hearing the footsteps, Jerrand ran down a corridor to find and embrace his son. For Tergiver, this was worse than seeing Robert.

Loren and Jason watched as Jerrand reduced their redoubtable chief to a child within seconds. Jerrand's fatuous grin smeared across his face like jam and he repeatedly cupped Tergiver's head within his hands, exclaiming, "My boy! My boy!"

Tergiver pried the hands away gently and said, "We should come in. Please, lead the way."

"Look at you! I still can't believe it, but here you are! My boy!"

Hoping to deflect his father's attention to the others, Tergiver said solemnly, "Jason, Loren, this is my father, Jerrand. He lives here in Northford. Father, these are two of the finest guards of the castle, Jason and Loren."

They bowed politely before Jerrand, and the act lit an immediate passion in him. Throughout the evening he thought of little but to whom he could tell that the best of the Royal Guard, *Tergiver's Guard*, would bow — in fact, did bow, to him at any given moment.

Tergiver noticed the change in his father's stature and speech as he accepted their courtesy.

Jerrand drew himself up into a pretense of nobility and strolled down the hall to the dining room, beckoning to them with a grotesquely familiar, "Follow me."

Feyton the magistrate was a tall, thin man with a soft voice. He wore a pale yellow robe striped with black. Short tassels hung from each of his shoulders. He greeted the guards politely and by name. As they proceeded through the dinner formalities and began to eat, he was gracious in praise of Tergiver's actions so far, and if he had any reservations about the Guard, he did not show them. The magistrate sat at one end of the thick oaken table. Behind him burned a high fire in a wide hearth beset by tall bookshelves. Robert sat at the opposite end; Jerrand and Loren sat across from Tergiver and Jason.

For most of the night, Tergiver found himself breaking eye contact with his father and noticing, more than he ever had, the oily obsequiousness of Jerrand's voice, and the false lift of his eyebrow whenever he addressed authority. Until that moment, the way his father acted toward Robert had never struck him as odd. Now he examined each of the particular inflections and gestures aimed at the magistrate. Tergiver understood his father's unctuous peculiarities, but they might not have lodged themselves so uncomfortably under his skin had Jerrand not begun to apply them to him as well. Now that Tergiver was figure of authority, he too was a victim of Jerrand's flattery, and he felt it with a painful clarity.

During the second course of the meal, Jason, who had been looking sideways at the magistrate for quite a while, addressed him. "I hear you think the Guard is to blame for what happened and that we should be disbanned. Is that true? Do you?" He gnawed on a bone and dropped it on his plate, awaiting the answer. Loren looked at him sternly, angry and surprised at his rudeness.

Tergiver was preoccupied with the strikingly hard angle at which his father repeatedly bent toward Councilor Robert when he spoke to him. He was also disgusted at how Jerrand would always nod his head up and down in agreement before the speaker had even come to his point. It was with a growing displeasure that he watched these mannerisms shifted toward the magistrate, who cleared his throat to respond to Jason's question.

Feyton took a sip of his wine, set it down gently on the tablecloth, and said, "To me, the question of the Guard has always been one of priority and finance, and I certainly do not think you should be disbanded. What you have heard is an unfortunate exaggeration, if not a deliberate one. Where I might disagree with, for example, our good councilor and host, is in the matter of how much money funds your great numbers on the wall, which might otherwise be manned in times of peace by lesser paid, though not necessarily lesser, men, thereby leaving the balance to be applied to the social welfare of," and here he nodded to Jerrand, "the good people of Northford, for example, to provide them necessities in times of seasonal or economic hardship."

Jason looked irritated, as if the man had tried to confuse him on purpose. He looked desperately to Tergiver, as if to ask his chief if he were going to allow this stranger to continue trampling the Guard with heavy words.

As Tergiver made a motion for Jason to let it go, Loren began to speak. "How would you settle the inevitable dispute and resentment that would arise from those who conducted our same work, but with lesser rank and pay? Despite one occurrence, our group is cohesive and loyal. Some would say your plan might create a division that could potentially threaten the security of the city in wartime — for those men who had kept watch the longest in peacetime would plainly be best suited to command, yet they would suddenly be forced to obey men that they would consider to be, at best, overpaid equals."

There was a burst of joyous laughter from Robert's end of the table, and he roared, "Loren the statesman! I never knew! I agree with you, by the way. What do you say to those questions Feyton? The young man has several excellent points."

Jason shrank into his chair and continued to eat, flashing menacing eyes at Feyton, who made several failed attempts to include him in the conversation before ultimately deciding to ignore him.

By the end of the night, another knot had fixed itself in Tergiver's mind. The magistrate was a decent man. He would report to Marscion that Loren had engaged him in a substantial debate. That, he decided, would ease Marscion's concern. However, that was not what troubled him.

The realization that his friendship with Charlie had been a manipulation from the beginning sat heavy on him, and it cast an even harder light on his father. Tergiver remembered the many trips to Robert's house when Robert was still only a Magistrate. He remembered, with a new perspective, the servile way in which he had been offered awkwardly and repeatedly as a playmate for Charlie. The boys had become friends despite what Tergiver now understood to be Robert's painful toleration of his father. He had always known that it was only because of his father's persistence that he had been taught to read and write alongside his friend, but he had not known the cost. However, now that he had achieved success in the kingdom, albeit by terrible circumstances, he understood that his father was still not happy for his son, only for himself. Tergiver felt used and disgusted by the man fawning over him from across the table, but this still could not detach him from the feelings he had developed before gaining this knowledge. As a result, he was ashamed of his thoughts. It was this difficulty that caused Tergiver to announce the guards' early departure shortly after everyone had finished dinner and moved into the main room.

Robert — and Jason, to everyone's surprise — protested loudly. The servants had prepared rooms for all the guests in the large house. Tergiver and Loren guessed that Jason simply wanted to stay in order to continue drinking by the fire. He had more than once disappeared into the kitchen with the servants and reappeared with new pitchers of wine, which he poured officiously and with an odd face. In the end, Tergiver gave Loren and Jason leave to stay, but Loren decided to follow Tergiver. This left Jason angry, still holding a half-empty pitcher of wine but obliged to follow his chief.

The wind was bitter as they rode south over the blue plains of Northford, their horses crunching snow under galloping hooves. The men could feel the alcohol still warm in their mouths as they breathed the night air into their lungs. The farther he rode, the more the tension in Tergiver's mind began to unravel, leaving him with a feeling of warm emptiness. The moon hung high and bright above the castle as it had a month ago, and everything shone with a pristine snow cover and jewels of ice. As his black cloak waved and flapped at his mare's sides, he questioned whether he should ever confess.

Every attempt he had made, to either clear his conscience or protect himself, had resulted in his advancement. He who had murdered the king was now hailed as the peoples' patriot benefactor. He noticed that Robert had not mentioned Charlie once, although the hallway to Charlie's room had seemed to extend around the corner and peer at him the whole night. Tergiver began to doubt that atonement for his actions could ever be possible. He allowed himself the thought that perhaps, although he could not bring his friend or the king back from the dead, if he simply accepted this new arrangement and devoted himself to it without remorse or fear, he might accomplish great things for the kingdom. Feyton the magistrate, for example, was not a threat as Marscion had feared. He was a fair man who had listened openly to Loren and asked several questions that showed his willingness to change his opinion on the Guard.

Tergiver felt that perhaps luck was now with him, regardless of whether he wanted it, and he concluded that his will to confess his crimes had become selfish, and perhaps the worst thing he could do for the kingdom. He realized for the first time that he was respected and needed by people other than his father — people who only needed him to be himself, and no one knew, or asked, what he had done in the past.

It was with a warm, bemused gratitude that Tergiver lay back in his bed and slept in sound, peaceful, dreamless sleep, for the first time since he had arrived at the castle.

19

Capitulation

Early the next morning, Agatha scurried down a stone hallway. Her pink dress swished in elegant folds about her legs as she went, and in her hand she gripped an envelope. She arrived at Sophia's quarters and entered without knocking. She found Sophia wearing the same plain brown clothes in which she had arrived at the castle. For a moment, her steps flattened, but then she clutched the envelope and crossed the room quickly.

Sophia had noticed the reaction to her clothes and said, "I was about to look for you. I would like to go home today."

As if she had not heard, Agatha pushed the envelope into Sophia's hands, saying, "This came for you. You should open it." Her head nodded in encouragement as she led Sophia to one of two chairs that faced each other under a broad patterned tapestry of brown and green.

Sophia took the letter and sat down. Then she set it in her lap, pausing to examine Agatha's face. "Your mother was calling for you again last night. I do hate to leave her. Promise me that you will stay with her when I go; she is sick, but she's also very lonely." Sophia noticed that the princess was not listening, but glancing desperately at the letter. This irritated her, so she continued to ignore it. "After I tell your mother good-bye, I would like to go. May I take a horse if I leave it at Eastport?"

Agatha was growing impatient and said, "Yes, yes — just open your letter!"

"Should I open it? Why don't you tell me what it says? It's plain that you at least know what it's about."

She frowned at Agatha for having read her letter, but the princess responded quickly, "It was already unsealed when I got it; the Guard has been checking everything since my father died. The flap was turned up when I received it."

"Then why did you fold it back down before giving it to me?" Sophia opened the envelope harshly and pulled the letter from inside. As the paper ruffled and unfolded, she smiled suddenly, seeing the signatures, "It's from Henry and Chess." She pulled the letter to her chest and said fondly, intentionally delaying her reading of it for a few more seconds, "I miss those two."

Agatha gripped the sides of her chair, and her hair hung forward expectantly.

Not wishing to prolong Agatha's apparent act of suffering any longer, Sophia looked at the letter, which was scribbled in large, almost illegible characters, with insertions and corrections made in her brother's neat script. She read aloud:

> Sophie, Tonight a man came into the Gos who Chess says had the same sword the man who came to get you had. But maybe *it* wasn't him because he had a beard anyway. He said he had lost all his friends he said he was living in Echmi~~dk~~ *ire* until he could go east when the snow melted. He said he had crossed the mounta*i*ns too and he was on a ship that wrecked. Chess said he

will show me the sword in a book if he can find it. We hope you come home soon and maybe he will still be around.

Henry —and Manchester

Agatha's face bloomed red while Sophia read the letter. Before she could finish, Agatha put her hand on Sophia's leg and said, "Do you think he could still be alive? Oh, I wished that things had been different and just maybe now it has come true. He would forgive me if I told him my side of things, don't you think?"

The chair creaked behind Sophia as she leaned back into it. Then she looked up at Agatha and answered, "It's not Herrick. My brother would have remembered him." She wanted to lie, to tell Agatha that the boys frequently came up with crazy ideas, but they didn't. "Let me read it again," she said, and pulled the letter gently from Agatha, who had taken it and was holding it as if it were hers. She looked over it again carefully, and concern moved through her face. "Who else has seen this?"

"No one, I mean, I don't know. I'm sure the Guard read it before Marscion gave it to me. He told me not to tell anyone about it —" Agatha stopped, realizing what Sophia had already shown on her face, and her hope dissolved into fear. "They know he's there don't they? That means that he's not safe."

"Who knows, Agatha?"

It had not occurred to anyone in the castle that the morbid scene on the icy shore of the Brumal Mountains had been anything but genuine. Sophia repeated, "Agatha, it's not Herrick; I told you. It must be the other one, Baelin was it? But then again, would Herrick have given up his sword for any reason? He was oddly protective of it. This doesn't make sense to me."

"Must it be Baelin, Sophie? He didn't have a beard." Agatha's head drooped, and her body sank weakly with a perceptible, defeated slouch.

Sophia knew at that moment that Agatha had become aware of her self-deceit. It was the beginning of a grief that Agatha had been allowed neither the time nor peace to experience.

She had been confused by her conflicting emotions about her father and Herrick. She secretly blamed each for the other's death, and felt that both had betrayed her by leaving her alone. These feelings, along with the resentment she felt toward her helpless mother, had made mourning impossible. She had been hounded constantly in her new duties to the kingdom, but it was her responsibility to the common people, with its deluge of tearful visits, sympathies, and commiseration, that exhausted her more than anything else. Her grief had no place in theirs, and mourning had become an irrelevant burden in the harried days.

Sophia also saw in this subtle posture the possibility of an Agatha too weak to maintain the tight clutch she had taken on everything else in her world, afraid that it too would slip away. Sophia rested her hand on Agatha's knee and said, smiling gently, "There are no mirrors for shaving in the Brumal Mountains, or in Etchmire."

Embarrassed by the absurdity of her statement, Agatha retreated from her emotions and straightened herself. She fought against the agony that had overwhelmed her the night she had sent Herrick away and promised herself that she would never feel so strongly again.

So Agatha sat, a portrait of a disappointed but honest child, unable to hide the fear in her voice. "Well, even if it isn't Herrick, maybe he can tell us what happened. I am only afraid of what will become of him if our people discover him first. If only Tergiver were there, we could trust that everything would be all right. I heard what the crowd wanted to do with Anson and Borleaf." She sniffled, and then said to Sophia, who was looking at her strangely, "OK, go, and take whatever horse you want, but just find him and then ... I don't know what to do next. I'm sorry."

Sophia sat still, wondering at the words. Agatha had admitted that the man might not be Herrick. It was unlike her. Sophia had prepared herself — even before finishing the letter — for a long argument that she did not have to make. They stood and embraced.

"No one said anything to you about the letter? Not even Marscion when you told him of it?" asked Sophia.

"No, not really."

"What did Marscion say?"

"He —" Agatha looked up and to the side, then answered, "He only told me to keep it to myself. He said it probably didn't mean anything, and then he went about his business."

"That's absurd! Did you believe him?"

The princess paused for a second, and then, in a defeated voice that matched her earlier posture she said, "No — because I didn't want to. This is all so difficult." After a moment, they moved quickly to the door and down the hallway toward the stables.

Sophia mounted a horse and prepared to ride for the East Gate. Then she leaned down and said, "This might not even be real. Someone could have simply pretended to be him; it might be a hoax designed to implicate more Guard members you know, to see who would respond to this kind of news, and more importantly, how they would respond. Tergiver is supposed to be some genius, right? Be careful, Agatha. I will stop by the inn before I go out into the forest and get a few things so I can protect myself. Be watchful here. I will let you know what I have found as soon as I can. Until then, if you do nothing else, please take care of your mother. You know she doesn't have long to live." Then without waiting for an answer, Sophia rode away in haste, kicking up clumps of snow and dirt in the city, leaving her friend leaning sad against the stable doors in heavy snowfall.

When Marscion found Tergiver on the East Wall earlier that morning, the daylight had scarcely broken. Tergiver stood, watching the sunrise with his hands buried inside his cloak for warmth. As Marscion approached, shivering and bothered, he noted Tergiver's face. This morning it did not seem to bear so hard the marks of his heavy conscience. In fact, Tergiver had slept through the night. He reveled in the thought that he had possibly helped the kingdom in his visit to the Magistrate, and he felt the pressure of his father's expectations begin to dissolve now that he could see his character more clearly. That night, for the first time in a month, he dwelt on subjects other than his guilt. A hot cup of cider steamed on the ledge of the wall, sending a pleasant smell into the air in front of his face, and as Marscion approached, Tergiver actually spoke first. "Good Morning, Marscion." He took a sip from the cup. "The trip to Northford went well. Loren is quite the speaker." Marscion's hand trembled a little, and Tergiver guessed it was from the cold.

"Follow me," said Marscion. Tergiver took up his cup and followed Marscion, who had turned abruptly and was already walking away. His white robe shone brightly against the grey stone, echoed by the lining of snow that huddled in the corners between the wall and the path. When Tergiver had caught up to him, Marscion said under his breath so none of the other guards could hear, "One of the traitors may be still alive, Tergiver. We have been made fools."

The stone walk before Tergiver seemed to stretch painfully from his gut, and he became dizzy and had trouble balancing the cup in his hand. In a rush, the first feelings of peace he had felt in weeks fled like startled birds. He had forced himself to believe that the four men on *The Dolphin* had truly been the conspirators, and that with their deaths he had brought closure to the search for the red-faced man — a search he had never started. That face was now reincarnated vividly in his mind. He felt like it was watching him, and he felt the presence of subtle footsteps walking near them on the wall, listening to his thoughts.

He stopped and stood petrified as he had in the clearing in the Pine Wood, and he imagined Baelin sitting in a high witness chair, staring down at him with Herrick's green eyes, pointing sternly in judgment, saying, *That's him. He's the one who killed Wiston. It was Tergiver of Northford!*

Marscion noticed Tergiver's transformation to his old, tortured form, and dismissed his earlier attitude as unimportant. He led Tergiver into the rear of the castle and down to the armory.

Here Tergiver had knelt before Agatha and accepted his position over the Guard. He felt as if he could still see the line of guards and councilors staring at him. He could still see Baelin's angry face. This image moved him to say, "Marscion, tell me what you mean. I thought everyone had died in the wreck."

Marscion watched him carefully as he answered, "We intercepted a letter from Talus that identifies either Herrick or Baelin. It was addressed to Agatha's friend Sophia, and it suggests that she was on the ship with Herrick and his men the morning they returned. If I read it correctly, fetching her may have been their errand, but we do not know why."

The barren room echoed Tergiver's deep breaths, seeming to inhale and exhale on its own accord, sighing through cracks and tiny passages Tergiver could not see. He felt that he could hear Charlie's whisperer for himself, listening, accusing, alive, expanding and contracting the walls around him. He did not try to help Marscion or voice any opinion about what should be done. He simply looked rattled and nervous.

A small twinge of annoyance showed in Marscion's face as he again assumed a parental role over one of the high rulers of Murmilan. "My questions to you, Tergiver, are these: What does this tell you? What does this information mean to you, and what action do you propose? This is your responsibility."

Instead of replying, Tergiver simply looked at Marscion with a concerned, but helpless expression, still wondering what it might mean if the conspirators somehow found a way to return and expose him. Then, overwhelming fear swelled into a quick reaction, "We should find this person, Marscion, immediately … and, then he must …" He wanted to finish, to say that the man should be found and punished like the rest, without trial and as soon as he was caught. His conscience, however, stuffed these words back into his throat, and he looked to Marscion to say it.

"And what? I can advise you, but this is your duty, Tergiver. We will do whatever you choose. For you, not I, are the Guardian of Mure Castle, and you must understand that it is your duty to protect it by *all* means, not simply by reputation and formal command."

Based on Baelin's flight with the traitors and his ostensible hostility toward the princess, Tergiver had convinced himself that Baelin had worn the red face. It had been easy to accept Baelin and Herrick's execution by the storm, but the thought of ordering it anew caused him great consternation. He understood that he was simply deciding whether to end another life in order to preserve his own. Finally, he said, without answering the question, "Who do you think it is, Marscion?"

Marscion's preoccupation with Herrick made the answer easy. "If anyone found a way off that ship it was Herrick. The letter identified the sword as his. Let me ask you something Tergiver, that sword, that symbol you carry at your side, would you ever give it to anyone, under any circumstances?"

"No, Marscion — of course not."

Tergiver followed Marscion's lead, hoping to push the decision off his shoulders. "Do you think we should send someone for him?" Tergiver hoped to be vague, but Marscion insisted on clarification.

"I would have to know what you mean, Tergiver. But since you are so reluctant to do your simple duty, I would say three things to you. First, the lack of courage you now display is shameful and unbecoming. One begins to wonder if you would stand protector over the living bodies of the king's murderers as you did the dead. You have already received commendations for this duty, yet you are now reluctant to make it certain. You were not so reluctant to accept the accolades."

This was untrue, but Tergiver had not heard it. A tiny flame of fear was spreading through his lungs as he heard Charlie's words in his head: *"If we do nothing, the people who did this will never pay for it."* Then he imagined himself hanging from a platform.

"Second, Tergiver, you should know, if you do not already, that our army consists not only of grand warships and foot soldiers. This kingdom, like all others, has in its employ the kind of people who are competent in carrying out complicated, quiet assignments such as these. Third, we are the living; we are the survivors, you, me, and Agatha. Let the dead remain dead, or we may take their place. Now give me your answer."

Marscion had done everything but execute the order in Tergiver's will. Tergiver spoke in fear, prepared by Marscion, but he was fully aware of what he was doing, "Send someone after him then — one of the people you mentioned. I know what they are, and … let the dead remain so." Then Tergiver felt something strange, something he had not felt the night he held Charlie in his arms; it was relief. There was no body or evidence in front of him, and he felt no attachment to either Herrick or Baelin. He swallowed whole the weak conviction that this remaining killer was being justly punished. Then, for a brief moment he did not feel responsible for King Wiston's death. He allowed himself to feel as if he were merely an outsider, correcting the situation.

In all these thoughts, he had wrestled with the worst parts of himself, and lost.

Marscion made no sign of judgment. Instead he raised a hand and said, almost dismissively, "Then let it be done as you have ordered. Now, let us think of how we may catch this traitor." He began to pace the room with his hand on his mouth. "Herrick is too clever to show himself in Talus without a purpose. He might be baiting us." Marscion made another turn and his mouth caught a bit of a smile, "He would meet Agatha if she wanted him, no matter her reason."

Although Tergiver did not speak, he was already growing uncomfortable with his decision. The sense of relief was souring. He had made the easy choice but he was not prepared to support it. He listened to Marscion and concentrated on feeling overwhelmed by the councilor's authoritative presence, until finally he felt that he no longer had any power to change his decision. This too did not last long, but it lasted long enough for Marscion to set things in motion.

"Obviously, the princess cannot go searching the forest to find him. She would send a representative — perhaps even a friend." He concluded with a gravid expression, "I know who to send for Herrick, and if by chance, this is Baelin, then her task will be even easier." Marscion stopped pacing and placed a hand on Tergiver's shoulder. "You have done the brave thing. A position such as yours is a heavy burden and only the strong can carry it. I am proud of you, for what you did was truly difficult." Then he turned his head and said, "Now, what have we left unfinished?"

Though full of anxiety, Tergiver was still sharp, and he wished eagerly to move to another subject, to pretend that he had not just ordered Herrick hunted and killed. He answered, "The princess's friend. If this is true, she was with them the morning they came to Tholepin Bay. It means that Herrick had sailed to Talus on the night —" and here his memories again cut into him. He started a new sentence, "We don't know why he went to Talus, but we know that she must be part of it." He thought for a moment. "We should let her read the letter, and then later tonight we will question her and see if she lies."

"It would appear that she has already lied," said Marscion.

"Still, let us see what happens and then question her tonight."

Having worked so hard to make Tergiver carry out his primary wish, Marscion allowed him to have his way in this decision, and so Sophia escaped arrest and fled the castle.

She rode to Talus hagridden by dread. With every gallop her fear increased, not only for the safety of the man in the woods, but for her brother and Henry, who might be subject to questioning in Murmilan. Most of all, she was afraid for Agatha, now alone in the castle. She crossed the Silver Channel by ferry and reached *The Gilded Gosling* just after dark. Then she slipped into her room unnoticed.

She knew that Manchester and Henry would keep her up talking for hours if they saw her, and she missed them and might not have turned them away. She was exhausted from riding, and the short ferry across the channel had not provided much rest. She looked, for a moment, out her window to the east and peered into the dark heart of Etchmire Forest. Then she fell into a deep sleep upon touching her pillow.

Tergiver spent that night sitting on the floor, awake in front of the fire. He watched it consume log after log. They glowed, lurid orange, until they were seared, weak, and grey, and Tergiver felt as if he too were being consumed. What troubled him more than having ordered the man's death was his brief sense of relief at having done it. The decision took the form of a staring, gaping mouth in the burning logs, which glowed bright, stared out at him listlessly from the fire. The jawbone of the eyeless face broke in half and fell against the irons, sending a rush of orange splinters into the air. So began another long, sleepless night for Tergiver.

20

Friends more dangerous than enemies

In the dim, grey light of dawn, a shadow nuzzled its way deeper into a pile of snow and disappeared beside a short scrub of dead boxwood. It stared ahead into a hollow below a granite overhang where a man slept, hidden behind a blue sheet of ice that poured over the top of the rock. He was wrapped in a thick horse blanket and his hand rested on the gleaming white pommel of a sword.

As the light pierced the canopy of the forest in soft, narrow rays, the man's eyes opened, and he remained absolutely still, peering carefully into every corner of the trees in front of him. Then he swung his legs out of the hollow and dropped into the streaky haze. He drenched his face in the icy water of a nearby stream, and then he drank, cupping the water in one hand while holding the sword firmly in the other. He returned to the tiny clearing in front of the overhang and looked up, careworn and gaunt. He stopped and listened again, as if he heard another sound against the tinny trickle of water sliding between the icy sides of the stream.

A short distance from the buried eyes, a rabbit shuffled through the brush, rattling the scrambled hedge. The man stood straight, startled and breathing heavily. He did not see the rabbit, which had disappeared into a hole, but still he kept his eyes on the spot from which the noise had come. His hairy face was haggard and tired, yet he drew it into a fierce expression and began to speak slowly, sweeping his eyes and speech in a wide arc to address the forest in front of him. His sword hand trembled. "I know you are there, you coward. I've heard you all this time, rustling the brambles, slipping through the snow, and I hear you now. Come out and tell me what you want!" His voice wavered in frustration, and he compensated by making it more gruff and menacing. "Come out!" He stepped toward the hedge and began batting it violently with the sword. Then he moved across the stream where he kicked at piles of snow and beat the sword against more scattered brush and foliage. He did this for several minutes, yelling and kicking fanatically until finally he fell to his knees in the snow, exhausted, cold, and trembling. There he dropped the sword, put his head into his hands, and began mumbling to himself, "I will go to Ashen as you commanded, but — how can I leave everything like this? I should have known. I have been so stupid."

Shafts of pale morning light poured through the holes in the treetops, and the stream shone with varying shades of blue. The man wiped his face with frosty fingers and sniffed. Then he dropped his head back into his hands and said, "I am going mad, that is all. Nothing follows me but regret. Why didn't I deal with her when she had only killed one man? Just once did I allow myself to believe in her, and now my king and brothers lie frozen in the ground." Then he looked down through his fingers and spoke to the sword that lay half-buried in the powder. "Can I go back now? Am I such a coward? Am I afraid to take rightful revenge? Your steps have haunted me since I lost you in the mountains. Are you angry? Is that why you follow me? I should not have shown myself in that tavern. I am so weary; help me to have courage."

Baelin sat in the small clearing by the overhang and listened to the stream for a long time, lost in his thoughts. Again, he heard the sifting of snow under foot and the breaking of dead stems, but he ignored it, thinking it his imagination. Then, over the ridge of a short embankment to his right, a girl appeared.

She wore a bright winter cloak that shielded her from the cold, and when she moved, the brown clothes she wore under it dampened her appearance. On her shoulder was a quiver of long arrows, and her blond hair was tied up in a knot.

The buried eyes watched her carefully.

She stood for a moment, studying the man and leaning sideways in the hope of seeing his face. Then she uttered softly, "Hello?"

Baelin stirred backwards, raising the sword in front of him and standing ready. He said nothing, but stared and watched her hands, which were empty and spread apart in a sign of peace.

She spoke carefully, "I heard yelling; was that you? Are you all right?" She descended the bank slowly and joined him in the small clearing.

He did not answer; instead, he seemed suddenly embarrassed by his behavior. He had been yelling at nothing, and he was ashamed. He lowered the sword point to the ground and sat down again, facing away.

The girl cast a deliberate look around the woods to see if there were any others in the area, then sat near him. She looked sideways at his face as if she were trying to place him, and then she examined the sword, which he was turning nervously in the snow in front of him. When she saw it, she knew for sure that he was the man from the letter. She looked again, up the embankments that surrounded them, and said in a quiet voice, hoping not to startle him, "You are not safe. People know you are here."

He turned quickly and asked, "Who are you?"

"I am a friend of Agatha's."

His expression turned dark and bitter at the name, and the girl frowned defensively at his reaction.

However, she continued in a placatory voice, "We have never met. Yesterday —" Then she stopped, startled and scared. Above the creek, on the far side of the man, there appeared another girl with long blond hair tied behind her head. She wore dirty brown clothes and an old leather pack. At her side she carried a long knife.

Suddenly everyone was standing. The new girl saw the two down in the clearing, then she drew her face into a fearful expression and screamed, pointing desperately at the first girl.

The girl behind Baelin was quickly drawing her bow tight, inches from his neck. She started to say something, but as he swung around, the blood froze still in his heart, and he could hear nothing at all.

First, he saw the girl, whose eyes were trained up the embankment. Then he saw a lump of snow behind a thicket erupt into a violent, furry spray of white, rushing like a shiver and leaping tall with horrible snarling jowls to tear the bow-wielding girl to the ground with a harsh yellow bite fixed deep in her shoulder. Baelin stumbled away as the animal's eyes flashed quickly up the hill to the second girl and took a step toward her.

The girl on the hill was breathless and terrified, but she read the situation quickly and tossed her knife into the snow a few feet away. As she predicted, the animal turned away from her and returned to the girl it had attacked. She narrowed her eyes and thought, *Marscion did not tell me he had protection.*

Baelin's hands shook with energy. He backed away from the beast, listening to it growl as it measured the standing girl with its deep yellow eyes. It was a large wolf with bristling silver and white fur that matched the snow around it, and a long tail that swished the ground behind its legs. It hunched its back menacingly and corralled Sophia to the base of a large, knotted tree, snapping at her with every sound she tried to make, leaving her to shake and bleed silently as it turned to watch the others.

Baelin's face was set in a hard, mixed expression of recognition, fear, and epiphany. He looked for the first time at the thing that had followed him since he had lost his captain in the mountains. He considered the place it had hidden, steps from where he had slept, and he regarded the ferocity with which it had attacked the girl. He stared at the creature that lay just a few leaps away. Even still, it was barely discernible, a mere set of yellow eyes in the silver snow. At once he shuddered and his throat gave way to a short exhalation of grief for the agony he had suffered in the animal's secret companionship.

In his weary state, he had not seen the nuances of what had just taken place. He wondered why he had not also been attacked. Then he felt in his tingling skin the realization that perhaps he had not been hunted all this time, but watched. He had unconsciously backed away and joined the rugged girl on the bank above the clearing, and he said quietly, as if they were alone and the entire event over, "Who is she?"

The assassin looked down to the paralyzed body against the tree, then back to him and thought for a moment. "The Guard in Murmilan found my brother's letter, and they know you are here. They sent someone to kill you; I guess it was her." She cast a glance at the wolf, understanding that she could not threaten the man as long as it was near. "You are lucky to have that friend of yours." Then she watched as Sophia tried to move, but was held in check by a sharp bite to her foreleg.

"I've never seen it before. It is no friend of mine and I do not know why it follows me," replied Baelin. Then he turned away from the animal in disgust, and looked on the standing girl as if she were a fellow survivor, or a companion during his long ordeal. "Who are you?"

"I am a friend of the princess," she responded quickly.

Baelin looked as if an internal wound had reopened. "Does she have more friends coming for me, or is it just you two?"

"What do you mean?"

The assassin reached into her pack slowly and carefully, and the wolf growled as she produced a small length of rope. "If we can, we should tie her up so she doesn't follow you. She is probably very dangerous, and if she escapes she could track you easily in this snow."

Baelin took the rope from her hand and descended the bank slowly, watching the wolf and keeping his hands in the air. The animal swished its tail once as if in warning, and then it lifted its haunches high as Baelin approached the body. Then it growled with a low and menacing sound that seemed to come from deep within the snow under its chest. After a few moments, Baelin capitulated, not with fear, but with the stronger desire to be rid of the animal's company. He backed away as slowly as he had come, and when he returned to his place beside the girl, he pointed away from the clearing, indicating that she should walk. "Now, what do you want with me? Why did Agatha send you?"

They had gone a good distance from the clearing before the girl answered. After considering his sword for a long time, she glanced again at his face, which was still hidden under a thick beard. "Agatha told me that she would only be happy if she knew that Herrick was safe."

"And you believe her?"

"She has been sick over it ever since the shipwreck, and … she thought that maybe he could tell her what happened on the night her father died. She is very confused." Marscion had prepared her well, but she had not expected the man to be so angry with the princess.

"So," he said with a smirk, "now she would make sure —" Then he stopped. His thoughts were circling around a decision. He wanted to say, *Now she would make sure that she has killed all of us for certain, and that is why she sent two of you,* but he did not care what Agatha thought or for what purpose she had sent for him. In that moment, Baelin made the decision that had tormented him since losing Herrick. He was torn between two pressing obligations. Herrick's last orders commanded him to press on to the east, and yet he believed that Agatha had simply acted a dramatic part on the night of the king's murder, skillfully crippling the head of the Guard, then tying Baelin to an empty chamber with a fake note and a brilliant performance. For this, he felt the greater obligation was to revenge his king and brothers in The Guard by killing her.

Then the girl took a risk. Marscion had told her that Herrick knew Sophia, but this man had not recognized either of them. It was possible that he had recognized Sophia but said nothing — this was the danger. She began to speak gently, hoping to lure him across the channel where she could kill him without the interference of the animal. "You may not remember me. My name —"

Baelin interrupted, his eyebrows furrowed in indignant determination, "I don't care who you are or who you think I am. Take me to the princess; I will see her. But know that I am watching you. I know every point of ambush in the Murmillian landscape. Do not betray me or you will wish you had traded places with your friend back in the clearing." With this, Baelin brazenly turned his back on her and walked westward.

She caught up to him after a few moments, afraid of the animal that she could no longer see.

They went in silence, side by side, until they came to the edge of the trees, where the mouth of the river emerged and ran through the middle of Talus. They heard a short scream from the clearing behind them, then the forest was quiet again.

21

The burning table

A purposeful knock on Tergiver's door rang hollow inside his chamber. He sat on the floor with his legs stretched toward a dead fire, sitting upright in a pile of ash and torn paper. The knock came again, followed by Loren's voice, "Sir, if you are ill, let us enter and we can bring help."

He waited for them to leave, but the knock came again. Tergiver rose to his feet and felt his legs aching under him as he lumbered to the door. He had been sitting on the stone floor all night and all morning.

Loren was surprised by his chief's disheveled appearance. He asked to be admitted, and Jason hovered close behind him. Tergiver stood aside and rubbed his sleepless eyes with dirty fingers as they passed.

"It is quite cold in here, sir," said Loren.

Jason took a silent and greedy inventory of everything in the room.

"I have been feeling ill, Loren, but I am sure it will pass," said Tergiver. Then he sat gingerly on the side of his bed, looked at the floor and repeated cryptically, "I'm sure it will pass."

Jason was excited about something, and though he tried, he was making a terrible show of hiding it. He nudged Loren and whispered, "Tell him."

"Sir," said Loren, "Feyton, the magistrate from Northford, is dead."

"What — when?" Tergiver stammered.

Jason's mouth hung open slightly and his eyes were wide.

Loren answered, "Councilor Robert told us that Feyton became ill that night after we returned to the castle. This morning we received word that he was dead." Loren bowed his head and looked sideways at Jason, who slowly understood that he was alone in his excitement.

A dull pain flashed through Tergiver's head. He felt unbalanced, as if the legs on the bed were wobbling and about to break. He saw the magistrate's face in his mind; he heard the graceful replies to his father's obsequious praise, and the friendly debate with Loren over the clinking of plates and glasses. Then he drifted, and imagined the same table, but it was darker, as if he were dreaming.

He heard King Wiston exchanging whispers with the magistrate, but when he strained to listen, he heard his name in grim accusations. Charlie sat across from the king, nodding in agreement. Then Tergiver heard a knock on the door, and everyone at the table looked at him. Herrick was trying to get in.

Another conspicuous knock came from Tergiver's chamber door, and Loren acknowledged the man who stood there, "Sir?"

Marscion gripped his white cloak, "Have you told him?"

"Yes, sir."

"Is he sick?"

"I don't think so, sir."

"Tell him to come to my office. I will be there until sunset."

"Yes, sir."

Marscion disappeared from the doorway.

Tergiver awoke from his daydream, looked up at the two men, and asked, "Was he poisoned?" He could tell from their eyes that each knew the answer, yet both were afraid to give it. Jason looked uneasy, unsure of whether he should say anything lest it displease Tergiver. Loren only stared at Tergiver, as if waiting for an unspoken sign. Tergiver stood and said, "Jason, thank you for your service. Please return to your post."

He bowed with a hint of disappointment and left the chamber. When he was gone, Tergiver said to Loren, "Speak, tell me what you know."

"Sir," he replied, "I am afraid that I do not know anything about this for certain, nor do I want to asperse my brother in arms, but Jason was delighted when he heard the news. He was aching to tell you himself. I would like to ask you, sir, although I know it is not my place to question your order, which I will not, but … sir, did you give an order for Feyton to be poisoned?"

"No." He spoke the word quickly and without sound, as if he were too weary to utter it fully. "I thought he was a good man. I even told Marscion about your debate, and how I felt you might have swayed him."

"Sir," said Loren quietly, and then he stopped, struggling whether to proceed. He trusted Tergiver more than he had expected. He felt compelled to tell him about his and Jason's part in the escape of *The Dolphin*; he yearned to gain his full confidence, but he dared not. He only knew that King Wiston had never allowed any kind of secrecy or perfidy among the governors of his kingdom. Loren suspected that if Tergiver had no part in this new murder, he might be trusted to understand that Herrick and Borleaf had been falsely accused. Then, Loren hoped, Tergiver might become an ally in his own quiet search for the king's murderer.

These thoughts, however, were too tenuously connected, and Loren knew that he was filling the holes with dangerous assumptions. He saw the intense struggle in Tergiver's eyes, and it convinced him to wait. He said, "Sir, please get well. It would seem that there are still some unknowns here at the castle, and I believe that if anyone can figure them out, you can." He waited for Tergiver to respond, but the chief only looked up at him, nodded gratefully with a subtle sign of dismissal, and walked over to the fireplace. Loren asked at the door, "Sir, did you hear Marscion's request that you meet with him?"

Tergiver turned his head sideways and down, and answered, "Yes. Thank you, Loren."

After Loren had left him alone in the chamber, Tergiver returned to the floor, and his tired, sleepless mind drifted again to the dark table where his victims sat discussing their murders. This time, Tergiver was seated at the end of the table, wearing his black cloak; his hands and face were painted dark red. The three men looked menacingly on him and began to hurl questions, while Herrick announced himself at the door with rapid, hammering fists.

King Wiston squinted. "I knighted you as a sailor didn't I? Is that the blue cloak I gave you, Tergiver of Northford?"

Charlie said nothing; he just looked up to Tergiver with confused, teary eyes.

Then Feyton addressed him, "You barely knew me, Tergiver, so surely this cannot fall on you, can it?"

Herrick pounded on the door.

"You and your guards presented yourselves as the embodiment of courtesy to me — at least you and Loren did so — and as you act, so acts The Guard, or is it the opposite?"

He saw himself at the table, trying to answer but unable. He could only move his red arms in the air before him as if they were not his, and they horrified him. Behind the magistrate, the fire grew larger and higher until it appeared as if it would soon spread and engulf the three other men at the table, yet they did not notice.

The magistrate continued, "My death could not have been your fault. Surely in your limited power you could have done nothing to prevent it. After all, your control is limited to the king's most influential forces — and your renown and respect within The Guard could not have helped."

At this King Wiston's gaze turned vicious and he said, "He has only what he has stolen."

Tergiver was frantic. He was pinned to the chair as the fire baked the red paint onto his face, hardening it into a shell. He felt it becoming a part of him, and his arms and feet burned as it clung to his skin.

"You knew didn't you? You chose not to pay attention, or did you think that by doing nothing you might save me?" continued Feyton.

The door rattled on its hinges and Tergiver struggled to leave the chair. Then the fire grew wider behind Feyton, and crawled forward until the individual hairs on his head were singeing, turning bright orange until finally his whole head was aflame. Tergiver was screaming for them to beware of the fire, but they ignored it, and King Wiston said, as flames engulfed his right arm, "Who else will you kill, Tergiver; how many more until you know what you want?" The black cloak hung about him heavily and he saw a flash of the black pall under which they had buried the king. The fire crept onto the surface of the table where it caught the cuff of Charlie's sleeve. Tergiver's face burned and he could no longer yell as the red paint had dried solid. He looked, as through a mask, at the others as they caught fire and burned before his eyes under the heavy thumping of Herrick's fists on the door, which shook the foundations and walls of the house; and he heard Herrick's voice, muffled, but deep and menacing. "Don't forget me, Tergiver; I'm coming for you!"

Tergiver awoke with a shout. He heard Marscion's voice coming from the other side of the door, mixed with intermittent bangs. Tergiver stood up, still frightened, and moved slowly to it. As he walked, he felt as if the burning table were still behind him, scorching his back. His body was shaking, and he wanted to confess. He drove everything else out of his mind to keep it clear for the task. Then, as he opened the door, the king's question resounded in his head: *"How many more until you know what you want?"*

Tergiver pulled the door open to reveal Marscion standing angrily in his white robe. Tergiver answered to himself: *I don't want this.* He would follow Marscion, and he would confess everything.

Baelin had not spoken since that morning, when the ferry had brought him and his companion across the channel to the city of Eastport on Murmilan's eastern shore. He had reminded her that he would kill her should he see any sign of ambush or arrest before he met the princess. To his surprise, she was not frightened.

After disembarking from the ferry, they walked up the long dock and disappeared into a thick crowd that worked its way in every direction and mixed thoroughly before a shoreline row of inns and taverns.

As soon as they were through the main thoroughfare, Baelin led them up a short ridge to the north of the city and into a long grove of pine trees that ran parallel to the road. They trudged silently through the snow for hours, and Baelin stopped them frequently, commanding her to remain still until a train of clopping horses or a caravan of rickety carts passed by. They traveled hidden in the trees but always within sight of the road, which ran all the way to Murmilan's East Gate. The snow was deep and they had to crunch through a thin layer of ice with every step before sinking into a foot of powder. However, they did not travel much slower than they would have in the open. The girl was fleet of foot, and Baelin marched with purpose.

When they had traveled half the way to the East Gate, the sun began to fade in the west. The sky, which had been a clear, cold blue all day, darkened around them. Baelin shivered with the new chill in the air, and addressed the girl companionably, as he had immediately after the attack in Etchmire, "Can you tell?"

"Can I tell what?" She had decided to pretend a sense of indignation at her poor treatment. She knew that the closer they drew to the walls of Murmilan, the easier it would be for Marscion to find the body and pay her the bonus for confirming its identity.

"I have heard these sounds and seen these same glimpses for weeks. It is there again, just off to our right."

She decided that he was lying, trying to scare her. She knew there were no bridges across the wide channel, and no way to cross but the ferry. Still, she pretended to be frightened, and she was so convincing that Baelin had a difficult time maintaining his threatening posture.

They moved on. He watched as she stepped lightly and skillfully through the snowy brush and deep drifts, and he found that he respected her. "You were going to tell me your name. What is it?"

The question caught her by surprise. She had been deep in her own plans for several hours, and she was unprepared. She stuttered, as if she had to grope for the answer. Then, she seemed to grow concerned, as if he might be testing her. Her hand moved to the back of her belt and thumbed the handle of a small knife. "It's Sophie."

The name meant nothing to him. "Sophie, why would Agatha send a girl after me when she could have sent any of her Black Guard? Did she think I wouldn't come by force?"

"She sent me because she trusts me. We're friends after all. She wants to meet with you secretly ... to talk."

"Before she hangs me?" said Baelin with a sneer.

"Are there any others left from the ship?" She asked. She felt that the situation was becoming dangerous, and she pressed one last time to find out who he was. Once she found out, it would be easy to cut his neck with the blade in her belt. She felt they were close enough.

Baelin did not answer for a minute. He had taken the question like a blow to the gut. After composing his response he answered, "You are not very subtle, are you. Would she like an official confirmation of Herrick's death? I can sign it for you personally, though I doubt my authority is what it used to be. Or, if you wish, we can go back and dig his body out of the ice on Allocausus where it lies." In her face he read that she had received the answer she wanted. She did not bother to feign sadness, but surveyed the wood ahead for the best advantage for her attack.

"What happened to the bodies of my friends? What happened to Borleaf and Anson? Did they find them?"

"The new chief of the guard had them buried in the cemetery."

Baelin contemplated the image of their proper burial, but he stayed any tears by focusing on the object of his revenge. "Did she erect the headstones in the cemetery, or has she hung them in her chamber as trophies?"

Her reply chilled him, and for a brief second, he stopped walking. "There is no stone for Herrick," she replied sharply. "But there is one for you."

Baelin looked at the girl stoically, and after a minute his face hardened with a new strength of determination. The thought of his name carved on a stone brought a sense of finality to his purpose. He saw his end clearly and he was prepared to face it. He began to bury the entirety of his feelings under the singular importance and duty of his revenge. He forgot his mission to the east, his personal hatred for Agatha, even his hunger. Baelin saved only one request, which he asked of the girl as if he had now surrendered all authority to her: "Before I see the princess, let me go to the graveyard and say farewell to my friends. Then I will follow wherever you want."

She held a long, serious face that hid the laughter in her heart. Then she turned her head away from Baelin and suppressed a little smile, wondering if she might also charge Marscion for the irony.

22

Three confessions

The queen's chamber had begun to grow dark. Servants had recently loaded logs into the fire by the bed, and it burned warm at Agatha's back. She sat in an embroidered felt chair with her hands on her lap, watching her mother's heavy, labored sleep. She had come the day before at Sophia's request, but only because it afforded a chance to hide from everything else. She had asked kindly not to be interrupted, and the castle servants had obeyed.

Agatha had not known what Sophia had expected her to do there. Most of the time she had stood, staring out the east windows, running her fingers around the inside of the ruby necklace she wore, and turning occasionally to find her mother still and unmoving in her shadow. She had made petty conversation with the servants, and she had counted the stitches in the queen's blankets, but she had devoted little attention to the queen herself. Only on the second day, after giving close attention to everything else in the room, did she turn her eyes to her mother.

She noticed, at first without interest, and then with a gradual curiosity, how her mother's nose, in earlier years, might have looked like her own. She began to compare other features, wondering if she might look similar when she was older, and she began, halfheartedly, to match parts of herself to familiar traits in the queen.

Looking at her mother for a more sustained period, Agatha also noticed how much her health had declined even in the last week. She was hollow-faced and gaunt, as if the folds of her skin were too heavy for her face. Agatha wished she had spent time like this with her father before he died. She wanted to ask him more questions, to make him explain himself, and she wished she could unspeak her last words to him. Then, for the first time since her mother had taken to bed, Agatha reached out hesitantly from her chair, and held her hand.

Queen Rose awoke several minutes later and her eyes rolled to look on the side of the bed where Agatha sat. They were set deep in her skull, and Agatha saw the sharp rims of her eye sockets protruding through her weak eyebrows. The queen's face had been free from bright colors for many weeks. She did not smile at her daughter, but reserved her strength for strained, soft speech. "Your father loves you. Tell your father you are sorry, Agatha."

The princess sat in the chair with sad eyes and pursed lips. She did not know how to respond. She did not know whether her mother was delusional or if she truly understood that he was gone.

"He was so glad you weren't going to leave us, but he didn't know why you were so angry with him. I told him I didn't know. I told him girls are girls."

Agatha did not understand. She had never discovered her option to leave, and she felt for the first time an odd longing for home, as if she had been threatened by the idea of leaving it. This did not last long, however, before she instinctually began to defend herself. "I didn't decide anything, Mother; there was a ship that was going to …"

"No, no," murmured the queen, "only if you wanted."

The queen's softness of speech was uncharacteristic and it made Agatha uncomfortable. "What do you mean?" she demanded, receding into her aspect of self-pity. "He never understood what I was going through; he had everything planned anyway."

Queen Rose closed her eyes and took a cumbersome breath, then looked back to her daughter and whispered in a weak voice, "He understood."

Agatha's spirits sank. She found the change in her mother confusing; she felt as if her father or Sophia were speaking instead. Then the store of Sophia's many reprimands began to collect into a thought, and it occurred to her that even on her mother's deathbed she could think of nothing to do but complain about her own misfortune. She knew she had slighted her mother by remarking on the king's understanding of love, a comment in which she had hidden an insult, and though she was barely aware of it, she felt ashamed.

She continued to feel sorry for herself, however. She wallowed in her grand, impossible struggle to be the royal personality everyone wanted her to be, and yet, within it she suddenly felt a new, dramatic awareness of her inability to talk about anything but herself. Agatha thought on this for a while before recognizing the irony of her self-absorbed contemplation. She squeezed her mother's hand in an attempt to shake free from her thoughts. "I'm sorry, Mother," she said, and then she waited, straining herself to avoid saying anything else.

After a minute of watching her daughter's struggling attempt at kindness, the queen smiled and said, "You look so much like her."

Agatha sat quietly, guessing that her mother had again slipped into waking dreams, from which she now seemed to speak so often.

"Let me tell you a story, my dear," began Rose. "Once there was a beautiful princess."

Agatha flopped her head forward and closed her eyes. She knew that her mother was drifting away again, relapsing into an old pattern from her childhood. Until Agatha had been old enough to send her away, the queen had put her to bed with the same story. It involved a beautiful princess who grew up in a beautiful house, married a beautiful prince, and had a beautiful life forever. Her mother had always lingered on the word *beautiful*, and it was a word that Agatha had come to hate. She settled in her chair to endure the long, repetitive story, and realized that perhaps this was what Sophia expected. In this, she decided, in listening to a story she did not want to hear, she might do something good, even noble, despite the truth that she did not feel noble, nor did she want to listen.

"And this beautiful princess wanted to marry a beautiful prince. And the prince sailed across the ocean to find her."

Agatha stared out the window, ready to suffer the long pause that always preceded the part about the *beautiful* wedding.

"But this princess had a little sister, who wasn't so beautiful, and she wasn't so smart, but this little sister loved her dearly and followed her everywhere she went."

This was new. Agatha turned her head with a glance, and though she retained her languorous affectation, she began to listen.

"The prince saw them both, and he saw how kind the princess was to her little sister, and he saw how lonely and afraid she became when the princess left her alone. So the beautiful prince asked the king if he could also bring the little ugly one home so she would be happy too, and the king said yes. The wedding was beautiful. There were beautiful flowers and beautiful clothes, and the prince cried when he stood in front of his princess. He loved her more than anyone has ever loved anyone in the whole world. She was so beautiful. Her little sister even got to stand by her and she got to hold her hand as they walked out of the hall, even though everyone knew she was ugly and she kept stepping on her dress."

Agatha was silent. She had never heard this version, and as her mother told it in raspy, wilting breaths, it slowly began to affect her. Soon her grief, which had until this time been latent and overpowered by fear, welled up within her. Agatha's eyes began to water in sympathy for the ugly little girl who had always been there, hidden away in the story, but never seen.

"There was a beautiful ship and a hundred beautiful people and they all said good-bye and cried and the prince kissed his princess. She was so good and wise and she loved everyone around her and she was so very kind to her sister. But on the sea, on the way to her new home, she became very sick. The prince cried and worried and pulled his hair and spent every night by her bedside with her little sister, who didn't understand what was happening, but cried with him because she was very afraid. Then, before the ship arrived at the beautiful castle, the princess died."

Agatha's eyes were full and her face was strained in sorrowful anticipation.

"The prince was so sad that he couldn't speak to anyone for almost a whole day. Then one of his guards asked him if he wanted to turn back and take the princess home to Ordon, but he said no. He asked the ugly sister, though she was stupid and afraid, if she would be his princess. He told her that he wanted to honor his love and her father. He said he had promised to take care of her. He said by doing so he would never forget his princess. And you look so much like her, Agatha. You always have, and I miss her so much right now. I am so afraid." The queen sobbed until her face was pale and awash with tears.

What strength she had left she spent on weeping and looking up at her daughter while clutching her hand tight. They cried together, and Agatha could not speak. Only then did she understand the cruelty of the words she had so often spoken to her father. The east light grew darker until the windowpanes were almost black. Then, as Agatha sat, matching her breaths to her mother's and watching her at rest, the queen's breath stopped.

Agatha held her hand for a long time afterwards. Then she rose wearily and rested her head against the cold windowpane, staring out over the dark Pine Wood to the statues and monuments of the cemetery, whose tips peeked above the East Wall. She left the queen's chamber somberly and walked down the hall in tears, carrying the words, "*Tell your father you are sorry, Agatha.*"

Tergiver followed Marscion down the dark hallway and stood aside as he turned the key in his office door. The room was ablaze and hot with an enormous, colorful fire in the fireplace. Marscion hung his long white cloak on a hook and closed the door behind them. In the windows, the sun was beginning to sink toward the horizon. Marscion stood in front of them, behind his desk, and faced Tergiver, who had refused to sit.

The fire kept the recent dream burning low in Tergiver's mind, and he tried to form the exact words he would use to confess.

Marscion spoke first. "You were told to meet me here before I left at sundown, Tergiver. I must speak to you before I go, and now I will arrive late." He leaned on his desk and said, "Feyton was dangerous. You need to understand that. Jason understood it."

"But did he have to die, Marscion?" Tergiver spoke as if he were still in his dream, as if Feyton were feeding him words, "Could there have been another way?"

Marscion was cold. "Did Herrick have to die? Just yesterday you sent someone to find and kill him, did you not? So I ask you, was there another way?"

Tergiver was trapped. He knew it had simply been his fear of discovery that had condemned the man in the woods, and now that he was going to confess, the decision cut him even more deeply. "Can we stop it? Is there anything we can do, Marscion? But there is something else," Tergiver sounded desperate, adding these words quickly, as if they were burning his tongue.

"I will not lead you like this for much longer, Tergiver. You must grow up and understand that sometimes, unpleasant things must be done for greater purposes. You are a soldier, yet you run from blood. Even the most meager peasant with a rusted scythe understands what he must do when his kingdom is attacked. Tell me you are ready. Tell me you understand, and then we can end all of this deceit, this killing — let us finally move forward. We are so close, Tergiver, close to moving on from all of this and starting anew, but I have to know that you are brave enough to do what must be done."

Tergiver didn't feel brave. He still grasped at circling words, trying to piece them together in his head. While Marscion had spoken, he had tried them silently, *I don't want to be chief of the guard anymore … I can't keep killing people, and Marscion … I killed King Wiston … and my best friend, and now Feyton …* Each sentence ended painfully. Nothing sounded right, and he had stalled in the middle of each one, understanding that once he admitted this guilt to Marscion, his life would change, and it would end shortly thereafter. The finality of the decision struck him dumb several times, and he found himself wishing again that he could discover some way to live without the guilt that wrung his conscience, and without facing the consequences of his actions.

As he battled these thoughts, Marscion turned around to face the windows, but he remained at a slight angle so he could still see Tergiver's reflection in the glass. "I told you we can stop all of this and I mean it. You are young, Tergiver, and I know that you have seen things that no one your age should have to see. Nevertheless, I have also seen you recover; I have seen your courage. Now, you just have to fight through one final endeavor, and then I think you will see an end to these feelings that trouble you."

Tergiver could not concentrate. He had not slept more than a few hours since the night he returned from Northford. He hadn't understood Marscion the first time he had said these things, and he didn't understand now. He listened more intently, momentarily putting aside his attempts at confession. Secretly, he hoped to find in Marscion's words some key that might either solve his dilemma or move him to confess.

The sun had sunk lower in the sky, and the clouds began to turn pink in the winter windows.

"I think we have all been naïve about the king's murder, and I am sure you would agree with me. What if I told you, Tergiver, that we know who was truly responsible?"

Tergiver was stunned and he felt his heart pounding. His words dried up completely.

Marscion saw in the reflection that he had Tergiver's full attention. "The case against Herrick is easy, but we have all had our other suspicions and theories. Correct?" There was no response, but he continued anyway. "Borleaf? Anson? No. We know the killer is still with us, Tergiver, walking these halls every day. This being so, we cannot feel safe ourselves, when the threat of constant guile and offense is ever at our backs, occupying our very castle, still with power to command and the authority to kill. Think on it from our perspective, and tell me what you would do."

Tergiver felt as if all the blood had drained out of his body through his feet, and he balanced the best he could. He did not know if he could stand much longer. He saw his free confession slipping away. After Marscion's accusation, his confession would sound like nothing more than a startled reaction from one caught in his crimes. His head dropped lower at the loss of this last chance to confess with dignity.

In the windows, the sun sank into the horizon and the entire sky caught fire. Marscion watched Tergiver's face and noted the fear and helplessness that passed over it. "We have cast guilt where there has been none, and perhaps innocents have died for the crimes of others. This is what we must stop. Do you understand? Yes, Tergiver. You know what I am talking about."

There was a knot in Tergiver's throat, but he took courage, and answered truthfully. His words struck out from his mouth as if he had been long choking on them, "Yes, and I am ready to face whatever may come." He held his hands out in abdication and dropped to one knee, bowing his head. He no longer cared what the punishment would be, only that he meet it courageously. "Marscion, I have wanted so badly to tell —"

Marscion did not let him finish, but spoke over his words purposefully, darkening his eyebrows hard into the glass, so that when Tergiver looked up he became uneasy at the sight of his reflected face. "Tell me then, Tergiver. Tell me of everyone involved, and let us see if we have come to the same conclusions. Surely we can understand each other ... but let me speak first, and let us be honest and clear." He waited until he was certain that Tergiver was listening. "You still have an opportunity before you; there is no soldier in the kingdom who commands more respect than you do. The common people believe in you, and this is a blessing we have not had for some time. They call you 'Tergiver the brave, the kind, the loyal ...' and I think you have earned those titles. But now, Tergiver, think on the one who has not earned their love or loyalty, and I think you will find the villain you are really searching for. You will find the answer to the question you have long asked yourself in secret. Who was it who set all of this in motion? Who put you in the position you are in today? Who has put me in mine?" Here Marscion's reflection appeared grim and menacing. "We have uncovered a horrible truth, Tergiver. We have discovered a traitorous serpent among us, one who has snuck and hidden and bitten and then retreated into a paling semblance of weakness. Did you know that we recently found a note hidden in a certain chamber of this castle, which warned of the assassination? Did you know that we have identified the handwriting of the boy who wrote it, and did you know that this boy disappeared on the same night the king was killed? Do you know who occupies this chamber, or that she received a visitor, carried to her that very next morning by Herrick himself — on that same stolen ship that later appeared in Tholepin Bay?"

Tergiver began to shake his head sideways in petrified disagreement and disbelief; he had avoided the princess out of guilt, but also because she still retained the mystical quality she had gained in the cloaking ceremony, and these things had combined to make him feel unworthy of her presence.

Marscion grew sterner as he pressed on, raising his hands in the air proudly as if he wished to illustrate the story with convincing passion. "And now that visitor has fled the castle, having realized she was caught. Yes, Tergiver. Did you know this person once told me privately, how she sent Herrick and Borleaf away, clearing the way for the king's murder? Did you know that several councilors and guard members heard her threatening her father just before he was killed? And when I visited our good queen's chamber later that morning, do you know the first thing she asked? Queen Rose asked me if the king had ever found their daughter that night, and when he was coming back to bed.

"You know all of these things are true, but one must be wise enough to assemble them, and braver still to say them." His words were grave and deep, and the sun began to burn dark on the horizon.

Tergiver's knees began to shake, and he put a hand behind him to catch himself from falling over on the floor. He continued to shake his head sideways, and said, "No, no — but it wasn't …"

The face in the glass hardened, watching him, and then it said,

"The courage to do one more thing, Tergiver. You have come so far, yet look at you, whimpering there on the floor." Marscion's face had turned up into a sneer and Tergiver could not breathe; the dying rim of the sun had painted the glass red, and Marscion's reflection burned deep with the same disgust and disappointment it had shown on the pavilion.

Tergiver lost his balance, feeling as if the walls behind him were pushing him forward. Marscion turned; then his face shone again in the high fire with flickering orange, red, and black shadows. He spoke in a strange and different voice, poisonous and vindictive.

"Were you going to confess to me, Tergiver? Do you think I don't know you — that I didn't remember the desperate, flattering boy from the first day of the tournament, or your face as you stumbled pathetically down the sculpture garden that next night? Look at you, again collapsing in sick fear in the grand moment in which you should be burning with triumph. Tergiver the weak. Who else were you going to accuse — and were you also to confess to hunting and killing innocent guardsmen and magistrates?" He walked forward, away from the desk and toward Tergiver.

Tergiver was paralyzed. The room had darkened except for the sunlight that colored the scene in sanguinary splotches of red, and the rumbling fire that splashed orange and black shadows high on the windows. His body shook, and he felt cold and limp as Marscion pulled him to his feet.

The red face was now dark and close in the shadow, and he knew it hated him. It hissed through angry eyes as the fire spit and popped behind it, "Tonight, before I return, you will kill Agatha."

Tergiver's eyes watered and he trembled under Marscion's grip.

"What is wrong with you! I have given you more chances than you deserve, but I will not tolerate your weakness any longer. I cannot imagine why he chose you — you who become so powerless at the sight of blood. I can't imagine why he has kept you alive." Then the face turned sideways and gentle, sickening in the light. "I have offered you a safe place with me, and I have told you that if you have the courage to do this last thing, we can be free of this whole issue. It will be finished, Tergiver. The story is solid, the council will believe me, and you are already a hero."

Still, Tergiver shook and said nothing.

Then the face regained its horror, and its breath fell on him like the heat from the fire. "Tonight I am going to appoint the new magistrate in Northford, and I am leaving Jason to guard him after the celebration." Then the face smiled falsely. "You should be proud; your family has become rather influential in this kingdom. You should understand that it is within your power to prolong these newfound lives, or to lose both of them. Now take courage and do what you are told, as you did with King Wiston. This is no different. After tonight, no one else will have to die. Think on the outcome; think of what it will be like. You will be renowned as the only man brave enough to have discovered and purged from this castle the secret wickedness that poisoned it for so long." The face lightened, rejoicing in the glory to come, and it nodded fitfully to the papers on the desk. "Then, as a show of goodwill, we will rescind the worst of these unfair, oppressive taxes she has suggested and endorsed over these last few weeks. We will be able to show the people proof of the horrible future Agatha had planned for them. Let them imagine the rest for themselves. Let them linger on the life of fear and slavery that would have come from serving a queen who hated them — and let them praise us, above all others, for having discovered this future and stopped it. Then they will love us, Tergiver, as they ought, but they will love you the most. Think on it. You have only to do this one thing and it will be finished. If you have doubts, remember the evidence against her, use it, and ask yourself if you truly know that she is innocent, because I know you cannot answer that question."

Tergiver involuntarily imagined Agatha's voice whispering into Marscion's office, disturbing the candle flames. As he did, Marscion rested a hand on his shoulder and held it for a moment. Then there was a knock at the door.

Marscion held him still with a confident look and then went quietly to the rack by the door. He pulled a heavy white cloak over his shoulders, wrapping it around the dark garments he wore, and cracked the door to reveal Loren's face. Tergiver listened, hidden from view.

"Sir, the princess has gone to the cemetery. I was concerned that she should be there alone so I posted two men to watch her. You were right, sir. She did look quite strange, and I might not have noticed otherwise. I am glad you asked me to watch her. I think she truly needs us right now. Is there anything else I can do?"

"Yes, Loren. I am riding tonight for Northford. Please find Jason and choose three other guards to accompany us. Bring full dress; there will be a ceremony in which you will play a part. Have everyone at the stables shortly. I will meet you there."

"Yes, sir. I will report to Tergiver to tell him we are leaving by your request."

"He knows," said Marscion. "That is all."

Loren nodded and turned back down the hall. Marscion closed the door and threw these words at Tergiver, "I will dismiss the men from the cemetery. You will be alone. Now you know what you have to do, and you know the consequences if you do not. I will return tonight. Be brave, and do not disappoint me."

23

The death of a princess

The ridges of the cemetery protruded from the hill like giant jawbones with chipped stone teeth, while the moon hung behind trawling clouds and cast inconsistent spots of blue on the snowy scene. Fog crept between the gravestones and the tall, wooden poles on which were hung burning torches that marked the sloping, frozen paths of the cemetery.

Agatha moved slow and dolefully along one of these paths, staring absently at her feet as they disappeared at intervals, engulfed by the darkness between the torches. Her father's monument stood at the northern edge of the graveyard, at the end of the highest row, but she walked east and west on the lower ridges, ashamed to meet him. After a short while, when the walking had warmed her courage, she climbed the torch-lit path to the Row of Kings, the highest ridge in the cemetery. She turned apprehensively and stepped past the tall granite statues of kings past, noble grandfathers who seemed to scrutinize her in the moonlight. Two torches burned on each side of a chiseled marble block that towered over King Wiston's grave. Agatha sat down lightly on a pile of pebbles and rocks in the snow, and put her head between her knees.

A rare night breeze nudged the flames lightly then disappeared. Agatha tried to recall the first time she had been angry with her father and what she had said to him. She remembered his kindness, the gentleness with which he had always spoken to her, and she remembered how he had tried to teach her to speak kindly to others. She remembered how he alone would carry the queen to bed when she was tired or drunk, and how he would let no one speak unfairly of her. She longed to see him again, and turned her hot face upwards to the slab of marble before her. In it she could see the roughly carved outlines of his long purple robe and the points of his crown. His great hands held the pommel of a sword with a blade that had not yet taken shape. Under his crown, however, the slab was bare. They had not started his face. Agatha was crushed.

She put her hands into her hair and put her head down again. She wore a thick pink robe that spread out around her, and the wind snuck through again, rolling tiny pebbles and pieces of broken rock onto its edges. She looked up to the faceless statue and began to speak. "You would have been proud of me today." She bit her lip, then continued, "I sat with Mother all day, and I held her hand. I can't remember the last time I did that, if I ever did." Then she looked up and to her left, where she could barely see the tip of the castle rising above the East Wall, behind which the queen's chamber was hidden from view.

Behind the Row of Kings, the spotty blue moonlight exposed a single set of tracks that led to the heels of King Wisent the Fourth, whose marble head had been knocked off one hundred years earlier. Crouched against the base, hidden from Agatha's view, was a black figure deep in its own dilemma, listening closely to the voice of the princess. Tergiver ached at the words, *"You would have been proud of me today."* He imagined the way his own father would be embracing Marscion tonight with too many compliments and telling everyone how lucky he was to have a powerful son like Tergiver. He remembered hiding on another cold hill, wanting his father's acceptance, and he looked down. At his feet again were four ironwood arrows with green tips.

He tried to drown the sound of Agatha's weepy voice in his mind. He told himself that he was a soldier, and that his was the work of a soldier, to be completed for the good of his kingdom. He also tried to tell himself that this would be the last time he would ever do such a thing. In his mind, however, his voice came not from his mouth, but Marscion's, and it dribbled blood with every word. His stomach twisted itself into knots and his head ached. *She sent everyone away on purpose that night*, he thought, *Everyone knows she hated him.*

He tried to remember all the evidence against Agatha, but her words ran across the snow to meet him as if they knew where he was hiding. The princess's open repentance for her selfishness burned in Tergiver's heart, and he longed to join her. Her words diffused each of his insecure thoughts, leaving him hopelessly resigned to honesty.

He looked ahead into the night and wondered if there was a point beyond which one could never be forgiven or rescued from his deeds. He wondered if he had already passed it. It occurred to him that no matter what he felt, or what he intended, he was fated to play this role. Even his honest confession had been met with anger and cast aside as unimportant. He felt as if he were riding blindly down a dark, evil river, unable to turn or to see ahead of him. He had not wanted Feyton to die either. He knew Marscion would simply have Agatha killed by someone else if he did not do it, and then he too would be killed, and his father soon after. Tergiver looked down at the arrows and fitted one quietly to the string.

Two forms disturbed the fog that gathered near the broad, stone-studded feet of the cemetery. They stayed close to each other, avoiding the lamps and torches, and spoke in barely audible tones. "Stay close and do not make a sound. I will be watching you," whispered Baelin.

The girl retorted in her own whisper, "Remember that I am trying to help you! If they catch you here it will be your own fault. I am tired of you speaking to me like this. Anyway, if that thing is still following us, you should be watching out for it, not me." She delighted in knowing that he still feared the creature, not understanding that it had protected him.

Baelin took her by the wrist and pulled her behind him, climbing the ridges and staying low to the ground with the sword bouncing silently against his grey garment. He moved irregularly, checking the patrol stations and searching the wall for movement. He found it odd that the cemetery was wholly unguarded. He looked with suspicion on his companion and whispered, "Where have they buried my friends?"

She shrugged, and Baelin stopped walking. Then he pulled her along the eastern side of the slope, passing between high monuments and wading upwards through headstones capped with snow. She bumbled behind him, pretending weakness and letting him feel as if he were in control. The clouds unfurled from the moon, leaving a thin veil through which it shone down on the blue hill. Baelin leaned quickly against a carved obelisk and looked up the hill. On the third terrace from the top he saw the wide space devoted to the Guard. Set apart from the rest were two new headstones and a small monument, on which was chiseled an inscription. He dropped her wrist and marched toward the stones, entranced.

Baelin's face was dirty and he still wore bits of twig in his beard. His eyes fixed on the hard black shapes carved in the stone, illegible in the fog. As he crept closer, the shapes resolved themselves into, BORLEAF, ANSON, and carved vertically on a short obelisk beside them, BAELIN. He fell to his knees, mortified by the sight of his own name alongside those of his fallen brothers in the Guard. Then he began to weep quietly for them, making audible clicks in his throat and swallowing hard. Clouds again covered the moon, and as Baelin knelt before Borleaf's grave, dropping his forehead to the snow in grief, Herrick's long sword swished through the powder and knocked against the obelisk with a loud ring. He started up nervously. The girl was nowhere in sight.

Agatha's face was drenched in tears as she continued to pour out her life on the faceless statue. Her eyes blurred and her tongue was becoming slow from the cold. She was trying to explain to her father why she had thought he was going to kill Herrick. Then she stopped, envisioning Herrick's body dragged down under icy waves with the same hurt expression he had carried away with him that night in the hallway. Agatha no longer believed in Sophia's note, and she was too worn to lie to herself any further.

Tergiver peered carefully around the corner to behold the form of the princess. It was huddled and sad under the wavering torches of the faceless statue. He felt his blood pounding in his head and his lungs burned with cold breaths. He began to mumble audibly, but his words remained with him, hidden behind the stone, "Charlie, forgive me, I am so sorry. I wish you were still here; I would do anything you said. Please help me." He paused, as if waiting for an answer. He raised the arrow, still half-drawn on the bow, and closed his eyes, resting its green point hard under his chin. Upon feeling the point, however, a distant ring broke the sound of rushing blood in his ears, and drew him out of his half-sincere self-pity. The feeling did not pass away quickly, but hovered about him like another failed resolution, and he began to feel warm and angry. *No, I wouldn't do whatever you said, Charlie. If I had listened to you, King*

The death of a princess

Wiston would still be dead, and so would we. He lowered the arrow from his chin indignantly, glaring hard at the Pine Wood. Then, another of Agatha's fervent apologies drifted over the snow to him, and he thought: *Well, my father isn't noble or good like yours, princess; I wish he had been on the pavilion that night instead.* Tergiver's face was bent hard in anger and resolve. He turned his face back toward Agatha, and then he rose to his feet behind the statue.

A noise rang out like a bell from one of the lower terraces, but Agatha did not stir. Slowly, she considered what it might be. She turned her crumpled face quickly to see where it had come from, and she was terrified. She peered into the blurry darkness down the hill and saw that the sound had come from the graves of the men she had sent to their deaths. Her throat contracted and tears ran afresh down to her lips. Something was moving below, rising shadowy and tall from the graves; it was staring directly at her with incredulous and hateful eyes that sparkled with the light of the two torches burning above her.

The snow spread under Tergiver's boots as he leaned against the front of the headless statue. He closed his eyes then opened them wide in angry disbelief; he felt as if he were dreaming the scene before him. The princess was splayed out with her head on the ground, and half-emerged from the shadows stood a violent outline with darting orange and black torchlight flickering weakly across its face. In its hand it carried a long blade, which it pointed hatefully at her. Tergiver closed his eyes and fumbled blindly on the ground for his bow. *Marscion has not even waited for me,* he thought. He considered the seeming inevitability of his circumstance, and the helplessness of the great king as he had twisted and fell before him on the pavilion. He considered his dependence on Charlie, and his regrettable need for his father's approval. His eyes flitted about the scene hurriedly, and then, in an instant, all turmoil was finished. Tergiver was calm and warm and he knew exactly what to do. He gripped an arrow, slid it easily onto the string, and raised it in shadow. He felt in the completion of that act a sense of resolution, strength, and finality, and for this new, unquestionable resolve, Marscion would love him. He watched the scene with the arrow half drawn, and slowly pulled the bowstring back.

Agatha was speechless when she saw Baelin appear in the flickering firelight, spectral and carrying the fog on his heels. After a minute under his wrathful gaze, she began to sob mournfully, and she reached a thin hand out to his astonished face, saying, "Oh, Herrick, what have I done to you? I thought they were going to kill you, but instead I have done it. Please forgive me."

Standing close to her, just out of the light, Baelin was full of fire. Before him lay the woman who had sped everyone he loved to their deaths. He raised Herrick's sword, pointed to the king's statue, and spoke through his teeth. "How dare you bring your tears to this good man's grave?"

She dropped her head, losing her breath under the blow. "I know," she wept, "it is my fault; I didn't deserve him. I am a wicked daughter. But please, let me tell him I am sorry before you take me away; let me tell him I am sorry for not trusting him. Please, Herrick, I really didn't know."

Confusion mixed with Baelin's anger, "Herrick is dead! I am the only one you have not killed — I am the one come to avenge them! Speak now if you have anything left to say."

Agatha sniffled and nodded her head forward in acceptance, dripping tears from her wet hair into warm circles in the snow. "Please tell Borleaf that I miss him," she began, "that I remember when he used to carry me on his back, and tell him I am sorry. Tell

Anson he always made me laugh, and tell Baelin that he was always right about me, that I am selfish and horrible. But tell him that I *did* love you Herrick — that I only sent you away because I was afraid — because I thought it was you they were going to kill. Finally," she concluded, "tell my mother, that I apologized." She sniffled again then wiped her hand across her nose. "It will make her happy." Then, still looking down, she crawled forward weakly and sat upright on her knees before Baelin, keeping her bent head low with her hair slung over her face, exposing her neck.

Baelin stared in shock. This was not the Agatha he knew, and her appearance suggested that she had been in this state long before he arrived. He whispered inaudibly, "You know Herrick is dead; why do you think I am he?" Then, looking back at his grave, he understood. Agatha's neck was laid bare before him, and he could not strike. He believed her. Her grief had persuaded him, but her bravery and resolve now overwhelmed him, and he felt like a coward in comparison.

Baelin thought he saw a subtle movement in a shadow along the row of statues, but before he could focus deeper, there was an eruption of snarls behind him followed by a crack and an indistinct yelp. He turned furiously and grabbed Agatha's wrist, pulling her up sharply so that her thick pink cloak fell away and settled behind her in a pool.

Her eyes shone as she struggled along behind him and looked up wearily, as one waking from a dream, "Baelin?"

They stumbled down the snowy slope in haste to the site of the noise, where they stopped, still and silent. Blood dripped off the top of a headstone where there had once been a thin cap of snow, and just beyond it stood the wolf, bristling white and silver, and giving a long, persistent growl. Agatha looked down to the other side of the stone, then clasped her hand to her mouth and turned back, burying her head under Baelin's arm. The wolf was low on its haunches, then it rose sternly and the growl grew stronger and louder. There was a gash in its right flank, and it was bleeding.

Agatha was convulsing and she felt sick. "Who was she, Baelin?"

He looked down at the girl and answered, "You sent her.... She said she was your friend." Baelin moved to look closer, still holding Agatha, who peeked her head out from under his arm.

"No," she said, looking down in confusion, "I've never seen her before." She held onto him tightly with closed eyes and said, "Have I done this too?"

Baelin's mouth fell open in a gasp as he realized for the first time the danger he had been in since the forest. He studied the wolf intently, then yelled, "What do you want!" Baelin stood like a madman, as if he would attack the animal for being mute, though he knew it could not answer.

Suddenly the fur on its back bristled higher and its tail shot straight behind it. Baelin felt light as his blood whirred through his body. He read the animal's eyes, shoved Agatha to the ground, and spun quickly to find Tergiver standing within a sword's length of his back.

"I sent her for you," said Tergiver. "Just as I have been sent for the princess." Tergiver looked on the wolf, and then on the body of the girl. His eyes gleamed and a smile worked its way into his face. A small knife lay by the girl's hand, and a broken black arrow protruded from her shoulder. "Wait here while I get a torch," He walked to the near path and returned with the torch. The wolf seemed to relax when Tergiver returned, but it followed his movements closely. Baelin kept the sword drawn and trained on Tergiver. Agatha remained in the snow, weeping over the destruction she had seen.

"What do you know, Tergiver?' Baelin demanded. "Who has done all of this? Tell me now or I will kill you."

The Death of a Princess

Tergiver walked within Baelin's striking distance and stopped. The smile that had glinted on his face was gone. "Should I kneel for you as she did?" He waited for a moment, then held his hands behind his back and leaned forward slightly. Baelin was again astonished and bewildered. Tergiver brushed past him and moved to the front of the grave where he held the light on the girl's face. Baelin looked over the stone to see her.

Her head had smashed against the rugged granite. There were deep bites and tears along her neck, and the wolf's blood ran down her right forearm. Blood stained the snow around the scene of the struggle, and discolored her pack, which was lying open beside her body. On the ground sat a corked green vial and several arrows whose tips were wet with a liquid of the same color. There was a tiny white container snapped closed beside the vial. Tergiver reached down to open it. In it was a thick red substance. At the same time, he and Baelin noticed a painted red stripe running downward across the girl's face. She lay on top of her crossbow, which, Baelin could tell from the disturbed snow, had been set momentarily on the top of the gravestone and pointed at him.

Baelin looked at Tergiver cautiously, and Tergiver looked at the animal that watched them both with keen eyes. "We all thought you were dead, Baelin."

He looked down at Agatha morosely, "I am the last."

"I have never seen a wolf do that, it's the strangest thing," Tergiver said blithely, "I don't understand why it would hunt alone, or why it isn't afraid of us. But I can't let it have its kill." Tergiver looked strangely at Baelin, as if they were friends. "Neither of you can remain alive — and I have little time."

Baelin looked at Tergiver, who was almost smiling again. "What is wrong with you? What have you done, and who would want to kill the princess?"

Tergiver reached into the snow and grabbed the arms of the girl, pulling her upward, and replied, "It looked like you did; do you want to tell me why?" Baelin did not answer, and Tergiver continued to lift the girl. Then he stopped and rested her on his knee. "Listen to me, soon there will be men here to make sure that Agatha is dead. I will only say that until now I have never seen good fortune in my life. Everything I have done — every time I've tried to do good, it has turned out badly. But tonight I finally realized that nothing matters except people's beliefs about what I have done. Pick up her legs, Baelin, and tell Agatha to give me her jewels."

Minutes later, the animal disappeared into the woods, and Agatha and Baelin stood in black shadows at the eastern edge of the graveyard, on the middle ridge.

Tergiver approached them without a torch. He held out a hand in which he held the assassin's pack and crossbow. "Take this. There is money in it, and I cannot have it found here. I have only kept one thing."

Baelin took the pack as Agatha shivered beside him, cold and clothed in the other girl's bloody garments.

Then Tergiver said to Baelin, "I need proof that our assassin has succeeded. Give me the sheath from your sword. I will tell him she offered it as proof. We never told her she couldn't sell your possessions."

Baelin hesitantly removed Herrick's sword from his waist, and gave the sheath to Tergiver.

"You will tell who?" Agatha asked weakly.

Tergiver looked hard into her face and said, "If you ever come back to Murmilan, or if anyone ever discovers that you are alive, I will be killed immediately, and then they will come for you." Then he turned to Baelin with the same grave, threatening expression. "If you return, you will be killed for treason — by my order and without question. We have all been fortunate tonight, but we must let the dead remain dead. Agatha, please consider my actions here as payment for the offenses I have committed against you. This is my last kindness and all I can give. Do not think I do this for your sake; I do this because it is my choice." Then he turned toward the king's statue and spoke, as if to no one, "Be gone by the time I reach the body."

Tergiver turned his back and began walking upwards to the grave where he and Baelin had dragged the dead girl's body. He did not look back.

Agatha could not see the castle in the darkness, only the high stones and mausoleums of the middle levels. She longed to see her father's face and to hold her mother's hand once more. She looked at the walls in the night, with their floating ship torches moving from place to place on the grey stone, and she realized there was nothing, and no one left for her. She felt truly alone in the world; then she asked, "Baelin, did Sophia, my friend, ever find you?"

He inhaled deeply and his eyes told Agatha that he did not want to answer. Instead, he took a step forward and offered his hand.

Agatha closed her eyes hard. Then she opened them and looked up to her father's faceless grave. She remained still for a minute, staring at the body lying in front of the king's statue, wearing her clothes and wrapped crudely in her pink robe. She saw her ruby necklace resting against the gored neck of the girl, whose crowned head was partially covered. Then she took Baelin's hand, and followed him wholly into the darkness.

An hour later, a figure on horseback stopped behind the Row of Kings and dismounted. He walked silently down the path to King Wiston's grave, where he found Tergiver sitting with his legs crossed and his head down. Before him, flickering in the torchlight, a young woman's charred body was laid on its back. Marscion knelt to examine it, running his fingers along the ruby chain stuck in the girl's black neck. Then he picked at the thin crown, which was melted into her head, and said quietly, "The queen is dead, and no one can find our princess."

Tergiver's voice was cold, "She was killed there, beside those headstones." He lifted his arm, but not his head, and pointed to the middle of the graveyard. "This was the only way to cover the wounds." Then his voice grew stiffer, colder. "But knowing that she suffocated her mother, it should surprise no one that in her remorse she killed herself here, in such a horrible way. No one who has done so much harm to others can live long without coming to such a resolution." He lifted his face, silent and hardened. It was covered in red paint.

CONTINUED IN BOOK TWO:
THE SEA OF THE MISSING

AVAILABLE 2010
WWW.CARIUSBOOKS.COM

Web	www.jehunt.us
Twitter	j_e_hunt
Facebook	cariusbooks.com/jehuntFB
Publishing	cariusbooks.com

A NOTE FROM THE AUTHOR

Thank you for reading. If you enjoyed this book, please post a review online to let others know. Positive reader reviews are one of the most helpful ways to show your support. I will include in the upcoming sequel a credits page, to thank everyone who posted a positive review or otherwise contributed to the success of these books.

If you would, help spread the word by becoming a fan of my Facebook page, and please consider lending this book to someone else, or even buying a copy to share. The first two novels in this series came to life over several years, and while the final two are under way, I am unable, at present, to devote my full attention to them. Every copy sold is a step closer to that goal.

I welcome any edits or corrections. Please send these or any constructive criticism to feedback@cariusbooks.com.

Finally, I'd like to thank the following people who reviewed this work and provided critical feedback: Anna Delaney, Chris Knox, Phillip Kelly, Linda Merkler, Sam Hunt, and most of all, my wife, Sherri Hunt, without whom none of this might have happened.

Alexandria VA, December 15, 2009